GRANITE OATH

GRANITE OATH

A Seamus McCree Novel

James M. Jackson

First Edition
Trade Paperback Edition: August 2022

Wolf's Echo Press
PO Box 54
Amasa, MI 49903
www.WolfsEchoPress.com

ISBN-13 Trade Paperback:	978-1-943166-32-9
ISBN-13 e-book:	978-1-943166-33-6
ISBN Audiobook	978-1-943166-34-3
Library of Congress Control Number:	2022941674

Printed in the United States of America
109876543

Valeria's Map

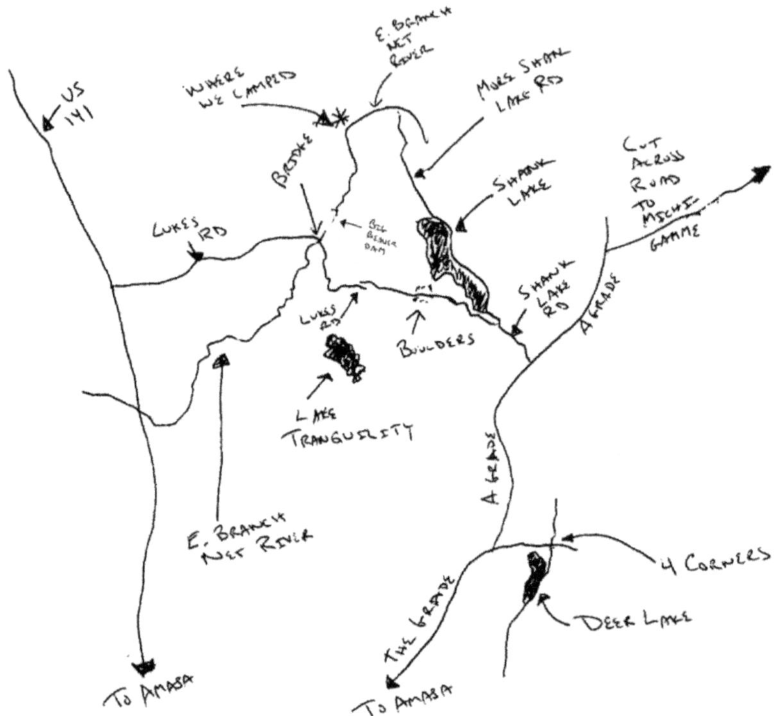

ONE

MY WORDS FROM THE MORNING shamed me. "Megan," I'd said when my granddaughter was dragging her feet. "People are late for two reasons. Either they think their time is more valuable than the other person's, or they don't care about breaking their promise." She looked at me like I was speaking Urdu. "Which one are you going to tell Mrs. Belanger when you're late?"

That got her moving. Now, I was late to pick her up at the Amasa Summer Creative Arts Academy. I boiled up the long gravel driveway and skidded to a stop in a parking area next to Kim Belanger's backyard, where she held the Academy. Megan and another girl sat at a picnic table in the shadow of an ancient yellow birch, their backs to me.

Kim was perched on the other side. At my approach, she folded a page corner of the book she was reading and shaded her eyes from the sun. "Seamus McCree." She drew my name out: Shay-mus Muh-kree. "You're the last person I *ever* expected to be late."

"I'm so sorry. I got stuck behind logging trucks coming down The Grade. That's no excuse. I should have left earlier. And I couldn't call because the card with your phone number is sitting on my refrigerator, and I never entered it into my contacts. Can I pay you for your extra time? Come on, Pumpkin. Put away your coloring book and pencils. We need to get out of Mrs. Belanger's hair."

Megan looked up, surprise painting her face. "Grampa Seamus, look at my unicorn."

She had finished the horn and was working on the mane, each lock of hair a different color. "Beautiful," I said. "How did you become such an expert?"

Megan laughed at our joke. She adopted a solemn face, wove her torso back and forth, and deepened her voice. "Practice. Practice. Practice." Then she giggled. "Can we wait with Valeria until her mommy comes?"

Kim said, "You know I was just busting your chops. You don't owe me anything. But you could do me a big favor and take Valeria home. Her mother works in Iron Mountain and sometimes can't get here until five. Problem is, I can't wait that late today because I have to cart my own kids to the library. The Friends of the Crystal Falls Library is sponsoring a YA author they want to see."

"I'm a little uncomfortable driving someone's kid without her parent's permission."

Kim waved away my worries. "I've taken her before. I'd do it again, except the road's tough on my Prius. If we could take your Subaru, I'll go with you." She asked if that was okay with Valeria, whose answer was a squeal of delight that she and Megan could play longer. We sent the kids in to use the bathroom before we left.

Kim handed me the coloring materials and Megan's backpack. "I'll be sorry when your granddaughter's visit is up. Before Megan arrived, Valeria was pretty much the outsider. You know, everyone else grew up together. Megan bullied her way past the cliques and brought Valeria with her. Those two are besties."

My face broke out with grandfatherly pride. "Megan is a force of nature. I was worried how to keep her entertained for an entire month while her parents are rafting down the Colorado. Your summer academy is perfect for giving her time with kids her own age. Before I forget, let me get your number into my contacts."

Kim dialed me, allowing me to capture her information, and then she called Valeria's mother. Her brow furrowed, and she left a message to say she was bringing Valeria to the trailer.

"Problem?" I asked.

"It's probably nothing, but Kat—that's what Valeria's mother wants me to call her—usually lets me know if she'll be late, which she hasn't this time. And she *always* picks up my calls."

Two

THE KIDS HAD A WHEE of a time bumping and thumping down two miles of a long-abandoned logging road to get to Valeria's trailer. Frost-heaved rocks threatened to dent a rocker panel or remove a muffler. How Kim brought a Prius in was beyond my comprehension. We drove through parklike areas of mixed mature hardwoods. As the road worsened, I slowed further and marveled at a stand of majestic hemlocks so large that, even with joined hands, the four of us couldn't have circled their trunks.

A mile in, we crawled through a section of road gullied by past spring flows from the surrounding tamarack swamp from which the dry spell had sucked any sign of standing water. Another mile of dodging rocks the size of Gibraltar and potholes deep enough to swallow a VW Bug brought us to a spot used as a turnaround.

Valeria called, "Mister, Mama stops here."

I pointed to the rutted tracks straight up a hill. "I can drive that. How much farther?"

Kim said, "She's right. It's maybe four hundred yards, but there's no place to turn around at the trailer."

Valeria unlocked her door. "I can get out here."

Not on my watch. Plus, we had the minor matter of the four gallons of water Kim had brought with her. I released everyone to bathe in mosquito dope and parked the car with one side scraping encroaching tag alders to allow Valeria's mother room if she returned while we were here. A horde of mosquitoes attracted by the car's exhaust buzz-bombed me before I could spray. I hate bug spray smell, and if I had known I'd be tromping through the woods, I wouldn't have worn shorts and sandals. Megan and Valeria skipped up the road. Kim and I split the water jugs and trudged after them.

The road curved past a vernal pond, then bent around a knob covered with mature popple. I smelled the woodsmoke before I saw the camp. Hidden in a dense thicket of white birch was a rusted travel trailer with an extended awning roped to the trees. A curl of blue smoke rose from a firepit with a saucepan on a grill perched on four legs. Sitting on rocks were a cast iron frying pan, a coffee pot, and a ten-quart kettle. Nearby was a stump with a hatchet embedded in it and a stack of branches lying beside it. A smaller pile of chopped wood waited, ready to burn.

The trailer looked level and had a couple of hundred-pound propane tanks covered with spider webs attached at the rear. Two card tables and four camp chairs had pride of place under the awning. Three settings of glasses with water, empty bowls, and spoons occupied one table. The other held a dish rack with various plates, silverware, and cooking utensils. Sitting in one chair was a knife, whetstone, and a maple burl partway to becoming a bull moose walking past spruce trees.

"Nana," Valeria called. She rapid-fired several sentences of Spanish. I caught only "*amiga* Megan" and "*señora* Belanger."

A middle-aged woman's distant voice responded in Spanish.

"Grampa Seamus," Megan said. "Valeria's grandmother won't come out while you're here."

Kim gave my hand a reassuring squeeze. "Megan and I will make sure Valeria is safe and meet you back at your car."

THREE

SOMETHING WAS BOTHERING KIM, BUT I couldn't ask because I needed to concentrate to avoid road obstacles. Once I was on pavement and no longer worried about damaging my car, I said, "Is their only source of water the containers you fill for them?"

"I know, right?" Kim glanced over her shoulder at Megan in the backseat. "When I found out Kat was using an artesian spring she found somewhere between here and Iron Mountain, I insisted she get water from my place. Each day I fill the empties Kat leaves with Valeria. Nana—Valeria's grandmother prefers I call her that—is worried. Kat came home in the afternoon all agitated. Refused to answer why she left work early. Changed clothes and drove away. I've found Kat very responsible. It's not like her to not call. I hope she wasn't in a car accident or something."

I sent a prayer skyward.

Kim continued, "Why was she home early? She should have been at the motel. She works like three different jobs."

I agreed it seemed strange. "You want to call hospitals? The police?"

Kim let loose a long sigh. "I'm just being a mom and worrying. She wouldn't want me to contact the police. She's a Dreamer, and she fears the authorities. Nana brought her here from Nicaragua when she was ten. Last year ICE raided Valeria's husband's job site. He was also working legally under DACA, but there were several illegal immigrants. ICE decided he had not reported a juvenile misdemeanor. Kat says the courts erased it from his record when he turned eighteen because he had graduated from high school and kept his nose clean. But ICE deported him anyway. The family didn't have the money or the wherewithal to fight it. Kat paid for a coyote by borrowing from one of those paycheck lenders. Her husband got caught crossing the Mexican border and deported again. Now he *does have* an immigration record.

"Long story short, the lender garnished her pay. Nana caught Covid and lost her job. Despite the national moratorium, Kat's landlord evicted them. How they ended up in that trailer, I don't know. Kat works all the time, has a truck that's held together with duct tape and prayer. The minister at my church is paying for Valeria to attend the academy. I can't imagine this will end well."

I supposed not. Given Kat was a Dreamer, Nana was obviously here illegally. Their concerns about police probably extended to any government agency. I doubted they were getting any of the assistance she and Valeria were entitled to—made harder by finding herself stuck in the U.P., where locals considered you a newcomer unless your great-grandparents were born here.

"Maybe you shouldn't have told me, Kim. If the wrong people learn about this, the family could suffer more heartbreak."

"I knew you'd think like that. I don't know how I feel about this illegal immigrant thing. It's complicated. But kids in poverty? That's easy to understand. My dad worked hard his whole life. Even so, I sometimes wore cardboard inserts in my shoes because we didn't have money for new ones." She rubbed her temples. "This is so not like Kat. I have a bad feeling, and so here I am, running at the mouth."

I suggested she try Kat's cell again. Still no answer.

Kim was not a bleeding-heart liberal, and I didn't think it worthwhile discussing my approach to solving the problem, which would be to put business owners who hired illegal immigrants in jail and fine them enough bucks to make it unprofitable to hire undocumented workers. And while she and I might vote for opposing candidates, she was a survivor whose instincts I trusted. My gut told me she was right to worry.

"Grampa Seamus?"

How much had Megan heard? "What, Pumpkin?"

"Can we invite Valeria for an overnight this weekend?"

"We can ask, but it might not work for them."

"Why not?"

How to explain to an eight-year-old that people might not trust a single man to take care of two young girls? "We'll have to talk with her mother, Pumpkin."

"Okay. Bring me early tomorrow. You can talk to her momma, and I get more time to play with Valeria. Win-win."

Yeah, two wins for Megan. Still, I liked her idea. Until I knew Kat was okay, I would worry about Valeria and her grandmother. Little did I know.

FOUR

I FIGURE PART OF MY grandfather responsibilities are to spoil Megan in ways that drive her parents nuts but don't do her any harm. We dropped Kim at home and stopped at Tall Pines Grocery. Dinner would be late and having dessert first made sense. Megan did not object to this plan and ordered a double-dip blue moon cone. No longer having the metabolism of my youth, I chose a single scoop of black cherry in a cup.

I held her cone above my head. "You promise to eat all your veggies?"

Megan raised a curled pinkie. We solemnly performed a pinkie swear, and I handed her the cone. The temperature was eighty-plus in the shade, and Megan's tongue worked hard to stay ahead of the melting ice cream.

The husband of the couple who own Tall Pines stepped outside for a breath of air. He asked Megan if she was enjoying her ice cream and received an enthusiastic "Yum."

"Me, too," I said. "What's news on the Amasa grapevine?"

"You heard about the break-ins over by Cable Lake?" I had not, and he filled me in. "Someone broke into nine camps. Took a generator, ATVs, some rifles and fishing gear, and propane tanks—the twenty and hundred pounders, not the big pigs we sell."

"I remember Sheriff Bartelle telling me a few years ago that neighbor kids are often responsible for clusters of camp break-ins. This sounds a lot more serious than that. How long has this been going on?"

"Couple of weeks. Trail cams caught two masked guys wearing night goggles—one big, the other small. Cops are holding information close to their vests, but I heard rumors of a truck towing a trailer. Maybe a side-by-side."

"Grampa Seamus, is my tongue blue?"

It was. As were her hands from the ice cream leaking from the cone's bottom. "Finish that up. You driving us today?"

"Grampa." She drew out the word and rolled her eyes. "You know my feet can't reach the pedals." She popped the stub of the cone into her mouth and smacked her lips.

"Okay, then I'll drive and you navigate. Now go wash up while I buy some double-A batteries for my trail cams. We'll check them tonight. Maybe we'll have a picture of a moose."

"We already had moose this year. I want a bear." Megan sprinted to the store, stopped at the door, and shouted, "And a wolf." She wrenched the door open, sending the bell tinkling, and burst inside.

I smiled after my little whirlwind of a granddaughter. "Whenever she visits, I sleep very well at night."

"I hear you, but if I were you, I'd have my eyes peeled. Cable Lake is no farther west of the highway than you are east."

FIVE

TO KEEP MY PROMISE TO Megan that I would speak with Valeria's mother about arranging a playdate or sleepover for the girls, we left camp the next morning earlier than usual. No logging trucks or downed trees slowed us, and we arrived at the Amasa Summer Creative Arts Academy fifteen minutes before camp drop-off started.

To keep dry in the steady rain beating a tattoo on our roof, Megan and I spent the quarter hour in the car playing a game I call, "And Then." We alternate creating a story. One of us starts with setting and characters and ends the intro with the words "and then." The second person picks up from there, ending their segment with "and then." Megan delights in twisting stories beyond all recognition, such as her contribution, "and then a dragon with flames shooting from its mouth flew down to the fairy village, and then."

I responded, "and then the fairy fire department extinguished the flames and brought the dragon to the fairy doctor who diagnosed the dragon with *flamous erruptus*, a hereditary disease passed on only to females who eat blue moon ice cream before dinner, and then . . ."

The fifteen minutes flew by in dragons and fairies and giggles and groans until the next camper arrived. Megan extracted a promise from me to wait and talk with Valeria's mother. Mission accomplished, she grabbed her day pack and lunch bag, and she and her friend sprinted to the massive tent Kim had set up in the yard for rainy days and to act as a midday sunscreen. I read the latest William Kent Krueger on my Kindle, losing my place each time a vehicle pulled up to discharge a child. Ten minutes after the camp's official start, I hopped from my car and dashed to the tent.

The kids sat in a circle and shared their morning check-in, their voices raised to hear above the rain pounding the canvas. Kim motioned me to the edge, where we had some privacy. "I called Kat Serrano," she said. "Still no answer. I'm getting really concerned something happened to her. I don't want to worry all weekend. Will you drive up and make sure everything is all right? I have two water jugs for them."

Six

THE STEADY RAIN BECAME A downpour, obliterating previous vehicle tracks and transforming parts of the two-track to the Serrano trailer into a stream. The Subaru's all-wheel drive worked like a charm, but I hit several rocks hidden by pooling water. My hope of seeing Kat's truck at the turnaround bore no fruit. I parked my Subaru pointed toward civilization, then zipped my raincoat, pulled up its hood, and pressed into the rainstorm. When I bent into the car to retrieve the two gallons of water, my slicker hitched up and drained cold water down the seat of my pants. *Dumb move, Seamus.*

Footing was slick going up the hill, but despite more than an inch of rain, the vernal pond remained dry. At least this precipitation would lessen the fire hazard, and there were no mosquitoes. At the trailer clearing, I called to announce my presence. The saucepan remained on the grill above the drowned fire. They'd have no fire until the rain stopped, and even then, it would take work to start one with soaked wood. I found no evidence of breakfast dishes.

The awning sagged with collected rainfall, straining the trees holding it up. Water poured through a slit in the awning over the trailer's steps. The force of the water running off had knocked over three empty gallon containers.

I called again. Valeria stepped out wearing a faded yellow raincoat with too-short sleeves and a broken zipper. She held the raincoat together, exposing the black bear attached to her wrist to the water dripping through the awning. Over the drumbeat on the trailer's metal roof, she said, "Grampa Seamus, you can't come in."

Her use of Grampa Seamus sent a shiver down my spine. I suspected she didn't know my last name—kids rarely knew surnames unless adults used them and they picked them up. "I'll stay here. Did your mother get home last night?"

She swiveled her head, as though she was listening to something from inside the trailer, then spoke rapid-fire Spanish. I wished Megan were here to translate. Valeria closed the door behind her. "Nana says we have everything we need. Can you please leave?"

Her quivering bottom lip gave the lie to her brave front. I was unwilling to depart until I knew whether Kat had returned. I framed the question in a way I hoped she'd answer. "Megan's worried about your mom and asked me to find out if she got home okay yesterday."

Valeria heeled water off her cheeks. She looked at her feet and shook her head.

Now what? I didn't know if Kat's no show was unusual or a common occurrence. Despite her grandmother not wanting me here, my Good Samaritan genes kicked in. "Okay if I take your water containers and fill them for you?"

"Yes, please." Valeria picked up the three jugs at her feet and traded them for my two filled ones. She scampered back to the relative shelter of the stoop.

Fine, smart guy, you gave yourself an excuse to come back. What do you do if Kat still hasn't returned?

SEVEN

Sheriff Lon Bartelle greeted me in the tiny reception area secured from the main facility and led me down a hall smelling of disinfectant. At his office, he said, "I'm fully vaccinated, so you can remove your mask. Long time no see. What's up?"

I ignored his offer to remove my mask since I didn't know who else had been in his office. I passed him a memory card. "This came from my trail camera on Shank Lake Road. I heard of the break-ins on Cable Lake and thought you should see these."

"Hey Tex," Bartelle shouted into the hallway. "McCree's here. Bring a card reader."

I had met Tex, then a deputy, now a sergeant, eleven years ago. Because of a hitch in his step, I had bestowed him with the Tex nickname. Others had picked it up. He entered and plugged a card reader into the computer. "What's up? Love the bird motif on your mask."

Bartelle installed the memory card and a new window opened, displaying a long list of files. "Point me in the right direction?"

"The six pictures from Tuesday."

Bartelle brought one up and whistled. "First time we've seen them on the east side of the highway." He tapped on a picture showing a blurry license plate. "Bet they're using an opaque cover to obscure the registration. Seamus, you mind accompanying Tex to check your neighbors' places, see if anyone was broke in? Knowing which trails to take or ignore will save him a bunch of time."

I bristled at the suggestion I required Tex's help. "Once the rain stops, I was planning to use my daily run to loop around the lake and do exactly that."

Bartelle crooked his arm over his head, which I knew meant he was thinking. "Normally, I'd say fine, but I want Tex to join you this time. When are you free?"

I wondered why, but figured he had reasons. "Anytime until three-fifteen when I leave to pick up my granddaughter in Amasa. Bring a four-wheeler if rules don't allow you to borrow one of mine. Got a plat book handy? I can show you which neighbor properties I know have cameras up. Maybe you can sweet-talk them into letting you download their memory cards."

Bartelle liked that idea and deputized me for this work. "So I don't lose a case on chain-of-custody or some such."

At his mention of handling things, I pumped his sanitizer dispenser and rubbed the cool gel over my hands. He was not telling me everything that was happening. Why?

EIGHT

MY MAPLE TREES PITTER-PATTERED THE last drops from the rainstorm while Tex and I unloaded the Sheriff department's ATV in my driveway. The sun already warmed my neck, and I enjoyed catching the earthy scent of moist woods in the shaded areas while driving the ATVs to the first trail camera. The fun stopped the moment we discovered a camera that covered a neighbor's gate was missing. It had been there for years, and I offered to call the owners to confirm it should still be there.

"Let's walk and see what we see. I sure wish it hadn't rained last night. Washed away any tracks."

Doors and windows locked. Nothing seemed to be missing from their boathouse, but I admitted I might not know everything that was supposed to be there.

Tex pointed to the grass at one corner of the boathouse. "The overhang protects that area and someone's recently trampled the grass. Yeah, call them."

The husband didn't answer his cell, but I connected with the wife. She was pretty sure the camera had been up, but she'd have her husband call me. They had another camera attached to the pole with the solar panels, and yes, we had permission to look at the memory cards.

We spotted the camera high on the pole. Tex and I dragged over a picnic table and a dented fifty-five-gallon barrel that we set on the table's top. I was taller and climbed onto the wobbly barrel and retrieved the memory card. Even though Tex steadied the barrel, I didn't think OSHA would approve our technique.

Tex inserted the card into his reader and skipped past deer and some of the fattest raccoons I had ever seen chowing down on corn dispensed from a timed feeder. On the night in question, a false trigger at 11:37 p.m. provided three pictures of nothing. At 11:41, the camera caught two people, one big, one small, wearing night goggles.

I said, "Those goggles use infrared, right? They'd see the infrared flash of the cameras?"

Tex chewed his top lip. "If they were looking at it, maybe." He checked the next picture. "They've moved to the window."

Several false triggers followed, which we speculated meant they were walking at the periphery of the camera's sensors. The final shots caught one of them striding away at 12:52.

I did the math. "What took them more than an hour?"

"Let me copy this card. We'll put it back and take another look around."

This time, Tex checked locks for evidence of tampering. He found scratches on the generator shed door lock. "What kind of generator do they have?"

"A portable they use for projects and a big one for charging the batteries that are part of their solar system."

"Call your neighbor again. Most people keep a spare key around. I want to know if anything's missing."

The wife told Tex where they hid the cabin key, and that the genny shed key was hanging on a hook inside the back door. The cabin looked fine, but the entire battery bank and the smaller generator were missing from the generator shed.

I left Tex at the crime scene talking on the phone to the distraught wife and walked up the driveway to open the gate for the crime scene guys. The driveway had to be 300 yards long. No way I would want to hand-carry those batteries that distance. How did they do it?

On my way back, I found where the crooks had cut through the woods on a four-wheeler to circumvent the gate. I back-tracked the path of broken branches to the road, where tire tracks suggested they had parked a truck. They had hauled the batteries out on the ATV. I showed Tex the damage. He agreed with my analysis. He wanted to secure the crime scene and sent me with his card reader to check the other camps around the lake.

They'd stolen one more trail camera, but others had caught their activities at three camps. At the nearest neighbor's, the truck and trailer had turned around in the yard. A camera at the second captured a blurred picture of two people walking through the woods at the road's edge. Sneaky. At the third, the truck and trailer were parked in front of a cabin for three minutes—long enough to check the windows and doors.

I returned with the news to find Tex with another Iron County deputy taking pictures of the generator shed and surrounding area. Using the plat book, I showed Tex what I had found.

"Thanks," Tex said. "I know you caught shots of these guys driving by your place. If they had scouted your buildings, would you have known?"

Goosebumps rose on my skin. "Not the cabin, but there's nothing there to steal. I'm guessing they skipped me because I had a night light on in the upstairs bathroom for Megan."

"Yeah," Tex said, "and maybe not. Make sure nothing's missing from your garage and generator shed. Let me know."

"My batteries weigh two hundred pounds each. It took two muscular guys to lift them off a truck and set them in place. No one would lug those suckers through the woods up to the road."

Tex blessed me with his you're-a-fool-Seamus stare. "Guys motivated by drugs do stuff no rational person would consider. Besides, don't you have an inverter, and controllers, and copper wire?"

TEX'S WORDS WORRIED ME ALL the way home. He'd mentioned drugs. Did they know, or at least suspect, who these guys were? Like every rural county, we have our share of drug issues between the opioid epidemic now featuring fentanyl-laced products, meth, and heroin. Just what I wanted were strung-out addicts needing money for their next fix.

My check of the garage and genny shed proved everything was copacetic. Walking past the Subaru, I noticed the empty water jugs on the passenger seat. I scrounged two five-gallon containers from my basement and filled them too.

I left early to make sure I wasn't late to pick up Megan again. Seamus's Corollary to Murphy's Law was in full force. My corollary states that if you have planned for every contingency, none of them will happen. I arrived with a half-hour to spare and opened all the car windows to catch the breeze. A distant fire brought a sniff of woodsmoke. I listened to a singing cardinal until it became background noise, then lost myself in the Krueger novel.

Megan opening the passenger door returned me to the real world. I asked if Valeria had ever gotten to camp. As I suspected, she had not. "Then let's take the water to them."

"And invite her for an overnight."

"You can ask if her mom's there, but I wouldn't get your hopes up, Pumpkin."

TEN

THE TRAILER'S TURNAROUND WAS DEVOID of vehicles. I handed Megan a one-gallon jug of water and grabbed two five-gallon containers. Megan's burden slowed her footsteps, but not her mouth. She was full of plans for what she and Valeria could do over the weekend. Schlepping forty pounds of water in each hand, I kept up with Megan, but my arms protested by the time we reached the clearing.

Since I had been there, someone had added freshly split wood to the pile near the firepit. But there was no fire nor any signs of food preparation. Megan called and Valeria appeared from the trailer. She squealed and ran to give Megan a big hug. I set the containers down and shook out my arms. "I brought some extra water."

It occurred to me that the kid couldn't lift the forty pounds, and I didn't know her grandmother's capabilities. "Let's find a place strong enough to support them off the ground." I looked for anything suitable other than taking up the limited table space. "I'll gather rocks to put under them. Where's a good spot?"

Valeria pointed to a level area near a rope swing similar to the one I had hanging from a white pine. I gathered rocks. The kids added handfuls of pebbles to my pile—too small to help. "How about you two go get the other two water jugs from the car?"

Valeria removed the stuffed bear from her wrist and wrapped its arms around the trunk of a sapling. Magnets clicked together to hold it in place. What will they think of next? The girls sprinted down the trail. My lack of Spanish forced me to dismiss my desire to find out how the grandmother was doing. I built the two rock piles high enough to work and placed the heavy containers on them. Rickety. I used the Swiss Army knife I carried in my front pocket to carve several stakes that I pounded into the ground with the hatchet. When I tried again, the containers were level and stable. Hooray.

From behind me, I heard Valeria say, "You ask him."

Megan responded, "No, you ask him."

The kids appeared, supporting the gallon jugs against their stomachs.

I stayed squatted next to my completed project. "Ask me what?"

Valeria put down her water. "Is it true you're a detective?"

"*Private* detective," Megan said. "That's what Seamus means. Momma says it's Yiddish for a private detective."

Valeria tilted her head. "What's Yiddish?"

Megan placed her jug next to Valeria's and put on the face of a college professor. "Momma says it combines German and Hebrew spoken by Jewish people. But Grampa Seamus isn't Jewish. He's Irish, which is close to the same thing, 'cause they sound alike, and he has a Jewish name."

I covered my smile, then controlled my expression. "Well, not exactly. They're spelled differently even though they sound the same. I spell my name S-e-a-m-u-s and the Yiddish word for private detective is s-h-a-m-u-s."

Megan shrugged. "Momma says it's because you solve mysteries for people. Valeria and I want to hire you to find her mother. I'll use my allowance." She misunderstood my frown. "If that's not enough, we can both pull dandy-lions."

Valeria nodded vigorously.

"Dandelions. Valeria, what does your nana say about your mother?"

Valeria's mouth formed words, but none emerged. Megan rattled off some Spanish; Valeria replied, looked at me and said, "Megan says if we hire you, you can't tell anyone things we tell you. Is that true?"

I caught myself rubbing my eyes until they hurt. I'm not a doctor or a lawyer or a priest. "Well, I don't gossip, and I won't repeat anything you tell me unless I must. Like if I had to tell someone something so they could find your mother."

That triggered another Spanish conversation between the kids. Megan said, "Valeria's worried you might talk to the police, and then ICE will deport her nana and put Valeria in prison because Texas wouldn't give her mother a birth certificate for her. You can't let that happen, Grampa Seamus. I promised you wouldn't."

My memory spit out a factoid that Texas had lost a suit about not providing birth certificates for children born of illegal immigrants. Valeria was three or four when the suit concluded, but Texas didn't track you down and say they were sorry for your trouble and here's your paperwork. Guardians had to apply for the documentation, and how many knew they could or how to do it? I could not imagine at their age knowing what deportation meant. What must it be like to live in fear of the government? When I was eight, my father was a sergeant in the Boston Police Department, and jail was a place I visited on take-your-child-to work day. Even as a teenager, after he died on duty, and I joined a gang and didn't want them to catch me, I never feared the police.

"Valeria," I looked her square in the eye. "I promise I will not talk with the police unless your nana gives me permission. Your mother has left you with your nana before?"

Valeria hoisted herself onto the swing and set it to a comforting rock. Three, maybe four, times since they had moved to this trailer, her mother had been gone for a weekend. Those times, Kat had picked up Valeria from the camp Friday afternoon and brought groceries and ice for the weekend. Without a refrigerator, they couldn't keep food long because the ice melted. Kat had always hugged Valeria goodbye and returned before Valeria went to bed on Sunday night.

"Valeria, I know your nana is in the trailer. Will you ask her if she wants anything from the store? I have to shop anyway. If there's something I can pick up?"

"We don't need anything. Just Mama." Tears streaked down her cheeks.

Megan tugged my arm. "Grampa Seamus, do we sign a contract?"

The kid knew about contracts? "Pumpkin, the laws say you have to be an adult."

"I knew that," she said. "We can pinkie swear."

ELEVEN

I WAS THINKING AND NOT paying attention to the rocks in the road on the way out. My right front tire caught the edge of one and nearly jerked the steering wheel from my hand. The seatbelt snapped tight, and I instinctively threw out my arm to prevent Megan from getting hurt. She squealed from some combination of delight and fear. I was going slow enough that I didn't lose control, but I recognized it as a precaution that I should not think and drive.

A minute later, Megan pointed to a jutting rock. "Grampa Seamus, don't hit that."

"I already hit my quota of rocks for the day, Pumpkin. We're good."

We weren't good. The low tire pressure light glowed soon after we reached paved road. I found a level spot and pulled onto the shoulder. Megan offered me the tire gauge from the glove box. We agreed I had no use for it. The front right was fast becoming a pancake. "Ever change a tire, Pumpkin?"

We made it a team project. I showed her where to position the jack, and she ratcheted it up until it met the frame. At that point, the car's weight was more than her muscles could handle. She stomped on the tire iron to loosen the nuts, but was too light. I loosened the nuts and jacked the car high enough for the task.

Megan untwisted the nuts and kept them in her pocket, waiting for me to remove the flat and install the donut. She threaded and tightened the nuts. We took turns lowering the car, and once it was down, I cranked the nuts tight. We stored the tools and tossed the tire into the hatch. Job completed. Now she knew how to change a tire and had the dirty clothes to prove it.

It was after five o'clock and past normal closing time for the repair place in Amasa. On my arrival, the owner and four dogs the size of buses boiled from the house. He found a slit in the sidewall and declared it dead. He could order one, but it would take at least a week. With the price of gas, I preferred the Subaru over my F-150, and had another idea to get the car roadworthy again.

TWELVE

I HAD PRAYED MY WAY home on the donut and wouldn't risk driving the Subaru until it had new treads. The next morning, I secured the dead tire in my F-150's bed, boosted Megan into the cab, and, with promises of a restaurant meal, pulled out before seven-thirty.

The store in Iron Mountain tried to sell me four tires because "with all-wheel drive vehicles, they should have the same wear." I insisted I would buy one and keep it slightly under-inflated to match the other three. Suddenly, my tire was out of stock. I'd have to order it. You bet I would—from my guy in Amasa.

Megan and I chose a local restaurant for breakfast. While she scarfed down French toast loaded with a "mixed berry" syrup that was thick, sweet, and sticky, I ordered my replacement tire. It would arrive in seven to ten business days. The Iron Mountain tire dealer might be quicker, but they had lost my business forever. I next tried Kim Belanger. "Which motel did Kat work for and what did she drive? I'm going there to see what I can learn."

Kim gave me the place's name and told me Kat drove, "a rusted Ford Ranger, originally red, but now it has black fenders and a blue door."

The motel belonged to a national chain. We surveyed its lot, saw nothing resembling the multicolored Ranger, and parked. We entered the lobby and detoured to the hand sanitizer stand inside the door. Megan bathed her hands in the stuff. I used one squirt to minimize the rotten garbage stench from its denatured ethanol. Didn't help.

Megan delighted in tapping the bell—only a fairy could hear her first try. She nailed it the second time. Its ding brought a harried woman running from the office, tucking a loose hair behind her ear, and arranging her face into a smile. "Do you have a reservation?" Her hand hovered above a slotted rack with pages poking out like porcupine quills.

"Looking for information on one of your employees. Kat Serrano? I understand she works in housekeeping."

She froze like she was playing the game "Mother May I" and did not have permission to move. "I'm sorry, sir, we can't provide information about our employees."

I gave her my friendliest smile. "My granddaughter, Megan, is best friends with Kat's daughter. She and Kat's mother begged us to ask you if Kat left here on time on Thursday, because she never made it home." That wasn't accurate on several accounts, but the clerk didn't need to know we already knew Kat had arrived home early, left, and *then* disappeared.

Management had schooled her well. "I'm sorry, sir, but I'm not allowed—"

"Actually, although we're friends, I am asking as a deputy of the Iron County Sheriff's department." I pulled my shield from my pocket and allowed her a good look. "I'm trying to do this with minimal fuss. You know, no one wants an *embarrassing explanation* written up in official records."

Her flush suggested she could imagine several embarrassing explanations. "If you'll leave your name and number, maybe the bosses will call you back?"

Leaving my information did not strike me as my finest plan. "I can make it easy on you and call them." What a kind person I am to offer.

"Oh, I don't think the Crenshaws would want me to give out their numbers."

"Understood." I memorized the name Crenshaw and squatted to Megan's level. "Shake the lady's hand and thank her for her time."

"Momma says we're not supposed to shake hands because it spreads germs."

"She's right. Mind if we use the restrooms before we leave?" I tilted my head to show I was asking for my ever-so-smart granddaughter.

"No problem. Turn right at the elevators."

I snagged Megan's hand and led her past the elevators, peeked back at the receptionist, and saw she had returned to the office. "Come on, Pumpkin," I whispered. "Let's hurry upstairs."

She slammed on her brakes. "The bathrooms are here." She pointed to the marked restrooms.

I put my finger to my lips and whispered, "We're being detectives and need to be quiet and fast." That did not seem to register. I added, "It's what you hired me to do."

Magic words. In a silent flash, we were down the hall and into the stairwell with the door closed behind us. The motel had three floors. I figured we'd start at the top.

THIRTEEN

A HOUSEKEEPING TROLLEY STOOD OUTSIDE an open door four rooms from the stairwell. The whoosh of a vacuum suggested the housekeeper might be close to finishing that room. She—I had met only a few male housekeepers and those only in the fanciest hotels—probably had a certain number of rooms to finish in a fixed time. If we waited by her cart, we could talk and minimize interrupting her work.

I told Megan we would ask about Valeria's mom and hope we found someone who worked with her Thursday to learn what happened that day. The vacuum cleaner silenced after a death rattle. The housekeeper, a thirtyish Hispanic, wheeled the beast into the hallway.

"Excuse me. We're trying to find Kat Serrano. Her daughter is—"

"No English." She said and turned away from us.

Megan ran in front of her, blocking her way into the room. "*Por favor, señora,*" which I understood, followed by a bubbling stream of words. The woman smiled at my granddaughter and replied in a flood of Spanish. They conversed for a minute, ending with Megan saying, "*Muchas gracias, señora,*" and giving the woman a little curtsy.

Megan clued me in. "She knows Mrs. Serrano, but she wasn't working on Thursday, but Gretchen was." She pointed toward the trolley at the other end of the floor.

We found a ropey white woman dumping bedsheets onto the carpet outside a room. From down the hall I called, "Excuse me, are you Gretchen? Can we talk a minute about Kat Serrano?"

She kicked the sheets to the wall, crossed her arms over her chest. The sleeves of her uniform top rose, exposing blue butterfly tats. "Who wants to know?"

"I'm Seamus McCree and—"

"My best friend is Valeria, who is Mrs. Serrano's daughter. She left after coming home early on Thursday, and she's missing, and everyone's worried sick for her, and Valeria and I hired my Grampa Seamus to help us find her, and he drove us here to talk to people who worked with Mrs. Serrano, but he doesn't speak Spanish, but I do, and I talked to Juanita and she said you were working here with her on Thursday."

Megan ran out of breath. Gretchen's wide smile showed gaps from missing teeth. "Girl, you talk faster than a used car salesman. I gotta keep working, but you can come in. Your Grampa Seamus needs to stay where he's at." She looked me up and down. "Safety. Door will be open. I'll mute the TV. He can listen. You help me dust. Deal?" She held out a duster.

Megan scrunched her face. "Is this a trick to get me to do your work?"

Gretchen's laugh was deep and changed into a coughing fit. Her face grew red, and I worried she would hack up a lung. Eventually, she regained control. "No trick. They pay me to work, and you're slowing me down." She shook the duster at Megan. "I heard a lot of names, but not yours."

"Megan Nelson McCree." She accepted the duster and followed Gretchen into the room.

I leaned against the door frame and listened to the two-way interrogation as Megan and Gretchen traded questions. Gretchen knew of Valeria because Kat often showed pictures of her daughter. Thursday, Gretchen and Kat had started at opposite ends of the floor. Some time before lunch break, the boss lady came and taped shut one room in Kat's half. Kat seemed upset at lunch, but wouldn't talk. Then mid-afternoon, Kat apologized to Gretchen for sticking her with extra work, but she had to leave early. They hadn't been full, and Kat was such a nice lady, Gretchen didn't mind cleaning a few extra rooms. That was the last Gretchen saw her.

Gretchen's questions of Megan elicited information I didn't know: my granddaughter wanted to become an astrophysicist and discover where black matter went. How she learned of black matter was a mystery I'd explore on our ride home.

The two of them returned and stored their dusters in the trolley. Gretchen unwound the cord for the vacuum. I hurried my questions before she turned the beast on. "Did Kat have any close friends? Boyfriend?"

"Not that I saw. What with working three jobs, that girl didn't even have time to join me and Juanita and the others for any fun. But she dances at the Silver Fox. You know the place?"

"I've driven by it. Never been in."

"You don't want to go in by yourself? You could buy me a drink after my shift. But not with your little chaperone. They got a pole and nude lap dances. I hear there's private rooms, but I don't know how private."

"And you think Kat?"

"All she said was she hated working there. I got to get at it, honey." She plugged the vacuum cord into the wall socket.

"Thanks, Gretchen. Do you know what her third job was?"

"Kat joked once that she got to dress up instead of down. Kinda like it was super hush-hush?" She bent down to Megan. "I hope you find your friend's momma, sweetie." The vacuum's whoosh meant I'd have to find my own answers to my remaining questions about Kat's third gig.

Fourteen

THE FORECASTERS CALLED FOR GREAT overnight weather. Clear skies, low of fifty—perfect for sleeping in a tent. We set up one in a grove of cedar trees a few feet from the lakeshore. I lugged down sleeping pads and bags. Megan carried a book to read with her flashlight. A fresh breeze brought water lapping against the shore, and the kid was soon fast asleep, giving me time to research the motel's owners.

The official owner was a limited liability company controlled by Randolph Michael Crenshaw, who went by "Mike." He was a former board member of the Dickinson County Chamber of Commerce and through his LLC also owned a grocery store, bait shop, the Menominee Rapids Resort, the Silver Fox, and a gazillion acres of land in Dickinson, Iron, and Baraga counties. I'd often wondered who was behind the R M Crenshaw Family Trust I saw while flipping through the plat books looking at land to buy for a trust I had created for Megan.

His local home was an eighty-acre property outside Randville. The satellite view showed two big blobs on either side of the driveway where it met the road. Google's walking man hadn't made it down his country road, meaning I couldn't get a ground-level view of what I guessed were stone pillars. His drive ran through well-tended fields and led to a house, garage, and barn. His official residence was in the Moorings area of Naples, Florida, with easy access to the Gulf through Doctor's Pass. The satellite picture showed a private dock and a boat large enough to swallow my house. I exaggerate, but the dude had money.

He had married Anita Palumbo two summers ago, wedding and reception at his resort. My first thought seeing her picture was "trophy wife." Calling her that does not reflect well on me. It's caused by my deep skepticism about reasons a woman with a Barbie-doll figure would marry a rich guy forty years her senior. She might be a wonderful person and the couple deeply in love. Really.

She had no children, but he had four kids split between two former wives. Three daughters, all married, lived in expensive houses in Naples.

One son, Randy, owned a modest mid-century ranch in Iron River. There had to be a story about the disparity.

Questions buzzed in my brain. Why was a room on Kat's half of the floor taped off? We knew she left early on Thursday, but why? She had not returned to work. Where had she gone?

Something upsetting had happened at the motel. I tried out the idea that the reason Kat had not said goodbye to Valeria before a long weekend away was because she had to leave earlier than usual and Valeria was at camp. Possible, but she would have told Nana. Nana appeared upset. Was that because Kat was missing or because she knew why Kat wasn't at home? How could I know if she was lying when I couldn't speak her language?

With luck, Kat would show up tomorrow with an explanation. In my gut, I didn't feel that was a winning bet.

I WOKE TO A FAMILY of otters breakfasting on the lake. They were a chatty bunch. I peeked out of the tent and spotted one flipped on his back, chomping on a fish like it was a corncob. My stirring woke Megan, whose first words were, "Grampa Seamus, will you call Valeria's mom? I want her to come home."

Five-thirty was way too early to call anyone. We had time to enjoy the otters. Then I'd cook pancakes and bathe them in the maple syrup I had created this spring from my sugar maples. Given most kids wake by seven, that was the earliest we would try her mother.

At 6:59 Megan handed me my phone. My call to Kat Serrano dropped into a filled voicemail box. Who else had been calling her? Megan wanted to drive immediately to Valeria's trailer. To prevent us arriving before eight o'clock, I prolonged breakfast cleanup. Sunday was Megan's day to wash the dishes and mine to dry. A good drier can make up for spotty washing, but that morning I insisted Megan rewash until I couldn't find anything to complain about.

They say, "timing is everything." I do not know what would have happened had we left earlier, but I'm thankful we didn't.

Fifteen

WE MET A BLUE SILVERADO with super-sized tires and a jacked-up frame on the two-track leading to Valeria's trailer. I pulled my F-150 far to the right and retracted the side mirrors. I risked mosquitoes and stuck my arm out the window and offered a friendly "after you" wave. The truck squeezed by us. Sun reflected off its windshield, and I couldn't get any sense of the driver. I hoped this meant our timing was perfect, and Kat had returned.

I drove to the turnaround. No sign of Kat's Ranger—not surprising, assuming the Silverado brought her home. My hopeful feelings tanked seeing new tracks continuing up the rough grade to Valeria's trailer. If Kat were with them, she wouldn't have directed a truck that big to drive up there because it was too large to maneuver easily. Either she wasn't with them or something, like an injury, necessitated driving to the trailer. I didn't care for either option.

I kept my fears to myself and had Megan lug a one-gallon jug while I carried two more. Our approach hadn't been silent, but the woods we were walking through were. No fire smoke, no chopping wood, no kid playing. My feet dragged to a halt and Megan rammed into my legs. The clearing containing the trailer was a war zone with smashed-in windows, deflated tires, shredded tarp, overturned outside table, and plates, glasses, and mugs shattered against a boulder. Someone had smashed the antlers from the bull moose carving. Valeria's swing hung in two pieces, chopped in half by the hatchet.

Deep ruts gouged the earth where the Silverado turned around.

"Valeria." Megan's wail expressed her angst.

The wind shifted and the smell of propane gas reached me. "Megan," I employed my rarely used do-not-mess-with-me-right-now voice. "Go back to the truck. Now!"

She dropped the gallon jug and flew down the path to my F-150. I ran toward the trailer, making a megaphone of my hands and yelling, "Valeria. Valeria's nana. It's Seamus McCree and Megan. We're here to help."

Propane hissed from the severed line between the propane tanks and the trailer. I shut down the gas at the tanks. It hit me: propane in the tanks meant the attack had to have been by the occupants of that blue Silverado.

I pulled open the trailer door. More destruction: mattresses slit; dishes broken; orange tree paint sprayed on everything. I came back out and again called for Valeria and her grandmother. "It's Grampa Seamus. Megan and I are here to help."

Not even a curious chickadee responded to my calls. With a chest tight with fear, I rushed around looking for bodies—nothing. Had the Silverado taken them? I leaned against a tree to calm my racing pulse and consider what to do. Make sure neither Valeria nor Nana were around and needed help.

My next call for Valeria brought a scuffling of leaves in the distance. Too steady for a squirrel or deer. I cupped my hands behind my ears and swiveled my head as owls do to determine the sound's direction. I soon spotted Valeria leading her nana through the trees. As they came closer, I kneaded my hands to burn off the worry of seeing the child dressed in a thin nightgown. Her grandmother wore a shapeless dress. Neither wore shoes.

I waited until they were in conversation range and tamped down my urge to ask what had happened. "Are you hurt?"

They were not, but they shivered in the morning's cool air. With Valeria giving me her grandmother's permission, I entered the trailer and found their coats—slit by knives. I recovered shoes and socks for both, a sweater for Nana, and jeans, tee shirt, and sweatshirt for Valeria. "Megan is in my truck. I'll get her while you change, and we can decide what to do."

Valeria translated, and her nana gave me a curt nod.

Megan waited for me inside the truck with the doors locked. I told her how proud I was of her mature actions. "If this happened to us, we'd call the police. These folks won't want to have cops look into this because Valeria's nana isn't supposed to be in the country. They'll worry the police will arrest her or at least report her to the immigration service."

"That's not fair." Her face flushed in anger. "If they arrest Nana, what happens to Valeria?"

She gets swallowed by the bureaucracy of child care services, which, despite their best efforts, couldn't help but add to the child's trauma. And I would not add to Megan's by telling her that, at least not now. "The first thing is to get them to safety. Whoever did this might return and trap all of us. I need your help to convince them. Can you do that?"

We climbed the hill, Megan silent, me strategizing. I could check them into a motel. Across the border into Wisconsin might be better. But if we couldn't find Valeria's mother, how long would that work? And then what?

At the sight of Valeria, Megan raced ahead of me, and the two girls met in a long hug. Nana was sorting through the broken dishes as if they were a jigsaw puzzle she could make right. "Valeria, is there any place you can go for several days?" At my question, Nana stopped sorting through the pottery and asked a question in Spanish to which Valeria and Megan both responded. The three engaged in a rapid-fire discussion that involved hand-holding between the girls. Nana crossed her arms, shook her head. When she hid her face—I suspected to hide her emotions—Valeria ran and threw her arms around the woman's legs.

"Megan, what's everyone saying?"

"There is no safe place they can go, and Nana refuses to leave with Valeria's mother still missing."

I understood the sentiment, but they couldn't stay in this wreckage. The three resumed talking. I zoned out until I realized they were staring at me. I felt guilty, of what I didn't know. "What happened, Megan?"

Valeria answered, "Nana says to tell you thank you."

I asked Megan for an explanation.

"They'll stay in our guest cabin if we promise not to tell the police anything, and I can stay with them while you find Valeria's mom, and tomorrow you can take Valeria and me to the arts academy."

I should have seen that coming. Megan had made logic leaps I couldn't fault since I hadn't mentioned my plan to find a distant motel to keep them safe. If the shoes were on other feet, I would want someone to make sure Megan stayed safe. Ah crap, Sheriff Bartelle still had me deputized. Michigan has no law against not reporting a crime, only for actively concealing one. Was that true for deputies? I could claim I didn't know *for a fact* that Nana was an illegal alien. Anyone could see this was a crime.

A cynic's line goes "No good deed goes unpunished." I would pay for whatever decision I made. I chose people over the law. It was only temporary, I told myself. I'd find a better solution once I got them away from the present danger by their trailer.

Sixteen

IT WAS AFTERNOON BY THE time we settled Valeria, Nana, and their belongings in our cabin. Everyone was hungry, but Nana refused my suggestion for all of us to walk to the house where I could make something. The kids explained Nana had only agreed to come here because we had the guest cabin. She would not consider entering my home. She had a line that she wouldn't cross—and that I didn't understand.

Nana used a camp stove to heat cans of soup we had rescued from the trailer. While we ate, I created a shopping list for two days' supplies. Nana shooed me out of the cabin proper and onto the screened porch to get out of her way while she washed dishes. Megan went to collect coloring books and pencils from the house for the girls to use while I traveled into town.

Valeria followed me and tugged my elbow, motioning for me to duck my head. She whispered, "Grampa Seamus, is my mother dead?"

The possibility was real, but we had no evidence of what had happened to her. I matched her tone. "What makes you ask that, Valeria?"

"Mama's never been gone this long before. What are wetback horses?"

"Wetback horses? Where did you hear that?"

"The woman was yelling before they. . ." Her lip trembled and a single tear curled down her cheek. "Before they wrecked everything. She kept yelling for the—she used the f-word, Grampa Seamus. For the f-word wetback horses."

F-ing wetback whores. "Were they all women? Did you hear men's voices?"

"No. Just her."

The destruction had all the rage of male testosterone. I hadn't considered that women had done it, but I knew better than to think rage was the sole province of men. What had Valeria's mother done? They were looking for something. How did they know where Kat lived? She might have told them, willingly or under duress. Or was this housing some kind of *quid pro quo?* I told Valeria I had heard the word before. "Telling me what they said is okay. Can you remember their exact words?"

Tears streamed down her face. "Why were they so angry? What does it mean?"

"Can I give you a hug? I know it won't make it better, but it might help a little." She gave a nod, and I wrapped her against my chest. I would not tell her what they were saying, but I owed her some kind of answer. "Some ignorant people call people who come to the US from Mexico wetbacks. Did you see any of them?"

Her head shook a no against me. "We were hiding. Grampa Seamus, please find my mama."

"I will do my best, sugar." I wanted to take her mind off her mother. She had been wearing the stuffed bear around her left wrist. I pointed to it. "You haven't introduced me to your friend."

"Mama gave him to me. He doesn't have a name."

"Oh, we need to change that," I said. "Everyone should have a name."

Seventeen

I STOPPED AT THE END of the cabin's driveway to install the chain to prevent the off-chance of someone pulling in and spotting Nana. I unwrapped the chain from around the quaking aspen where I stored it and stretched it across the driveway, looped it around a second mature aspen. Instead of locking it, I hooked a link on a nail to keep it tight. The point was to make it uninviting for any looky-loos without being a pain in the butt for me when I returned.

I used the half-hour drive into Amasa and its reliable cellphone coverage to plan how to ask my ex-wife for help. I didn't know for sure that helping Valeria's family was dangerous, but given Kat's disappearance and the trailer trashing, the potential was obvious. My first responsibility had to be Megan's safety. Her parents wouldn't reemerge from rafting the Colorado River for another two weeks. A drunk with six previous DUIs who was driving without a license had killed Megan's maternal grandparents. That left my ex, Elisabeth Lane, as my best shot. After years of a broken relationship, we were friends again. Plus, Lizzie loved spending time with Megan.

Her first words were, "Is Megan okay? What trouble have you gotten yourself into this time, Seamus?"

Busted. "Good afternoon to you, too, Lizzie. She's fine, and I'm trying to avoid trouble." I related recent events regarding Valeria and her family. "I don't understand what's going on, but I'm concerned I've created an unsafe environment for our granddaughter. She'll hate me for it, but can you take her? Could be just for a few days, but it might have to be until Paddy and Cindy return from their vacation."

A long sigh came down the line. "One of the most lovable and most frustrating parts of you is your willingness to take on other people's battles. Megan has you wrapped around her little pinkie-swear finger. I don't want to be the one to point out the obvious, especially since I want to congratulate you for thinking of our granddaughter's safety, but Valeria's nana may not be comfortable staying with you if Megan isn't around. I agree, you can't go to the police."

So far, so good.

"You should contact organizations that provide sanctuary to illegal immigrants under threat. Your silence right now means you won't do that because you've promised not to tell anyone."

My silence was simply me waiting to find out if her self-talk would lead her to accept my suggestion.

"You damn McCrees turn a pinkie swear into a granite oath that nothing less than a glacier can crush. Given all that, have you considered that instead of shipping Megan out, bring someone to your camp to look after and protect the kids until you spirit them away?"

"You're willing to come here?"

"A chance to visit the Holy of Holies? I'd love to, except I'm traveling all around the state organizing voter registration drives. I can't come there, and I can't have Megan here on such short notice."

A twitch of disappointment surprised me. "I understand."

"Ask Colleen Carpetti. She's dying to spend more time with you since you guys discovered you are half-siblings—or whatever you're called when you have the same mother and different fathers. Thanks to you, she's got a job she can do from anywhere. She speaks Spanish. Megan thinks Colleen is cool. Coming from a law enforcement family, she knows how to use guns a lot better than I do. Not that I hope it comes to that, but with you, it often seems to. A woman might convince the grandmother to seek help in a way you can't."

Everything Lizzie said made sense, and I kicked myself for not trying to put myself in Nana's shoes and look at this from her perspective. Her daughter was missing—although I still kept a smidgen of hope that Kat could return this evening, ready for work on Monday. People had destroyed most of their possessions. Nana was under threat of separation from her granddaughter and deportation. I'd fear making waves, too.

"Look, Seamus. I'm training trainers in all-day meetings next week. If there is absolutely no other way, of course, I'll take Megan and deal with the consequences. But you have alternatives."

"Thank you, Lizzie. I'm sure it won't come to that. And thanks for your suggestion to try Colleen. If you don't hear from me, assume I have it under control. Good luck with your voter registration training."

"Wrong, Seamus. You created my worries. Now you owe me the courtesy of telling me your solution. Unless I hear from you otherwise, I will assume you *don't* have it under control."

Ex-wives know too much.

I liked Lizzie's suggestion of bringing Colleen Carpetti here. I'd enjoy spending time with her, but I knew someone with more skills and experience dealing with the shit I routinely found myself in. Ashley Prescott, whom I thought of as Niki, was a former FBI undercover Special Agent who now worked secret assignments for the government. To my knowledge, she was between missions.

Eighteen

Niki answered my phone call with, "If this is a booty call, I'm in St. Paul, not D.C."

I took her booty call mention to mean she was not in a relationship, but her reference to D.C. didn't compute and I said so.

"My cellphone says you're calling from D.C. Where are you?"

"At camp. I just figured it out. When the cell signal is bad, I use the internet to make calls, and I set my VPN for Washington. I'm glad you're in St. Paul. It means you're closer and I have a favor to ask."

I gave her the lowdown on the situation, mentioned Lizzie's suggestion for my sister to help, but if Niki were available, I'd prefer her assistance.

Niki cleared her throat. "You and your ex still trying to work things out again?"

"Like I told you before, that experiment failed. The entire clan is just glad we're friends after decades of being estranged. So what do you think?"

"That you should have left a note for the mother to tell her you have her family and they're safe. When you correct that, why don't you set up a trail camera on the road in to the trailer so we can monitor visitors."

I cringed at the thought of being Kat and returning to find my home destroyed and my child and mother missing. I had been too worried about getting Valeria and her grandmother out of there before the Silverado returned to think through the ramifications. "I'll take care of both things. Does that mean you'll come?"

"I am *bored out of my skull.* And will be until I get my next assignment. Next thing on my calendar is dinner a week from Tuesday with three Pendergast Holdings board members. The meeting's the next day. I can do the prep work from your place."

I considered it prudent to keep quiet. It sounded like she was thinking out loud, not that she had committed to coming. At least she wasn't yelling at me for pushing her to join the corporate board. I waited for her to continue.

"Yep. That'll work. Need to rent an SUV for your roads and pack a bunch of stuff, 'cause I never know what will prove useful. I should get there before nightfall—by midnight, anyway. Regardless, you'd better be up for me. Double entendre intended."

Message received.

Megan acted happy to hear Niki was coming and translated to Nana my intention to correct my blunder of not leaving a note for Valeria's mother. Nana agreed to my plan for her to watch Megan and Valeria while I was gone.

I stopped first at the Iron County Sheriff's office to return the deputy badge. Given it was a Sunday afternoon, neither Sheriff Bartelle nor Tex were in. No one knew how to do the paperwork, so they didn't let me leave the badge. Wasted effort.

I found a perfect spot on the two-track to the Serrano trailer for the trail camera. It had cell coverage, provided a clear view of the road, and was not obvious to someone driving past it. I triggered the setup. Moments later, a notification whooshed on my phone. I opened the app to see a triptych of myself. Perfect.

To avoid getting trapped if the Silverado showed up, I parked on a skidder trail a mile before the trailer and hiked through the woods. The stench of propane had dissipated. Otherwise, everything looked the same. I reread the note to make sure it would reassure Kat, but not point other people to my place.

Your family is safe. They're staying with your daughter's best friend from the summer creative arts academy. I'll bring the girls there tomorrow morning.

I used a broken plate to force the door to stay shut and tucked the note under the plate. She couldn't miss it—if she returned.

Nineteen

Niki arrived after everyone else was asleep. We unloaded the bare minimum from her rental SUV and fell exhausted into bed. I awoke twice to the buzz of my phone announcing pictures from the trail cam I left monitoring the route to Valeria's trailer. The first time a doe and fawn sauntered up the road. The second captured a barred owl in flight, carrying a rodent in its outstretched talons. No trucks or cars or people meant Valeria's mother had not returned.

With breakfast dishes washed and put away, Megan and I took Niki to the cabin to introduce her to Valeria and Nana. The four chatted in Spanish, making me a fifth wheel. Nana's shoulders relaxed. Good, Niki was having a positive impact. Then they all shifted their gazes to me and laughed.

A secure person wouldn't care what had caused that laughter. I plotted how to get Megan to let me in on the joke.

"Okay, you two Munchkins, meet me at the road in ten minutes to leave for the Arts Academy. It's looking like rain. I'll tuck your raincoat into your backpack, Megan. Anything else you need?" She didn't.

On the drive to town, the kids stuck with Spanish. Since I couldn't eavesdrop and the day was warm, I lowered the window and bird-watched. Chickadees called their names, nuthatches ank-anked, an undulating flight of a dozen goldfinches twittered past. I startled a broad-winged hawk into the air and flushed a covey of ruffed grouse. I encountered no delays and had time to pick up mail at the Amasa post office—all junk.

At the intersection to Kim Belanger's, a kerfuffle of turkey vultures worked on the remains of something medium-sized—raccoon? If I hadn't looked in that direction, I wouldn't have noticed a blue truck semi-obscured behind a patch of red pines a hundred yards from the road. And a guy watching us through a spotting scope.

Maybe the turkey vultures interested him, and maybe it was not the blue Silverado responsible for trashing Valeria's home. Or it could be as bad as my imagination made it.

I accelerated and ignored Megan's shout that I had missed the turn.

TWENTY

NOT REMEMBERING WHERE THE MICROPHONE was in my F-150 to pick up my voice for the Bluetooth connection to my phone, I pointed my words to Niki toward the screen display. "It may be nothing, but I'm not taking any chances. We're headed back. I don't think they're following me. But if they know where I live, they might beat me there because I'm returning the long way."

Niki made humming noises like she often does to show she's thinking and doesn't want you to interrupt. "You're saying Nana may not be safe here. Where do you suggest I take her?"

"Remember the Deer Lake Campground? Let's meet there. I know a spot to hide our guests until we come up with something more permanent."

"Got it. On my way in last night, I spotted a perfect surveillance spot on The Grade. Nana and I will watch from there to see if instead of following you, they're headed to your place using the normal way. If we pass them before we get to our spot, we'll head directly to the campground. Call me when you get there. And Seamus, make sure they aren't following you."

We signed off. Thank goodness I had called Niki for backup. How could I make sure no one was following me other than stopping and waiting for them to catch up? Even with the rain we had three days ago, dust boiled up behind us. Someone could follow my dust cloud, and I'd never spot them. I couldn't make a quick turn off the roadway and watch to see who passed because the dust would give me away.

Got it. I'd wait to encounter a vehicle going the other way. It would create its own dust cloud and provide cover for me to find a place to turn off and park out of sight. I could run back to the road and watch for followers.

Brilliant plan, except I reached the campground without encountering any traffic. The idea to meet there had been lousy. It had only one entrance, which doubled as an exit, making it a potential trap. I drove past, continuing to the Four Corners intersection, where I had multiple routes I could take to escape if the Silverado showed. I pulled to the road's edge and called Niki. We kept the connection open while I waited for the dust to settle and learn if I had escaped their surveillance.

In a minute's time, the dust cloud had thinned sufficiently to see nearby shapes. The kids were deathly quiet. "It's okay to talk, you guys. No one can hear us." Sixty seconds later, I flicked on my turn signal and reported to Niki. "Looks like I overreacted. I hope I didn't scare you—"

Niki's voice boomed in the truck. "Hold on, Seamus. Something's coming."

The kids hugged each other, fear painting their faces. If Niki didn't say something soon, I might have a stroke.

"False alarm," Niki said. "This one's dirt-covered silver with a GMC logo on the front. Pulling a trailer with a side-by-side. You're good—hang on."

The tick, tick, tick of the turn signal measured the time. Thirty seconds. A minute. The connection remained open, but I heard nothing from Niki. I reached behind me and patted the kids on their knees. Ninety seconds.

Niki's laughter burst from the truck's speakers. "Well, isn't that special? I thought I had a situation. That GMC stopped, blocking the little trail I used to get to my observation post. Two guys got out. One's a hirsute bear eight feet tall and the other one is your size. They started up the two-track I'm parked on, each taking a side. I had my gun drawn when they unzipped and took a whiz. Let me tell you, neither of those guys has a prostate problem. Sorry for the delay. I couldn't say anything until they left."

"You damn near gave me a heart attack. I'll head home with the girls and start packing. How long will you hang to watch our back?"

"Half-hour should do it. If they were coming, they should already be here by now." She cleared her throat. "Unless they're waiting for reinforcements."

Twenty-One

HALF-WAY TO THE INTERSECTION FOR Shank Lake Road, we caught up to the truck towing a long trailer carrying the side-by-side. I dropped back as an extra precaution to prevent anyone from seeing the two girls. The kids were oblivious, making plans for constructing a schoolhouse in the "fairy village" Megan had built near the white pine by the lakeshore where her swing hung. Good, that would give them something to do while I packed supplies to go along with Valeria's and Nana's scant belongings.

Intruding on my creating a mental list came Niki's words describing the truck as a silver GMC. I peered ahead but did not see a trailer plate. I dialed Niki's cell and asked, "Did you catch a plate number on that silver GMC?"

"Nope. Why, they look suspicious?"

I slowed to put more distance between us and filled Niki in on the break-ins and the trail cameras showing a light-colored GMC towing a trailer with a side-by-side UTV.

"And you think it might be them? Pretty bold being out mid-morning."

"Not if we have nothing to ID them with. If they drive down Shank Lake Road, then I'll keep going north. I realize it sounds paranoid, but I'm getting that way."

"Makes sense. Let me know."

The trail cam images of the thieves had captured a big guy and a little guy. Those were relative descriptions. If the big guy was huge, then the little guy could be my size. Did Bartelle already know that?

When I reached the Y for Shank Lake Road, the dust assured me the truck and trailer had continued up the A Grade. I drove to my house and told the girls to have fun at the fairy village. "Take turns on the swing and no going out on the dock without an adult. I'm sorry this is scary for you guys. We still have to be careful. If you hear my horn honk—" I gave it a blast to demonstrate, "—there's trouble." Their eyes widened in fear.

I hated to make them fearful, but it was better than being complacent. "You hear the horn, Megan, I want you to take Valeria by the Lake Path to the log bench we sometimes sit on to watch the trumpeter swans. Go slow and be quiet. You *do not* want anyone to see or hear you. Got it? And stay there until Niki or I come and get you. Or I send someone who knows your secret word. Do not come if I call or Nana calls or Niki calls. Repeat it to me so I know you heard me correctly."

Megan's eyes were owl big, but she had paid attention. I sent them on their way with, "And take your raincoats."

I loaded the bed of my truck with the portable generator I use to run a window air conditioner when it gets too hot, three full five-gallon gas containers, sleeping tents, a twelve-by-twelve screened tent with rain screens, all my sleeping bags and air mattresses, a camp stove and two 20-pound propane tanks, two long folding tables, a bevy of camp chairs, water purifier, a picnic basket with dishes, and silverware for six.

What important things had I forgotten? I toured my garage, spotted water pails, and packed two, along with a portable potty, a skein of rope, and a couple of tarps. I dumped the ice I had in the freezer into a cooler and added food until it was full. Not perfect, but it would suffice for several days, after which we'd need more supplies.

I drove the loaded truck to the cabin. Niki's call caught me packing Valeria's and Nana's stuff. I asked if she was ready to head in.

"Negative. I'm following a gray Tundra and big blue truck with huge tires that make it look like it should be in some kind of mud race. Each vehicle carries two white suspects. Going slow. Michigan plates, and I've recorded their numbers."

"Their ETA, assuming they're coming here?"

"Six miles away, traveling twenty to thirty miles per hour. So—"

"Twelve minutes. I can block the road with my Bobcat and get the kids to a safe spot. Tell me your plan while I'm moving." I ran to my garage, where I stored the skid-steer.

"Park it where the road narrows at the top of your highest hill. They can see it from the earlier hill and turn around okay. If they keep coming, I'll have them covered from a distance."

"Roger. What do you want me to do?"

"Get the kids the hell out. I don't want any collateral damage."

"And Nana?" I engaged the Bobcat's ignition key. The machine generated a piercing warning pitch, telling me to wait nine seconds for the glow plug to warm the engine. I should have donned ear protectors. Deafness arrives on a series of such mistakes.

"I've got a rifle for her. Make sure you block that road."

The nine-second countdown finished, and I fired up the Bobcat. Without letting it warm up, I pushed the throttle from turtle to rabbit and roared up the driveway at its maximum speed of seven miles an hour.

Five minutes later, I parked the skid-steer perpendicular in a narrow spot between two banks that wouldn't allow any cars or trucks to pass. I stuck the key in my pocket. Niki had chosen the placement well. The surrounding trees were sufficiently open that she could see from the other hill. Given her expert marksmanship, she outmatched the guys, provided Nana could provide covering fire.

I ran to the cabin, hopped into my truck, and drove it to the house. I left the motor running and raced down the path to the fairy village.

The girls weren't there. They had constructed a new building in the fairy village, walls, a door, not yet a roof. The susurration of rope on wood drew my attention to the swing, still rocking slightly from earlier use. I peered past the swing to the single dock section poking into the lake. Empty.

I cupped my hands to my mouth and bellowed Megan's name.

Twenty-Two

I'D TOLD THE GIRLS NOT to answer, and they didn't. Had they gone into the house to use the bathroom? I flew up the trail, ignoring the sting of branches slapping my face. The basement door remained locked, and those lights weren't on. I sped up the hill to the kitchen door, stuck my head in, and yelled for the girls. Not there.

Where the hell were they? Megan knew the property well and could have taken Valeria to see the hollow tree, or the blue-headed warbler nest we'd found with the mother still on the nest, or the bald-faced hornets nest attached to branches of a sugar maple, or—too many choices, too little time. I ran to the pickup and honked two long blasts, grabbed the fob and sprinted toward the agreed meeting place.

My phone rang, and I slowed to answer it. Niki said, "Unless they take Ned Lake Road, they'll be to you in four minutes."

"Kids are missing. Try to stall them if you can."

"Roger that. Niki out."

I paused at the main dock. The girls weren't there, and I didn't hear them moving in either direction along the path. The corner of my eye caught sight of the boathouse, a roofed structure with open walls. I changed plans and dragged the canoe to the lake, dumped in two kid's life vests, three seat cushions, and two paddles.

I shoved off and paddled toward the meeting spot. Assuming the girls were waiting for me—I sent a prayer heaven-bound—I'd take them across the lake to a neighbor's camp, which was safe behind a locked gate.

The girls were not at the meeting spot. I tied the bow rope to a yellow birch and clambered onto land. The shoulder of the hill blocked anyone on the road from seeing the shore, making this spot excellent for hiding from the guys in the trucks.

Where the hell were the kids? They should have gotten here.

A horn honked a friendly toot-toot—what I would do if someone blocked my way and I figured they hadn't seen me. I scrambled up the hill, keeping low to the ground, and found a spot in a group of cedars where I could observe both the Bobcat and the meeting site. I crawled under the lower branches, browsed bare from the deer, and crab-walked sideways until I nestled against an uprooted tree and peered around the root ball.

The top of my Bobcat and most of the jacked-up blue truck were visible. The same horn sounded a five-second blast, then multiple vehicle doors slammed. I could only see the gray truck's roofline, but I thought its doors were open. I scanned for Niki at the top of the other hill. No furtive movements. No flash of light catching a scope. If she and Nana were there, they were ghosts.

The click of the Bobcat's door latch returned my attention to it. Someone was climbing in. "No keys," a guy yelled.

"Anyone got a screwdriver?" another asked.

To jimmy the lock. Why not? What's felony vehicle theft if you had come all the way out here to—do what? Why were they here?

A third person tossed something to the guy in the Bobcat. Moments later, the high-pitched beep announced the glow plug's nine-second countdown. I'd focused on what was at my front and had ignored what was behind me. I spun around, expecting to see the girls. No kids. What had gone wrong?

The skid-steer turned on with a throaty roar. I texted Niki, "Game plan?" The phone claimed it had sent the message, but I wouldn't know if Niki got it unless she responded.

Where the hell are those girls? We should be safely across the lake. Now, my only choices were to wait for Niki to engage the four guys or play dumb and apologize for leaving the skid-steer on the road. I could say I had a case of the shits. Sorry for the delay.

No text from Niki.

No idea where the girls were.

The Bobcat lurched like a drunken stock market as the operator struggled to point it forward. Whether by random luck or learning, he succeeded. In thirty or forty feet, he could leave it in a wide spot and allow the trucks to pass. Time for me to intercept them and pretend to make nice.

I used the fallen cedar for support and hauled myself to standing, then proceeded up the hill. No sense calling. They couldn't hear me over the Bobcat's diesel. I was halfway to the road when the Bobcat shut down.

A whistle, like a football coach trying to get his team's attention, cut through the quiet. I couldn't tell where it came from. Two guys got into the blue truck. The gray truck's driver ran and closed its passenger door and circled around to the driver's side.

A rifle shot cracked the air, causing me to flinch and duck. A maple tree branch dropped onto the road in front of the lead truck. "Yo, dudes," Niki called, "Next time won't be a warning. Turn those trucks around and leave. Now!"

I dropped to the ground and hoped no one saw me.

"What the hell, lady? We're just trying to get to our fishing spot." The gray truck crept forward.

"Tell that to the Sheriff's deputies when they get here. Last warning." Another crack of her rifle brought a second branch down, this time on the gray truck's hood. "Back out now. I'll forget the felony you boys committed taking that Bobcat. I'll flatten your tires if you move another inch forward." Seconds later, Niki yelled, "You realize this is a dead end, right? And don't even *think* about trying to flank me if you want to see tomorrow."

That must have convinced them this was a fight they did not want to have. The guy who had moved the Bobcat walked up the road holding his empty hands above his head. Got into the gray truck. The rear lights of both trucks engaged, and they reversed in a hurry.

With rear cameras, it was easy for them to stay on the road and reverse at speed. Were they trying to catch Niki in the open?

Nothing I could do to help. I shifted my thoughts to my other concern: what had happened with the girls?

Twenty-Three

I TRIED THE MEETING PLACE again—no kids. Returned on the lake trail to the fairy enclave. The swing had stopped moving, and the area was deadly quiet. I retreated to my house—no kids. My phone dinged. Niki's message reported the trucks had retreated. She planned to wait and watch, and Nana was walking down the road to the cabin.

I texted: *The girls are missing.*

Niki responded: *Didn't interact with the dudes in the trucks.*

I opened the house door and called, "Megan? Valeria? You guys in here?" Only the ticking clock answered.

I ran down to the tree house. No kids. Nana would get to the cabin soon. I didn't know how to communicate to her that I had lost the kids. Google Translate wouldn't cut it. I could get Niki on the phone, have her translate—I should have learned Spanish.

I met Nana coming down the cabin driveway. She carried the rifle comfortably, and a brief vision of her shooting me for letting our granddaughters out of sight flashed through my brain. I asked, "*¿Cómo estás?*"

"*Bien. ¿Dónde están las niñas?*"

I figured she was okay, remembered *dónde* meant "where" and guessed she was asking where the kids were and responded with "*No sé.*"

Her eyes widened. She nearly dropped the rifle. "You not know, señor?" She tilted her head and called in a powerful voice. "Valeria, *¿dónde estás?*"

"*Aquí,*" came a tearful voice from the direction of the cabin.

I ran ahead of Nana, yanked open the screen door. They weren't on the porch or in the cabin itself. I called their names. From underneath me came Megan's strong, "Grampa Seamus, Valeria's stuck in the basement."

Only then did I notice they had moved the picnic table on the screened porch, and the trapdoor to the half-basement under the cabin was open. I reached the opening in two steps and squatted. Below me, Valeria lay on the cement floor gripping her ankle. A plastic step stool lay shattered next to her.

Nana stood over my shoulder and flung spitfire Spanish at the girls. Ignoring Nana, I dropped into the hole and asked Valeria what hurt.

"I jumped wrong and broke the stool and my ankle hurts and the back of my head where I hit the floor but mostly my ankle and I can't stand on it and then—"

"And then," Megan said, "I couldn't get her out. We heard the horn, but I couldn't leave her here. Are we in trouble, Grampa Seamus? It's all my fault. Please don't send Valeria away."

"I'm not mad at either of you. I need to look at Valeria's leg before I move her. Pumpkin, once I boost you up, get me a flashlight. And tell Valeria's nana what's going on." I gave her a hug. She refused my offer to help, jumped, caught the opening edge and hauled herself out, all the while jabbering Spanish to Valeria and Nana.

I performed the how many fingers routine with Valeria. She was seeing fine, tracked my finger right, left, up and down. I tapped the minor bump on her head to judge her pain. She sucked in a little breath. I asked her how badly she hurt—from a little scrape to the worst pain she could imagine. Her head felt like she'd run into a door, but her ankle hurt like the time last year she broke her arm falling off her bicycle.

Megan handed down a flashlight. I had Valeria lie on her back and stretch her legs. I gingerly pushed up her pant leg. No protruding bones. Her ankle was twice its normal size, but she reported more pain from the fleshy parts of her leg than the bone. I'd experienced sprained ankles as a kid and broken ankles as an adult. This seemed to me to be a sprain.

An x-ray could tell for sure, but it would raise all kinds of issues if we went to the local emergency room. I had nothing to show I had permission from her mother. Nana probably couldn't prove she was Valeria's grandmother and even if she could, she probably couldn't prove guardianship. Plus, they had no insurance—I could pay the costs, but anything that exposed Nana to scrutiny was a problem.

"You have a sprained ankle, Valeria. You're a big brave girl. I'm going to lift you up. It might hurt a little because we're putting some pressure on your ankle. Tell me if it hurts too much, okay?"

She nodded.

"I'll place one arm under your legs and the other behind your back. We can't both fit through the hole. I'll lift you straight up and set your bottom on the edge. Then hold your hurt foot up and scoot away from the edge. I'll hop out and carry you inside the cabin."

The picnic table covering the hole complicated the process. Valeria gave one little yelp when I bumped her ankle on the trap door frame. "Sorry, sorry," I said. "Almost there."

Megan continued talking with Nana. Whatever she said worked. I hauled myself up and found Nana sitting on the floor supporting Valeria, and Megan shoving a pillow under the knee of Valeria's injured leg.

I scooped Valeria up and laid her on the futon, arranging pillows to support and stabilize her leg. Megan followed my instructions to wrap a hand towel around ice from the cooler I had in the truck's bed.

Nana gently poked and prodded Valeria's ankle, causing the girl to suck in air. The kid was tough. Nana reached for a shoelace. I stopped her hand and shook my head. We needed to control the swelling with ice before we removed the shoe or she wouldn't get it on for a week.

Time was ticking away. Kat had done something that had caused people to go ballistic at her trailer and to bring two trucks and four guys out to my property. Did they think Kat was here? If so, that meant maybe she was hiding somewhere. Or had Kat stolen something they wanted back? Under that scenario, she could be hiding, or they could have her, or she could be dead.

I didn't know what the guys in the trucks planned to do, but we needed to assume they'd return with reinforcements and act accordingly. The number one priority had to be to get Nana and the kids somewhere safe.

Nana kept the ice firmly on Valeria's leg while Megan and I packed the truck with their belongings. I kept a line open with Niki to give me as much lead time as possible if the bad guys returned. She again encouraged me to contact Iron County's Sheriff Bartelle. "We're outnumbered and probably outgunned. If they show up again, I can delay them. But if they have enough guys and are willing to leave bodies, I can't stop them."

"I've been trying to guess what could make them that desperate."

"I'm not saying this is anything close to the actual scenario," Niki said, "but imagine Kat disappeared with a shit-ton of drugs she stole from locals who are tail end of a long cartel supply chain. The cartel wants its money or its drugs, and they don't accept excuses. Saving your life is a big motivator. You see?"

"Too well. I want to move them to Lake Tranquility. Between here and there, a timber company's placed boulders on Lukes Road to block vehicle access. My Bobcat can move them, but it means I have to shuttle back and forth to move rocks, transport people in the truck, then replace the rocks with the Bobcat." I paused to give her a chance to offer to help. When she didn't, I said, "I had counted on you as the second driver."

Niki couldn't find Lake Tranquility on her GPS. I explained it isn't the name on any official maps. I had taken Megan on a tour of the 4,000 acres I purchased for the trust I created for her. She had fallen in love with a private lake. Displaying a vocabulary ten years ahead of her age—or so her proud Grampa thought—she exclaimed she loved it because it was tranquil, with no motors within earshot. She proved she knew what tranquil meant, and I agreed she could name it Lake Tranquility.

"Sounds good," Niki said. "Does Nana drive?"

Embarrassment burned my face at my implicit prejudice. Nana not knowing much English and being here illegally didn't mean she couldn't drive.

Twenty-Four

THE FIRST HITCH IN OUR operation was that the Bobcat's key would not start the skid-steer because of the damage they had done to the ignition slot. I knew the screwdriver blade on my Swiss Army knife solved that problem when the high-pitched glow-plug warning hurt my ears. I swapped the Bobcat's bucket for pallet forks to move the rocks. With Nana and the kids following in my F-150, I jounced at maximum speed down Shank Lake Road and hung a right on Lukes Road.

The Bobcat moved the rocks and replaced them to re-block the road once the F-150 was past. No longer needing the skid-steer until I brought it home, I hid it and drove the truck to the nearest of the three gates guarding entrances to the property. Megan unlocked the gate and closed it behind the truck. We soon arrived at a quarter-acre clearing I'd constructed on a rise overlooking Lake Tranquility, only a stone's throw away from a pier and boat house built to shelter a rowboat. I figured we'd set up the kitchen tarp near the firepit that I had surrounded with several stump stools.

I wasn't worried about Nana and her granddaughter camping. They had used the trailer only as a place to sleep, get out of the weather, and store their few possessions. With the tents and stuff I'd brought, they'd have more room, and the generator and propane would provide a few comforts they didn't have in the trailer.

I placed a camp chair and footstool next to the firepit for Valeria to rest her leg, although it was too warm for a fire. While Nana set up the serving tables, I re-iced Valeria's ankle. She'd kept it elevated during the ride. It had stopped swelling, and she flexed it a little for me. Both good signs, and I felt more secure with my diagnosis and decision that she did not require medical attention.

"Okay, Queen Valeria, where would your majesty like her tent set up? Megan loves it under those evergreens close to the lake. That means hopping. I don't want you putting weight on your ankle for at least a day. I can put it closer if you think that's too far."

She giggled at my silliness, and after conferring with Megan, agreed it was a fine spot. Nana chose my usual place: near her granddaughter's tent, but with enough separation to allow her granddaughter a little independence.

An hour's work had me sweating, but happy that I had thought of everything they required for at least one night. I left Megan to help Nana bring her clothes into her tent, and I walked to the bench bolted onto the end platform of the thirty-foot pier jutting into the lake where I had privacy and good cell service. I closed my eyes and let the sound of waves slapping against the shore relax me. When I almost dropped my phone, I jerked awake.

Niki answered my call. "I have to return my truck and Bobcat to camp, and you and I want to talk where little pitchers and their big ears can't hear us. Do you figure it's wise for you to leave your position and help me transport vehicles?"

Niki asked how safe I thought Lake Tranquility was.

"Nothing is as safe as Nana leaving the area. Lukes Road is the only road that provides access. The boulders I moved block the road coming from the east. You either have to move them or use four-wheelers. Lukes Road from the west has two sketchy areas that stop most people. Even if someone braved the obstructions, all three entrances into the property have locked gates."

"You're not convincing me, Seamus. A bolt cutter can take care of those locks in a flash. And all someone has to do is follow tracks from your house. Your Bobcat doesn't exactly hide where it's been."

I agreed. "Once I get the truck and skid-steer back home, we'll use ATVs to transport us. A couple of trips will help obscure the Bobcat tracks. To prevent wearing a trail they can follow from my place to the lake, we'll vary our routes using logging trails I know."

Niki said that was not good enough. "We'll pray for rain. I think I should remain on guard here, at least until dark."

In case they come back. "Understood. I'll take care of moving the truck and Bobcat."

"Excellent." She sounded chipper. "Leave Megan with Valeria for the night. You can join me here, and we can strategize. We need a plan."

"I have some ideas, but I didn't pack Megan's stuff."

"She's a kid. She'll be happy to share a sleeping bag with Valeria, sleep in her clothes, and pretend to brush her teeth with her finger. Ask Nana to cook dinner for the three of them. Given all you told me, I'll feel better if you and I overnight at Lake Tranquility."

An involuntary shiver tightened my back. "You're that worried?"

"I'm that careful."

I was just thinking that sounded reassuring when she added, "And that worried. Get your vehicles back home and then bring food so we can talk and eat. And keep your damn eyes open."

That was not reassuring.

Twenty-Five

IT TOOK DAMN NEAR FOREVER to tow the F-150 home with the skid-steer, but that was still faster than if I had shuttled them back.

I was hungry, and tired, and discouraged that the day had been a net negative. I filled all the ice cube trays with water to make more ice for Valeria's ankle, then packed the two-up with the supplies Niki and I needed. Besides an extra layer of clothes and a change of underwear, I included our toothbrushes, toothpaste, and her birth control pills. I reconsidered letting Megan wear the same clothes a second day and brought a change for her. I didn't bother with her toothbrush; she'd be asleep before we got there.

For dinner, I chose blocks of three different cheeses, a box of Triscuits, a bowl of mixed fruit, and two apples. Alcohol was a lousy choice given the circumstances. I packed two water bottles and a six-pack of Megan's apple juice boxes.

I grabbed my headlamp from its place on the hallway pegs and spotted a charger plugged into the wall. A sweep of the house netted various chargers, my laptop, and the burner phone that related to Niki's undercover work. I tossed them all into the computer backpack. What else would I need if I couldn't return here for a couple/three days? I packed Megan's and my passports, a guarantee we'd be back in the morning.

Niki's spot on a logging road used a curve to allow her to see vehicles driving toward my place, but hid her SUV from them unless they looked over their shoulder as they passed her. To prevent anyone noticing the four-wheeler, I pulled it deeper into the woods.

Niki delighted in the pop that came by stabbing the apple juice boxes with the miniature straw. Simple pleasures to reduce stress. Between bites, I poured out my concerns that my plan to locate Valeria's mother was like trying to follow cloud wisps. We had no clue who or what we were up against. My instincts told me Kat had not gone missing of her own volition, which meant every second we didn't find her was a second they could kill her.

I had tried to convince myself Kat might have left to protect her mother and daughter. Problem was, the more I learned of the Serrano family dynamics, the more certain I became that Kat would have warned them of the danger.

I rambled on. "Assuming those two trucks have something to do with Kat's disappearance, what do you think about us reporting the damage to the Bobcat? We could mention seeing the two trucks. Problem is, we probably don't want to mention you shooting at them, and officially, I'm still deputized, which means I should have called all this in hours ago."

She reached around and retrieved a camera with a telephoto lens. "That house of cards won't stand in a summer's breeze. I got pictures of three guys and their plates."

"I didn't realize you were a Nikon person, too."

"The difference is you buy yours, and I get mine from Uncle Sam. I prefer Canon, but I can't argue that black lenses make more sense than those white barrels of Canon. Back to business, check the pictures. Recognize any of them?"

I did not.

"Then answer me this: how did they know to wait for you in Amasa at that arts academy camp?"

Good question. "I didn't tell anyone I was bringing Valeria to the camp. Someone must have read my note outside the trailer and knew enough about Valeria to piece it together."

"Or," Niki said, "they saw the note, didn't know who it was, lay in wait, spotted her in your truck, and followed."

"Not directly, though. They waited for help and drove straight to my place."

"Which means they figured out who you are. I could ID you from your plate. How did they?"

"Maybe they asked Kim Belanger, the Amasa Summer Arts Academy owner? She's pretty protective of information, though. But the other kids all know who Valeria's best friend is."

Niki chewed on her bottom lip. "Meaning one of the guys has a kid at the camp? That's a stretch."

"Agreed. I'll call Kim and apologize for not telling her the girls weren't coming today and inform her they'll also be absent tomorrow. I'll slip the question into the conversation."

Niki rubbed her buzz cut. "You really should consider getting all the civilians the hell out of here and report the mother missing. Since the Iron County Sheriff's department is small and Kat worked across lines, they'd most likely call in the Bureau. They're good at missing persons."

"I gave my word I wouldn't."

"So we convince Nana."

"Feel free. Problem is, if we hide Valeria and Nana somewhere and report Kat missing, the first question is why are you reporting this and where's the family. I can't imagine your former associates at the FBI would take it well if I told them, 'Don't worry, I have the daughter and grandmother in a safe place, but you can't talk to them.' No—"

Her deep chuckle silenced me. "Got it. But I'm telling you, Seamus, if we don't figure this out PDQ, Nana will face two ugly alternatives. She sticks to her guns, stays until she learns what happened to Kat, and risks being exposed and deported as an illegal alien. She loses Valeria to the system. Two, she tries to find somewhere to raise Valeria when she doesn't even have a green card."

I agreed Nana was between the proverbial rock and a hard place. "Then we'd better discover what happened."

Twenty-Six

KIM PICKED UP MY PHONE call on the second ring and turned the table on me. "Any news on Kat?" I said I was not aware of any change and asked whether anyone had asked about Kat or Valeria.

"No one's asked about Kat. Some kids wondered where Megan and Valeria were."

"But no adults asked about Valeria?"

"Why would they? What's going on?"

Kat had trusted Kim enough to share that Kat was a Dreamer. I took a chance and told her someone had threatened the Serrano family.

"That's terrible. Are Valeria and her grandmother okay?"

"For now, but the kids won't be returning to the academy. Let's leave it at that." I hung up.

Niki patted my arm. "Good try, Seamus. I will ask you a question that you will answer yes. Got it?"

"Yes."

She swatted me. "Not that question, you jerk. This one: did the assholes in the trucks act like they might be part of a local militia?" She waved her hand to indicate I was to respond.

I squinched my face to let her appreciate I didn't understand what she was up to and dutifully answered, "Yes."

She pulled up a secure encrypted browser on her phone and entered a website I recognized as the one only five of us had access to: Niki, me, an FBI agent nicknamed Rick the Prick, FBI Deputy Director Ambrose, and Averell Harrington Park, the Assistant Director of National Intelligence. She typed a message for Park's eyes only but showed it to me before she hit send.

CI identified three suspects in a new domestic terrorist cell. Permission to use Rembrandt to identify.

"Rembrandt?" I asked.

"A super secret database and facial recognition software system. Not only can it identify most of the people in the US, it maps eighteen months of the target's whereabouts."

"Meaning what?"

"Any interactions with law enforcement reported to the federal government. License renewal, court cases. Social Media posts or tags with time or location stamps. I don't know what all else they access."

"Ignoring whether your *confidential informant* had his head up his ass when he said yes, isn't spying on Americans illegal?"

"National Director of Intelligence has authority to approve. If he wants to add information to the database from credit card purchases, bank account records, *et cetera*, he must get a special court order. I'm not asking for that."

"You know I contribute to the Southern Poverty Law Center, Amnesty International, ADL, and a bunch of other groups like that, right?"

"Yep. And I also know you are harboring an illegal immigrant and you've lied to local, state, and federal law enforcement. You and Rick the Prick are my cutouts to give Deputy Director Ambrose and ADNI Park deniability for my undercover operations. It's not like you're a virgin here."

I held up my hands in surrender. "I trust you, Niki. How long 'til we get answers?"

"Tomorrow, if they're in there. Hello, what do we have here?" She pulled binocs to her eyes and scanned the road. "Is this the GMC? It's pulling a trailer. Grab the camera and go take pictures. Don't let them see you."

I waited until they had passed before racing to the road. Using a tree as a blind, I took a series of shots as the truck and empty trailer pulled away. The brake lights flashed. I froze. Had they spotted me? The brakes released. Must have been slowing for a pothole.

Niki and I reviewed my images. Niki spotted red tape covering a hole in the trailer's right rear brake light. I didn't recall that detail from the trail camera pictures, but felt pressure to act. "I should alert Bartelle. If he has someone close to Amasa, maybe the officer can pull them over for a safety check."

"You do that," Niki said, "and you definitely can't *ever* tell him about the two trucks and what they did to your Bobcat."

It hit me. "Because even if I could come up with an excuse for delaying until now, I would certainly mention it when I reported this. I gotta call this in. Bartelle deputized me on this. I can't let—"

"So call."

I chose Sheriff Bartelle's personal cellphone number rather than going through the hassle of calling the office and having to bring someone up to speed.

"Lon," I said, "this might be nothing, but earlier today Niki—" *Oh crap, I hadn't meant to say her name.* "You remember the undercover FBI agent from years ago?"

"Of course, I do. Who could forget? Niki was like her childhood dog, right? What was her real name?"

Not my place to tell him. "She saw a silver GMC pulling a trailer with a big side-by-side UTV going north on the A Grade past Shank Lake Road earlier today. Just now, we spotted the truck returning toward Amasa with an empty trailer. Someone used red tape to repair the trailer's right taillight. Did any of the trail cam pictures of those guys stealing generators and propane tanks show anything similar?"

"Give me a sec." He put me on hold for two minutes. "Dispatch says we don't have anyone who can get to Amasa before that trailer reaches the highway. But yes, that was a detail we did not release to the public. Thanks for the heads-up, Seamus. What's Special Agent . . ." He continued after I didn't supply her name. "What's she doing up there?"

"A brief vacation to clear her head."

"Tell her that if it's a working vacation, I'd appreciate a heads-up."

"Nothing like that."

"Good. Why don't you make another circuit of the trail cams in your area and check for overnight activity?"

I should have ignored the receptionist and left the damn deputy badge on his desk. I agreed—how could I not without raising questions?—and ended the call.

Niki had a shit-eating grin on her face. "Oh yeah, just a brief head-clearing vacation. Score another one for white lies in the cause of justice."

Twenty-Seven

TUESDAY ARRIVED WITH MEGAN CALLING outside our tent, "Grampa Seamus, Niki. Time for breakfast."

"Be there in a minute," I said. I eased Niki's leg off mine. "We overslept," I whispered and kissed her neck.

"Amazing how well I sleep after a fine roll in the hay. So much for seconds." She whipped the sleeping bag off us. "Oh good, not broken. We can do this again." She rolled away, and we donned clothes and exited the tent to discover the sun scraping the tops of the trees. The air was moist with fog, no fire. Five-thirty, for Pete's sake.

"Grampa Seamus, are you going to find Valeria's mother today?"

Nothing like the focus of a kid.

"She had nightmares and was crying for her Mama during the night. I didn't know what to do and pretended like I didn't hear."

I squeezed Megan's shoulders and realized she was a coiled spring. "It's hard to know the right thing. Sometimes the best we can do is listen. It's not like you can understand exactly what she's going through, but you could imagine how bad you'd feel if your mother disappeared."

She could.

"Tell her that and give her a hug. I don't know if we'll find her mom, but we'll try. Won't we, Niki."

Niki knelt and looked Megan in the eye. "I heard your grandfather pinkie swore with you."

Megan grinned.

"Then that's your answer, isn't it? You two hired him, and I have every confidence he will do everything in his power to find Valeria's mother. I have something for Valeria to keep." She pulled a nickel-sized stone from her pocket. "Know what this is?"

Megan did not.

"It's pink granite. Your Grandmother Elisabeth told your Grampa Seamus that his pinkie swear was as solid as granite. It's not indestructible, but it withstands a lot of pressure. Give that to her to keep as a reminder.

I see Nana is about to start the fire. Maybe you and Valeria can help gather wood?"

Megan held the rock like a talisman and ran to Valeria.

I offered Niki a hand to stand. "You remembered me telling you that, and you thought to find a piece of granite? You'd make some child a wonderful mother."

"Oh, hell no. Nieces and nephews are more family than I desire."

"No ticking clock?"

She looked at me speculatively. "What, you want another kid?"

I tripped on a rock. That was the farthest thing from my mind.

"I see the answer is no. Then let's agree we never have to have this conversation again." She called to Nana in Spanish, and the buzz saw I had fired up marched away.

I'd bet good money Niki had been asking herself the exact question I had posed.

BREAKFAST CLEANUP COMPLETE, NANA REFUSED help washing the dishes. I sent the kids to catch dinner from the pier. Megan loved fishing and was a pro at baiting hooks and dehooking ones she caught. Megan raced toward the lake, raising the dead for a square mile with her whoops and hollers. Halfway there, she stopped and galloped back to take Valeria's arm and help her to the dock.

Niki declined to join me in fulfilling my promise to Bartelle to check the trail cameras around the lake. She wanted to run the portable generator, set up a satellite internet link, and download material Rembrandt developed based on her photographs.

"I'll kick on the generator for you. When I get back, we'll take the offensive and shake things up. Let's meet Mike Crenshaw and take his measure. He could prove helpful—or a danger. I assume you brought your supply of undercover disguises."

Twenty-Eight

NIKI AND I CHOSE ONE of the obscure tracks to drive the ATV from Lake Tranquility to my house. While Niki pulled together the supplies she wanted for this trip, I watched the road from the upstairs bathroom window to make sure no company surprised us.

"Ready?" she called up the stairs. For her outfit she chose short shorts, open-toed sandals, and a flowered bikini, covered by a sheer top that displayed her six-pack. A shoulder-length brown wig with purple highlights hid her clipped hair. She'd made up her eyes to look big and startled. She flashed her hand to show off an engagement ring with a rock the size of a softball.

"That's what you're wearing?" I shook my head at my inept way of phrasing my question. "The mosquitoes will love you."

"You said you planned to approach Crenshaw as fellow land barons. He has a trophy wife. You, my dear Seamus—" She batted her mascaraed eyelashes "—have a trophy fiancée. Don't you agree?"

Choose your words carefully, Seamus. "How much did that engagement ring set me back?"

"A quarter million at a Sotheby's auction."

"I went to an auction?"

A grin crept onto her face. "Well, a minion bought it for you."

"I sure can't tell the difference between diamonds and zircon or whatever those fake diamonds are."

She reached past me and scraped the ring down the edge of the bathroom window, leaving a scratch. "No, you can't. It's undercover bling I wear at high-end parties where I act as the dumb escort on the arm of some rich guy. Surveillance subjects talk freely in Mandarin because escorts are eye candy, not smart enough to understand their language. Try this on."

She handed me a shorter-haired blond wig. "It's just to get us out of the woods. You want to surprise Crenshaw, right? That means if those guys are working for him, we need to slip past, so they can't warn him. And if they don't work for him, we don't want to bring a tail to his house. We'll take my rental, but that won't do any good if someone recognizes you. Find an old pair of glasses with a different look. And put on a hat. You can return to your normal charming self before we meet Crenshaw."

"A quarter million? Really? They let you just keep it?"

"The diamond used to belong to a Mexican cartel until the DEA seized it. Sotheby's is a cover story. One more thing. You need to wear my ankle holster." She shimmied her hands down her bare legs. "I obviously can't, but I do not want to be far from a weapon."

"I don't have a concealed carry permit."

"So don't get caught. Let's go, Mr. Sugar Daddy. Time's a-wasting."

WE DID NOT SEE ANY suspicious vehicles during our drive to Valeria's trailer. Someone made finding my trail camera easy. They had tied orange logging tape to nearby branches to mark it. Huh. At least they didn't steal it. Maybe they thought it would transmit their location if they did?

I discovered another trail camera strapped low on a black cherry tree. Niki gave me a pair of evidence gloves, and I swapped its memory card with one of mine, slipping theirs into an evidence envelope. With the disguises, makeup kit, weapons arsenal, and evidence kits, it was little wonder she used an SUV to travel. There may have been more trail cams, but we agreed the risk of having our pictures taken outweighed whatever we might discover from their memory cards.

I left Niki in her SUV for my stop at the Iron County Sheriff's office. Bartelle was out, but Tex was there. I reported my morning survey of the Shank Lake area trail cameras and returned the deputy badge. He tried to get me to keep it, but I held firm and escaped before he pressed for my reasons.

While driving to Mike Crenshaw's place, Niki asked what it was I hoped to accomplish with this visit.

"He owns the two places we know where Kat worked, and maybe had something to do with the third. What better way to find out if he's feeling guilty than to observe his reaction when we show up at his door? If he knows me, don't you think he'll show surprise, give himself away?"

She tapped her lips like she was considering the idea. "And if he's not home?"

"He will be." At her skeptical head tilt, I added, "Irish intuition."

Twenty-Nine

THE GATE TO HIS ESTATE stood open. A good start. His half-mile driveway wound past fields planted in corn on one side and canola on the other. I caught myself licking my lips. Nerves. Niki patted my leg. "Just be your charming self."

The garage doors were closed, an older John Deere tractor, bucket resting on the ground, stood in front of the barn. The windows on the house were open to the gentle breeze and mid-seventies temperatures.

I helped Niki from the passenger seat. Like besotted love birds, we linked fingers and swung our arms on our walk to the house. Mrs. Crenshaw met us with a smile and a "Help ya?"

She wore a crop top a size too small. Her bleached hair was strategically messy, designed to make you think she'd just come from bed or wanted to take you there. Her stretch pants hugged stick legs, a wide belt drew attention to her pelvis. Unlike Niki, who was solid muscle, this woman bordered on anorexic. Whether she kept her weight low by starving or drugs, I wouldn't bet. I widened my eyes with feigned interest because she would expect that reaction. While I was sizing her up, she gave Niki the once-over.

"We were driving in the area, and I hoped to catch Mr. Crenshaw."

"Does he know you, Mister . . . ?"

Good. He was home. I dropped Niki's hand like a dead fish and offered mine to Mrs. Crenshaw, along with a big smile. "McCree, Seamus McCree. I'm interested in talking to him about some land. Won't take but a couple of minutes."

She didn't shake my hand so much as allow a touch. From inside the house came the rumble of a voice scratched by years of tobacco smoke. "Who is it, Bunny?"

I called past her, "Seamus McCree, Mr. Crenshaw. I hoped to steal a minute of your time to talk about our mutual interest in land. If my proposition intrigues you, we can discuss details later at your convenience."

He appeared behind her shoulder, a suntanned face carved by fault lines. His smile, a knife slash over his square chin. His gravestone eyes performed a CAT scan of my upper half. A big man, maybe an inch taller than my six-two, he had a broad chest and massive arms furred with gray hair. He offered a hand with the distinctive tanning of a lefty who plays a lot of golf. "It's Mike. Heard you're buying up land in Iron and Baraga."

His handshake was solid, with no extra pressure to show me he was the stronger of us. My immediate reaction was relief that I was meeting him as myself. He'd lay bare any act I tried to put on. I hoped he couldn't see through Niki's.

He released my hand. "Still have big northern in Shank Lake?"

So he knew where I lived. I assured him my fishing neighbors said the pike were plentiful. "Not a good year for perch, though."

"I got some time now. Bunny, why don't you give the little lady a cocktail on the veranda while Seamus and I talk business in my study? I was about to get something to wet my whistle. What's your poison?"

Not a time to ask for a glass of wine. "Beer would be great."

"Follow me."

Bunny stepped aside. He led me into a country kitchen, opened the refrigerator, and pointed to a shelf of beer. Miller Lite outnumbered the other choices two to one. Not my favorite, but likely his, so I chose a Lite and twisted off the top. He pointed under the sink for the trash can. I'd guessed right. He grabbed a Lite and drank from the bottle.

He led me through a living room dominated by dead animal heads, down a hallway into a dark-paneled office that featured a burl-wood desk, which I admired. "Had that made from a sugar maple I found on my land." He pointed to a pair of two-seater couches framing a coffee table. "Grab a seat. Did you have a particular property in mind?"

No idle chit chat with this guy. "I've been acquiring land to leave something for my granddaughter. The U.P. forest tracts are being chopped up, and I wish to keep the open space that brought me here. I donate the development rights to assure it stays the way we love it—and I get the tax deduction."

He chuckled at that. Good start, one businessman talking to another.

"My long-term plan is to improve the woods to combine sustainable timber harvests while increasing plant diversity. Probably too much information. I wanted you to know that if you ever considered selling, I'm interested in buying. For now, I'm adding land only in northern Iron, southern Baraga, and the southwest sections of Marquette County."

He took a long pull of the Lite, and those captivating eyes held mine like a tractor beam until I blinked and looked away. He set the bottle down. "That's interesting. I couldn't tempt you to buy a motel in Iron Mountain, could I? Good cash flow, recently updated. Wants a better manager than my son."

I used drinking beer to cover my surprise at the non sequitur. "Not his thing?"

"I'm a nuts and bolts kind of guy. He's developed all kinds of package deals for the resort, but the motel is too mundane for him. I'd be willing to price it based on current cash flow and share what we were doing before I put him in charge. Maybe add that to a few sections in Iron and Baraga?"

I matched his earlier pull on the bottle. "Only way I could do that is if I had a buyer for the motel lined up. I have zero interest in learning that business. Especially now. Getting workers must be tough."

His wave dismissed my concern. "Not if you know where to look, but I hear you." He drained his beer and set it down on the coffee table. "Well, keep your eyes open for someone interested in a motel, and I know we can make a deal."

I finished my beer and placed the dead soldier next to his, making sure not to let his eyes capture mine. "I appreciate your time, Mr. Crenshaw."

"It's Mike. If I'm willing to tell you that my son sucks at managing the motel, you can call me Mike, don't you think? Let's rescue the girls from each other before they tear themselves apart with their kindness."

Thirty

Knowing Crenshaw was watching us walk to the SUV, I maintained my possessive fiancé role and tucked my hand in Niki's rear pocket.

She wiggled her butt, leaned in, and nibbled my ear. "Having fun, are we?"

I kept my voice quiet. "All for show."

"Yeah. A bulge in your jeans says otherwise." She laughed and twisted away from me, slapping my hand. "I'll give you a show." She ducked herself under my arm.

Ruh-roh. Niki had an exhibitionist streak and a devil-may-care attitude. "Remember, we might have to deal with him again."

"Seamus, would you put the sunroof down? I think I'll work on my tan."

I assisted her into the passenger seat. By the time I got in on the driver's side, she had removed the sheer top and was arching her back in a stretch, fingers locked behind her head. I turned on the engine and opened the sunroof. Niki unfastened her bikini and tossed it and the top behind the seat, giving Crenshaw a fine view of her firm breasts. She lowered the seatback and stretched out with the sun caressing her.

"Drive, Seamus. And lick the drool off your chin."

I stopped before Crenshaw's driveway reached the street. "Better get decent."

"I must be losing it if you're not planning to jump my bones."

"Such a sick attempt to solicit compliments. Learn anything from Bunny?"

Niki retrieved her clothes from the rear and dressed. "Close the damn sunroof. I don't want to lose my wig in the wind. Bunny's Bloody Mary was high on vodka, low on tomato juice. She either has the metabolism of a shrew or she's doing drugs."

"Her eyes looked fine to me. She could be anorexic or bulimic."

"Could be. She'd be disappointed that you were looking at her eyes and not her rack. She's originally from Illinois. Hates winter. Is not fond of the U.P. Loves the yacht crowd in Naples and can't wait for their return at the end of August. Her mouth smiled a lot. Never made it to her eyes. I would not turn my back on that woman. On a brighter note, she wanted to know if we were 'friendly' with other couples. You into wife-swapping?"

She cut her eyes toward me and laughed at my raised eyebrows. "Not leaping at that opportunity? I told her you were a prude and left her the impression I was up for other possibilities."

I related my discussion. "You don't trust Bunny, and the hair on my neck tingled every time I caught Mike's eyes. That's a scary combination. You up for a visit to his resort on the Menominee river?"

She browsed their website on her phone. "Strikes me more like a party than a family place. I'm dressed fine. What's your cover story?"

"Party place? Somewhere Kat might dress up for fancy entertaining? Cover story—how about we're shopping for a place to hold my bachelor party?"

"Oh, you handsome devil you, and you plan to talk to the manager while the little lady is not in earshot. Well, that might get you thrown out on your ear."

"Bet?"

"Sure. You win, I'm on top."

"So now who's the horny one? And if you win?"

"I'm still on top. Twice."

THIRTY-ONE

THE MENOMINEE RAPIDS RESORT INCORPORATED a main building, a maintenance area, and twelve "rustic" cabins.

An overly endowed barmaid gave us a tour. I wondered if Mike Crenshaw had hired her. The main building housed reception in the middle, the public dining area on the left, a taproom on the right and through it, a separate private room that could accommodate a couple dozen folks. Tour complete, she led us to the office.

Randy, as he introduced himself, was not impressive. He was golfer tan, several inches shorter than his father with none of his old man's solidity. At thirty, he had gone to flab.

Rather than walking to the cabins set a quarter mile from the main building, Randy insisted we use a golf cart. The cabins fit the definition of rustic only in their exterior rough-cut half logs. The inside had hardwood floors with underfloor heating, wide-board pine walls and ceilings, and a cedar-lined sauna. In the one we toured (the guest was rafting today, a friend of Randy's who wouldn't mind if we took a quick peek), a real bearskin rug had pride of place before a crackling wood fireplace that provided a whiff of woods smoke. A stocked bar featured premium beers and liquors. A massive flat-screened TV with satellite hookup covered most of a wall, with a love seat and two recliners providing the viewing spots and access to an entertainment center. "Just got Starlink," Randy bragged. "Faster internet than in town."

The single bedroom had enough room to walk around a king-sized bed. Mirrors covered one wall. A skylight above the bed allowed for star gazing or, as I discovered when I twisted a knob, converted into ceiling mirrors for viewing other delights. Randy gave me a wink. *Really?*

The bathroom was the same size as the bedroom and provided a two-person jacuzzi that looked onto the river if you raised the blinds, and a shower with two showerheads and grab bars strategically placed for non-cleansing activities.

Niki oohed and aahed her way from room to room, squeezing my arm at each new discovery, shooting me lustful looks. Given our earlier conversation, I wasn't sure how much was acting. Since Randy had to show us an occupied room, I assumed there were no vacancies and risked asking if they had a room available for tonight. Alas, they were booked until after Labor Day.

"Hey honey," I said, "want to check their fire ring and barbecue pit?" Niki wiggled her ass out the door. "So," I tried to sound conspiratorial, "do you ever book the entire resort, like for a bachelor party?"

His wide smile grew wider. "When were you looking at?"

"Next year. Sometime around bird season. Ten, twelve of us."

His smile faded. "Well, we haven't started taking reservations, so it's wide open. We'd have to insist on a minimum three-day stay, and at that time of year, our residents typically book guide services, that sort of thing."

"We were thinking four or five days. Time to do some hunting, some fishing, run the river." I thought he would pee his pants. Time to jiggle the line and hope he grabbed the bait. "Do you supply entertainment or is that something we'll have to arrange ourselves? Hunting and fishing are better without female company, but you know, a little dance-band combo to go with a little dancing." No bites yet. I dropped more chum into the water. "And no one wants to waste water showering by themselves." I gave a shrug. Like what could you say?

He could respond that they did nothing of the kind. Instead, he rubbed his hands like he was already feeling the money. "We'd reserve the private dining room for your group. The band is no problem. We have an arrangement with an escort service to supply dinner companions. The main area is family friendly, but what happens in the cabins is between consenting adults. Once we determine what add-ons you want, we'll require a fifty-percent deposit. The rest paid a month before the event. That does *not* include tips." He flashed a shit-eating grin. "Our escorts prefer their tips to reflect the services they provide."

I knew his kind from Wall Street. Hookers were not a problem, and for the right fee, I suspected nothing else was either for this guy. Making money was all that counted. I would not want to stand between him and a dime lying in the gutter. Niki burst in, glowing with excitement. "I'm so pissed you guys found this first. Randy," she drew out his name. "Do you have any sister facilities I could use for a girls' weekend?"

The minuet played out with our good buddy Randy buying us a beer at the bar, ogling Niki whenever he thought I wasn't looking. I apologized that I couldn't commit today. We had one place to visit in North Dakota, where we could combine elk hunting with other activities. I promised to talk with him before I decided. And Niki hinted she'd be the one talking to Randy if I chose North Dakota. He gave us both brochures and his business card. Written on the back of mine was his private phone number to "continue our discussions to make sure we fully satisfy your guests."

On our exit, Niki surreptitiously used her phone to photograph all the visible vehicles and their license plates. No gray Tundras or silver GMCs, jacked-up Silverados or rusted Ford Rangers with different colored doors. I asked which car she figured was Randy's.

"The blaze orange Caddy Blackwing. Not prime for U.P. winters, but it's the only vehicle registered to him."

I did not ask how she had learned that. "He strikes me as sleazy. I wanted to wipe my hand on my pants after we shook. He bears investigation."

Niki drove away from the resort. "Have you asked yourself why he works in Iron Mountain but lives in Iron River? While we know he's here, let's pay his house a visit."

"You think we're going to find Kat's truck parked in his garage?"

"Doubt it, but who knows what we'll learn until we get there?"

Thirty-Two

RANDY CRENSHAW'S HOME WAS AT the edge of what locals still called Stambaugh two decades after it and Mineral Hills had both merged with the city of Iron River, making it the most populous city in the county. During the last decade, Iron River's population had shrunk six percent to 2,800, leaving a lot of scars.

A screen of planted evergreens shielded his vinyl-sided split level from its neighbors. One story in the front, its rear showed two stories overlooking a patch of woods. No vehicles in the driveway. A two-car garage featured a solid garage door and a pedestrian door with a clear window at the top. Not what I'd want if I were hiding something in my garage. Occupying the half-acre yard were a few mature trees and a metal swing-set with twin worn tracks under the swings. At the edge of the yard stood a solitary outbuilding, large enough to store a ride-on mower and a few tools—or act as a crude prison.

My quick online search had found no marriages, but that didn't mean he didn't have a girlfriend or children to explain the kids' equipment.

We pulled into the driveway. Niki ambled up the concrete walk to the front door and rang the bell, prepared to ask about children in the neighborhood and the house for sale down the block. I sidled to the garage and peeked in the window. Crammed to the gills, leaving barely enough room to fit his car.

We saw nothing unusual through the house windows and called into the storage shed. A scared robin flew off her nest under the roof, squawking in protest. A bust. Nothing suggested Kat had ever been here.

On the way home, we picked up crutches to replace the heavy branch Nana had crafted for Valeria, a block of ice to use on Valeria's ankle, fresh veggies and salad makings, and worms at Luckey's Sports Shop for the kids to drown or catch fish as luck determined. On the first straight section of Shank Lake Road, we set up the trail camera I had retrieved from the road to Valeria's trailer. Creeks and marshes created a pinch point, assuring that if someone planned to get to my camp or Lake Tranquility using Shank Lake Road, they had to pass that spot.

I asked Niki, on a scale of one to ten, how productive she thought the day was.

"A solid three. Could have been a four of five if I'd gotten laid this morning."

"Still time." I waggled my eyebrows.

"Not if you want ice, not water, to put on Valeria's ankle."

Thirty-Three

WE CHECKED TRAIL CAMS NEAR my house on the way in. Nothing had passed while we were gone. Niki again stored her rental SUV behind the garage. We took separate ATVs to Lake Tranquility to provide more flexibility. Besides the supplies we brought from town, I grabbed two decks of cards and a cribbage board.

"Let's strategize about tomorrow," I said. "I plan to take the kids on an ATV ride and in the process create tracks all up and down Lukes Road to obscure the ones into Lake Tranquility."

"Smart, but every time we go to town is one more chance for them to spot us and follow us to Lake Tranquility."

I granted that. "But Nana won't leave until she knows what happened to her daughter. On a scale of one to ten, with ten being severe danger and one being minimal, what do you think our current risk is?"

"What's this with the number quizzes?" She squinted one eye and tilted her head. "Another three. But it could go up in a hurry. After we get back, I'll check to see if Rembrandt made any matches. That may inform our plans. After dinner you entertain the kids—you're better at that than I am—and I'll have a woman-to-woman conversation with Nana. Even though she's a grandmother, I'll bet she's only a few years older than me."

I gave Niki a look of confusion. "She looks older even than me."

"She's had a much harder life. Regardless, you represent authority to her. I bet I can do better."

"Plus, you speak fluent Spanish, and I need a translator." And not to mention this eliminates you discovering that the kids love doing stuff with you.

I led the ATVs to the third, most western, approach to Lake Tranquility from Lukes Road. To get there required crossing corporate forest properties before looping south and east to enter Megan's land through another locked gate—the only green one I owned.

We found everything fine at the camp. Nana had skinned and filleted the perch. She sat on a stump, carving a stick of wood. Megan was reading her Kindle to Valeria, who was icing her ankle.

Niki handed Nana the groceries and slipped away to learn what Rembrandt had found.

"Look what I got you, Valeria." I held up the crutches. "How's your ankle? May I look?"

She unwrapped the dishtowel, spilling a few remaining chips of ice onto the ground. Her face contorted into worry lines.

"We're fine, Valeria. I brought a block of ice. You tell me if it hurts." I poked the purplish swelling and triggered only one "Ooh." Terrific progress. I had forgotten how quickly kids heal. "Have you put any weight on it?"

"Nana said I shouldn't."

I offered a white lie. "That was good advice, but now you have crutches. Make sure you take it easy with them and put only a little weight on that foot. It shouldn't hurt. And when you're not active, still keep your foot raised. Megan may have told you I've had ankle injuries before."

Her eyes grew curious. "Do you really have metal holding your ankle together?"

"You want to feel it?" I removed my boot and sock and twisted my foot to expose an edge of the plate where only a little muscle covered it. "Go ahead. It doesn't hurt."

She was reluctant, but Megan poked it, then lapsed into giggling. Emboldened, Valeria prodded and asked me to rotate my ankle to see how it worked. Both girls' curiosity satisfied, I put one of my clean socks on Valeria's foot and set her up on a blanket near where Nana was starting the evening fire. I should have grabbed more pillows from the house, but I hadn't thought of that. I collapsed two of the camp chairs and used them to support her legs.

"Whatcha reading, Pumpkin?"

"Momma gave me the first Harry Potter. I'm re-reading the beginning for Valeria because she hasn't read it."

I'm no dummy, but I am amazed at how Megan speaks and what she knows compared to me at her age. Some is because of the times. What was X-rated in my day is practically PG these days. But it's more than that, and joy fills me watching her engage with the world. Glass ceilings are higher and more fragile now. Good thing, because I suspect that girl carries a sledgehammer with her. I do not envy anyone who tries to stand in her way.

I heeled away drips at the corners of my eyes. Sentimental Grampa Seamus. Concentrating on something other than Valeria's missing mother gave my subconscious time to work on a plan to determine if the Crenshaws, Randy in particular, were involved in Kat's disappearance.

I had the gray edges of an idea and knew just the person to call to bring it into focus.

Thirty-Four

COLLEEN CARPETTI GREETED MY CALL with, "Elisabeth told me to expect your call. Before I forget, Robert Rand offered me a fifty-thousand-dollar bonus to convince you to come back to Criminal Investigations Group."

Never happen. "His hope springs eternal. You're still enjoying your work?"

"Oh God, yes. I can't believe how fast the time flies. Do you realize it's been nearly five years since we met and discovered I'm your half-sister? I am forever grateful you introduced me to forensic accounting and CIG. I am many, many times happier than if I had stayed with the accounting firm and become a partner."

"That's why—"

"Elisabeth tells me you have Starlink. I can work while my grandniece is at day camp. Grandniece makes me feel so old. Elisabeth said you were worried Megan might need protection. She says you don't have guns. I'm sure I could borrow one from my dad. When—"

I wanted to get in front of this conversation. "Hold on, Colleen. Everything has become much more complicated in the last two days. Let me tell you the story. After, you can decide whether to risk your ass in another of my convoluted messes."

"You can tell me why I should say no, but the answer will still be yes."

Colleen, who had been adopted through private channels, had been delighted to discover she had blood relatives. We have the same mother. Last I knew, Mom had not told Colleen who her father was. I was curious as all get out but had kept my nose out of that. If either wanted to tell me, she would. An only child, Colleen's enthusiasm for her newfound relatives meant she had a tendency to discount the danger. I emphasized that facet of visiting me. The only thing I left out was what went on in my tent with Niki. I ended with, "Questions?"

"Okay, I'm booked on a flight. Leaves Logan tomorrow morning at five twenty-nine and gets into Iron Mountain at nine twenty after a stop in Detroit."

"Wait. Wait. Wait. I need to contact the guy who owns the motel and see if he'll agree to let me have someone review his books. I'll look anxious if I do that tonight. Even tomorrow morning is pushing it."

"Hey, old man. Cool your jets. The first aspect of any forensic audit, as someone I admire once told me, is to understand the business and how one might manipulate it. I'm online now, booking a room. By the time you receive permission for me to talk to them, I'll have done the legwork. Am I correct you think the Silver Fox might be the source of the party girls?"

Using my own words against me wasn't playing fair—but it was playing like a McCree. I needed to keep that in mind. "I have nothing to indicate that. But the Silver Fox is the only business of its kind for many miles around. It wouldn't surprise me if they and the resort share employees or clientele."

"Excellent. I'll introduce myself there as a down-on-her-luck girl who is living off credit cards."

"Colleen, *that* was not what I had in mind."

"Are you implying I'm not attractive enough?"

"I'm saying my mother and my son and my ex-wife, not to mention your adoptive parents, would string me up if I let you take that kind of risk. May I remind you, the reason we're looking into this is because a woman is missing?"

"Hold on. Let me check something. Look at that, would you? My driver's license says I'm thirty-seven. Which means you don't get to tell me what risks I will and will not take. I'm single. No partner. No kids or grandkids. Tell me the truth: don't you want to know if there is a link?"

Of course I did. Talk about the law of unintended consequences. "How about Niki goes with you? It gives you someone to go to the ladies' room with, since women always travel there in pairs."

"Deal. Once I'm settled, I'll call you, and we can agree on a safe place to meet. See you soon, Boomer."

I clasped my hand to my chest. Not that she could see my dramatics. "That hurts. Flap your wings hard to keep the plane up."

I told Niki what I had done.

Niki loved the idea of Colleen reviewing the motel's financials and didn't think Colleen ran any danger by checking out the Silver Fox. "It's not like she's pretending to have experience as an exotic dancer or anything. There's nothing that ties her to you. I'll wear a different disguise from the one I used for the Crenshaws and Bunny. We'll make sure Colleen doesn't ask questions about Kat. Maybe we learn something. Maybe it's a waste of time. But we need leads if we're going to find Kat."

I had no winning arguments and pointed to her computer. "Rembrandt?"

"Two out of three ain't bad. We have a local boy, no arrests, no warrants." She tapped her screen and pulled up a social media picture of Glenn Korpi. I remembered his name from his high school days. He'd been a big-time athlete at West Iron High. Drove logging trucks for a local outfit. Married, no kids. Owned a two-year-old blue Silverado registered to him and his wife. Had she been part of the group who trashed the trailer and called the residents wetback whores?

At my nod, Niki pulled up the second individual's mug shot. "Different kettle of fish with this one. Name is Aaron Rogers. Alias Aaron Robinson. Alias Aaron Riddle. Busted as a teenager for drinking and driving, and dealing dope. He earned several domestic abuse arrests in his early twenties. Last one sent him to prison where during a huge brawl, he stomped a guy to death. Clean since his release eighteen months back."

A shiver hit me when I looked at his mug shot. Hard flat eyes. I could see him as a killer. "Just means no one has caught him."

"Most likely. Last known address was Chicago. No known vehicles registered in his name. Makes me wonder what he's doing up here."

I tapped his mug shot. "How did he link up with Korpi? The third guy's a mystery?"

"I took that photo through a windshield at an oblique angle. Too much distortion for Rembrandt to make a match. Rogers/Robinson/Riddle isn't big enough to hit the FBI's database of known associates. And we have the fourth guy, who we never got a look at, let alone a picture."

"Okay, we got an asshole from Chicago working with a local boy. I assume Korpi is still local?"

Niki referred to her computer. "Dude is an Instagram nut. I've got him renting a house in Iron River in Randy Crenshaw's neighborhood. Korpi loves hunting, fishing, trapping. One interesting change. Several months ago, his social media feeds stopped showing other people. Now he's all scenery and fish."

"You think that's when he hooked up with Rogers and/or the Mystery Man? Assume it is. How do you think we should proceed?"

"While you do your grandfather thing with the girls, I'll help Nana clean up from dinner and try to convince her the best way to learn what happened to her daughter is to let us contact the police. It's been what?—five days since Kat and her truck disappeared. That trail is getting cold."

"Good. If you understand the root of Nana's worries, we can figure out how to address it. I sense a big part of her thinks Kat is dead and fears the government will deport her and take Valeria away."

"You're a good man, Seamus McCree, but in this fight, even that may not be enough."

Thirty-Five

THE NIGHT WAS CLEAR AND cool enough that I wore another layer to prevent goosebumps. Megan begged me to take her and Valeria onto Lake Tranquility to see the Milky Way, spot satellites, and maybe catch a shooting star.

Sometimes Megan's requests to stargaze were an excuse to delay her bedtime. Her father had used the same pretext as a kid. I aided and abetted, eager to let them view night skies with so little light pollution you could believe that, if you were only a foot taller, your fingers would touch the necklace of the Milky Way. If it distracted Valeria from missing her mother, they could stay awake until dawn.

The girls lay in the cocoon of sleeping bags and blankets I made at the bottom of the skiff. I sat in the stern and rowed into the lake.

Megan pointed Valeria to the W of Cassiopeia. They worked together to locate the Big and Little Dippers. Cepheus was the only other constellation I could find. I couldn't remember the Greek mythology surrounding it. Besides, it's not all that impressive. I gave the girls a break from Grampa Seamus education and let them ooh and aah at the satellites that streamed overhead.

I zoned out from their chatter and considered Niki's report of her conversation with Nana. In the week before she had disappeared, Kat had grown more worried and remote. Nana thought Kat's distress was caused by something more serious than the everyday worries all Dreamers had, despised by one political party, ignored by the other, and used by both to score points. Nana believed Kat was dead. If her daughter were alive, she would have contacted her family. She was certain that if the police knew Kat was missing, they would rip Valeria from her arms and put Nana on a plane to the drug-torn countryside of Nicaragua, from which they had fled many years ago.

Niki had nailed Nana's age. She was sixteen when Kat was born. Married at eighteen, the family slipped across the border into the US. A roundup at a meat-processing plant ensnared Nana's husband, resulting in his deportation. An uncle later reported the drug cartel had killed him because he refused to be their mule.

Nana had remained under the radar, using a fake Social Security card and a legal individual taxpayer identification number to pay federal taxes. Kat graduated from high school, attended college, fell in love with another Dreamer, and got pregnant. Catholics, they would not consider an abortion and were married in a simple church wedding. Kat quit college to earn money to take care of Valeria, named for her husband's mother who'd drowned crossing the Rio Grande.

Kat's husband had a good job lined up as an engineer for an automaker but made the mistake of celebrating with friends and getting nailed for OWI. ICE was on a mission to deport everyone they could and kicked him into Mexico within a week. Kat sent him money to hire a coyote to sneak him back into the US. The coyote left him to die in an Arizona desert. A rancher found him. ICE deported him again. Kat heard once from him in Mexico. Silence for the last year.

Their close relatives were dead or missing. Valeria probably had cousins still in Nicaragua, but Nana didn't know for sure. Nana knew families where Immigration had deported the mother for a minor crime and deported the grandmother when she tried to gain custody of the child. She believed that if the police searched for Kat and found she had done *anything* illegal, no matter how small, they would deport her.

How could Niki or I argue against Nana's justified fears? I might make a different decision, but that was not the point. Nothing we could say could give her peace of mind. We had no sanctuary to offer.

All those galaxies and stars and orbiting planets, and yet on this blue orb we call home, Nana had no safe place. I had to ditch that train of thought, or I would slip down depression's siliconed slope.

I focused on bright Venus, which stared back, unblinking. My watch said we'd been on the lake for three-quarters of an hour. The kids would sleep in the boat if I let them. I'd give them another fifteen minutes before I brought them in and sent them to their tent.

A minute later, Niki's shrill whistle sounded over the water. "Seamus," she yelled, "your trail camera just sent a photo of a side-by-side towing a big trailer running down Shank Lake Road."

THIRTY-SIX

NIKI MET US AT THE dock and lit our way in with a headlamp. I lifted Valeria to Niki, steadied the boat for Megan and asked her to help carry bedding. The girls did not utter a sound. The intruders had spoiled the tranquility of the lake's sky viewing, and I wanted to wring their necks.

We tucked the kids in and planted kisses on their foreheads. Niki handed Nana a rifle and provided rapid-fire instructions that had her looking determined.

I threw on a vest to counteract a chill caused by anger and nerves. As Niki strapped two rifles across her chest, I prodded her for a plan.

"Depends on what they do. If we see them on Lukes Road, I want you to lead them on a merry chase away from here and somewhere we can ambush them."

My face must have projected my alarm at the thought of her shooting guys because they were chasing us. She flicked my scalp with her fingers. "To make them stop and identify themselves, you dumbass, not to kill them."

Why had that not been my initial assumption? "I have a couple of spots in mind."

"If we don't see them or their tracks on Lukes, we'll assume they're going to your place and follow them on Shank Lake Road. Whatever happens, follow my lead."

The trails from Lake Tranquility looked different at night. Twice at intersections, I had to slow to get my bearings. We lost more time unlocking and locking the gate behind us. Niki ground her teeth so hard when I fumbled the gate lock, I could hear them. Tough, I thought. I will not permit anyone easy access to Megan, Valeria, and Nana.

We blasted down Lukes Road, past the rock barrier, and all the way to Shank Lake Road, where two sets of fresh tracks ran toward my place.

Niki doused her ATV's headlights and shouted for me to do the same. "We'll see theirs before they see ours."

"Maybe," I said. "No way they won't hear us."

"I'm counting on that."

Say what?

She putt-putted a quarter of a mile to a straight section of road and pulled her ATV into the woods on the right. She pointed me to the left. I followed her example of leaving the engine running and ran across the road to her in a crouch.

"Plan?"

She released the safety on her rifle. "Forty-five minutes until we have decent night vision. We wait. If they are anywhere on the lake, they'll hear our ATVs."

Ah-ha. She wanted the psychological pressure on them of knowing someone was around. "You giving me the other gun?"

"Have you stopped shaking yet?"

I held out my hand. Almost steady.

She checked the load on the second gun. "You willing to shoot it?"

"If they fire first."

She handed me the rifle, reminded me how to disengage the safety. "Keep in mind, I have the easy part. I get to kill them after they perforate you when you tell them to stop."

THIRTY-SEVEN

AN HOUR LATER, WE MOUNTED our ATVs and crawled forward, following their tracks. As we approached Ned Lake Road, I crossed my fingers that they had gone that way. They had not. Nor were they stopped at the next two camps before mine. I motioned for Niki to stop. "Isn't it safer for us to park and walk in to check on my camp?"

She agreed, and we tucked the ATVs down one of the many trails crisscrossing my property and walked in using what I called the ridge trail—my son and I had constructed it years ago running along a ridge that paralleled the lake and was never more than five hundred feet from the road.

We kept low to avoid presenting a target above the horizon and jogged the trail. My heart raced much faster than the exercise justified, and I cautioned myself to remain calm and not react if I found people taking or destroying my property. I did not like even the *idea* of carrying the rifle because in the heat of the moment, it was too easy to use it and become prosecution, jury, judge, and executioner.

And yet, my parents had taught me to stand up against the bullies of the world. These days, adult bullies relied on semiautomatic weapons. All my life, I had refused to own a gun. Despite that, I had used one to defend myself or others more than once. I mentally slapped my head. *Pay attention to where you're running and leave the angels-on-pinhead discussions to the theologians.*

The trail ended at the guest cabin driveway. We reached the cabin, having heard and seen nothing. As it became more likely my place was not under attack, my anxiety dropped several notches. I motioned for Niki to follow me to the hill overlooking my house.

Everything quiet. While Niki remained on top of the hill, I clambered down and checked the doors. Buttoned up tight.

That left the camps at the foot of the lake. One part of my brain argued that since my neighbors weren't around, any crimes being committed were only property crimes. Bartelle would tell me to stay away and check the camps in the morning and call in anything I found.

Years before, I had suffered the mental anguish of having my Cincinnati property destroyed. If we proceeded, we might prevent my neighbors' experiencing that sense of psychological loss of no longer feeling safe that comes with a break-in. My parents had instilled in me before I could walk the philosophy that "If not me, who? If not now, when?"

Niki would support whatever decision I made, but her training made her prefer stopping the crooks—if that's what they were—I didn't know for sure.

Our eyes had adjusted to the dark, and we had no difficulty following their tracks down and around the foot of the lake. Before we reached the outlet, I led us off-road, and we parked the ATVs behind a short rise screened by a growth of balsam fir.

I quietly let her know the layout of the camp and that the road would reach a pinch point where a bridge spanned the outlet creek. We could follow the road, which kept to high ground, or cut into the woods beyond the bridge and work through an area that, although dry this time of year, flooded in the spring, leaving holes and root tangles to navigate.

A barred owl hooted from a nearby tree. Its mate responded, and soon a pair farther down the lake joined the chorus. We used their caterwauling to cover our footsteps and followed the road across the bridge. Niki stopped and crouched without warning. I nearly plowed into her.

Silent as a stalking cat, she flowed from her crouch to lying flat on the ground. I did the same and saw the reason for her actions: a headlamp shone from the far side of a pole barn building. Its glare exposed a massive guy—Niki's hirsute bear—holding what looked like an automatic rifle. He paced near the camp's 500-gallon propane tank.

He had to be close to seven feet tall, had a barrel chest, and weighed 350 pounds. My mouth went dry. Any physical tussle with these guys would not go well for us. If he even got a paw on me, I was in trouble. I checked Niki's reaction. If she was feeling the same fear as me, it didn't show.

Nature's conductor signaled the cut-off, and the two pairs of barred owls silenced their verbal duel. The headlight moved toward the giant, the crunch of gravel marking his progress. Part way there, he said, "Nothing at that other camp. You finish filling the tanks?" The baritone voice had a local accent, but not someone I recognized.

"One twenty-pounder left, but there's not enough pressure. You hear those engines? Sounded like two four-wheelers. Stopped not far away."

"Huh. I thought it was you turning the trailer around. Well, whatever. Let's load these suckers and get the hell outta here."

The four-wheeler's headlight flicked on, displaying a dozen 20-pound propane tanks and four 100-pounders. That's how they transported so much stuff: they piled their stolen goods on the same trailer as the four-wheeler. My recollection was this camp kept one or two twenty-pounders for their grill. They never had a hundred-pounder and ran their generator using propane from a 500-gallon tank. The thieves were stealing propane from that tank to fill the portables.

Given current propane prices and the cost of the portable tanks, the total theft had to exceed $1,000—the minimum loss in Michigan to justify a citizen's arrest. Walking up and politely asking them to submit to arrest was not an option. The more armed people they thought we had, the less likely they'd choose to fight. And we had to catch them with their hands full of something other than automatic weapons.

Thirty-Eight

As though acting on my mental suggestion, the big guy set his gun down, picked up a hundred-pounder like it was a cigar, and carried it to the front of the trailer. The second guy used both hands to tip another tank and spin its bottom on the ground. It would never get better than this. I let the smaller one get halfway up the ramp and yelled, "Stay where you are. Let us see your hands."

The smaller guy fumbled the cylinder but held on. The giant put both hands on the trailer rail as though he planned to jump off. Niki fired a round over their heads. "Next one goes into those tanks, and you can roast in hell. Get on the ground. Now!"

I pointed my rifle in their direction. My rapid breathing and the adrenaline coursing through my body made it hard to keep the gun steady. The whole fire-a-bullet-into-a-propane-tank-and-make-it-explode was overhyped. I knew it, did they? What am I to do if they made a break for it? We should have agreed on a plan.

I sucked in a lungful of air and held it.

Niki barked out, "Now, assholes."

Whether these two were less sanguine about their chances of burning to death than I, or Niki's command voice and shot over their heads scared them, they lay face down on the ground and on Niki's order, spread their arms and legs.

"I have them covered," Niki said in a quiet voice that wouldn't carry to the men. "Move far enough away so these assholes can't hear you and call Iron County dispatch. Don't mention me. Okay?"

It wasn't a question. I ducked behind the pole barn building to shield my voice and report I had under control two suspects caught stealing propane. I guessed the dispatcher knew my name and thought I was acting as a deputy. She recorded my detailed directions to get to the scene and kept me on the line as she contacted the available cars. A state trooper was closest. He would arrive in forty minutes. Iron County deputies were at a two-car accident with injuries. She was alerting an on-call deputy. Be an hour-plus for him.

Figuring Niki would prefer to tie the guys up—at least their legs—I found an old piece of rope hanging on a game hoist and another piece underneath the cabin's deck.

Niki laughed at my offered rope and directed me to retrieve four zip-ties from her backpack. "Do the beanpole first. I don't want him to escape if the bear tries something. Make them tight, but not too tight."

I knew what too tight felt like on me, but what did that mean when I was the one putting them on someone else?

The bear turned his head to look at me. "If you know what's good for you, you'll keep the propane and let us go free."

"Shut up, douchebag," the beanpole yelled.

Beanpole gave me a wicked grin. He may have been thin, but his arms were corded with muscles. I secured his wrists first, fearing his arms more than his legs, and made sure the ties were plenty tight. Then I zip-tied his ankles. As I approached the bear, Niki moved closer to us and changed her angle. She laid down her rifle and pointed her pistol at his head.

"You're right," she said. "You think when my partner gets close enough you can grab him or knock him down with a leg kick and use him as a hostage. And you can."

What the hell? I stopped five feet away on wobbly legs.

"Thing is. It's the last thing you'll do." Her voice had the edge of sharpened steel. "Tasers are for pussies. You so much as twitch, and I will put a slug in your skull. Your buddy won't testify because I'll gun him down and claim he was trying to escape. No jury will convict me." She let loose a maniacal laugh that put a shiver down my back. She nodded me over to him. "Truss him up like a pig. Wish I had an apple to shove into his mouth."

Niki sounded so feral, so wicked, if I had been the bear, I would have pissed myself. I formed the zip-tie into a loop and approached from his side, eliminating the possibility of him butting me with the back of his head or whip-kicking me. His hands were the size of catcher's mitts and pressed hard into his back. Menace flowed off him like steam from boiling maple sap. I loosened the zip-tie loop, leaving only enough tail to pull it tight. Even with that adjustment, I had to get him to lift his hands to lasso them.

"Keep your hands together and lift them off your back."

The bear snorted and grabbed his shirt, making it hopeless for me to secure him without wrestling his hands. Trained police might know how to overcome his tactics. I could try to pry his arms up, but unless I could keep them up, how could I tie him? An idea popped into my brain. Make him think I was crazy, too.

"Listen asshole, raise your damn hands or I'll kick you in the head and do what I want. Your thick head won't stand up to my steel-toed boots and a soccer kick that made me a pro." I walked around to where he could see me and practiced taking corner kicks. "Make your choice."

Beanpole yelled. "You can't do that."

I backed up a dozen paces and began my sprint.

Thirty-Nine

I'D TAKEN THREE STEPS WHEN the bear raised his arms over his back. The extra distance I'd given myself was for show and to give him time to stop me, so I kept coming until he screamed his submission. I broke off my attack and secured his hands, which were shaking. He offered no resistance when I tied his feet. A guy that big had maybe never been in a position where he was helpless.

"Okay guys," Niki said. "Let me read you your rights." Niki recited the version of the Miranda statement I assumed she learned in FBI training. "You have enough stolen stuff to warrant a felony charge. For you, I have a limited time offer. Tell us who you work with and where you're cooking the meth, and we'll recommend the prosecutor knocks it down to a misdemeanor. With your cooperation, you'll get a suspended sentence. Worst, a little community service."

"Don't say anything," the beanpole said. "We'll bail out before breakfast."

Niki continued like she hadn't heard him. "Don't talk, and once we take down the operation, we'll consider you full partners. Fifteen to twenty years for manufacture and distribution. Probably get out in ten if you behave yourselves and don't leave feet first with a shiv in your neck. The State guys won't agree to this. That means you need to deal with us before they get here and take charge of the scene."

She waited. I don't know whether she wanted to discover if they would start talking or arguing between themselves or if she wanted pressure to build. I kept switching my headlamp from one of them to the other. Partly, I wanted to gauge their reactions. I also wanted to make it difficult for them to learn what Niki looked like. I guessed them for early twenties. The big guy looked like he would crap his pants. The beanpole looked at ease. They didn't bother to deny they were cooking meth.

Niki broke the silence. "It could be worse, I suppose. You don't tell us anything and after we nail the leaders, they decide you ratted them out. No reason for us to protect you then. Probably end up in the same prison.

Normally, we'd separate you two. I'd talk to one. My partner would talk to the other. We'd compare stories. We might lie and tell you the other one was spilling their guts even if they weren't. But I can tell you guys are too sophisticated for that kind of bullshit."

She clucked her tongue. "If you talk to each other, we'll separate you. Once you're separate, only the first one who talks gets my deal. Half an hour until the state trooper gets here. That's your window. My friend is going to document your crime with his cellphone, but I'll be right here if you decide to save your asses."

To my surprise, they remained quiet. I shot photos of each propane tank, the tubing and gauges they used to siphon the fuel from the 500-gallon tank, the side-by-side, and close-ups of their faces.

With time available until the police came, I figured I'd collect my ATVs. I sidled to Niki and explained my plan quietly to prevent the culprits from overhearing.

"Here's the thing," she said. "I do not want any personal publicity. Before the state trooper gets here, I'll fade into the woods. I'll leave you a rifle to make it look good. Since I don't want the trooper to hear me leave, I'll walk to your house and take the spare ATV to Lake Tranquility. That means you need to bring your ride here. While you're at it, hide the ATV I used somewhere they won't find it. You and I can pick it up tomorrow."

"And what am I supposed to say if the guys mention a woman reading them their rights?"

"I doubt they'll say anything. Someone has scared the bejesus out of them, and it's not either of us. If they do, suggest they get tested for psychedelics. You've got a fast mouth, you'll come up with something. I'll talk to Bartelle tomorrow—well, later today. You'd better get going."

I stored the ATV Niki had used at the next camp, which was less than a quarter mile away. On the way to ditching that four-wheeler, I thought better of collecting my ATV. If I was supposed to be alone, how could I have collected it and kept the crooks under guard?

Lying is such hard work. All I wanted was to hand the miscreants to the pros and curl up and sleep. Never having performed a citizen's arrest, I didn't know how much paperwork was involved. A lot, I'd bet, and I had to make the details hang together. Oh joy.

We heard the faint sounds of an engine a mile or more away. Niki pecked my cheek. "That's my cue. Do not provide any personal information if those guys can hear. Their lawyers, who they will talk to, might work for whoever runs the operation. The bosses might decide to take revenge."

I hadn't considered that minor detail.

FORTY

LATER THAT NIGHT, TWO CARS from Iron County—guys I recognized but had never worked closely with—joined the state trooper's car, flooding the crime scene with their headlights. I kept out of the professionals' way while they verified the thieves had not broken into any camp buildings. I answered questions and avoided using the word "we."

Because I could not say for sure which propane tanks belonged to this camp, they would need to contact the owner to go over everything with Tex, who would perform the official crime scene investigation the next morning. One sheriff's deputy stayed behind to secure the scene.

After four hours, they told me I could go home. "Tex will pick you up and bring you here. Be ready by seven."

The fresh air smacking my face on the ATV ride home woke me up. I unlocked the chain to my driveway and realized I might want a handy reason to explain my locked driveway if any of the police officers had noticed—more lies to anticipate and remember.

The eastern sky was lightening, and the first robins were already cheerily singing. I wasn't sure whether I'd be more alert if I grabbed a cat nap or toughed it out until Tex showed up. I chugged a pint of water to stave off a dehydration headache. Then I had to pee and decided I was up for the duration.

Tex found me sawing wood, slumped in a rocking chair on my screened porch. "I gotta say, McCree, I am impressed you nabbed these guys. When did you start toting a gun?"

Tex knew I had not owned guns in the past. This conversation was a slippery slope I did not wish to take. "Have the guys talked? They didn't say boo to me."

"Lawyers don't get up this early. Hop in. You can catch me up on the way down to the crime scene."

"I need caffeine. Let me grab a soda, and I'll catch up on my ATV. That way, once we finish talking, I can come home and grab some proper sleep. You know your way?"

He had directions, and I avoided the first bullet. Temporarily.

Diet Dr Pepper in hand, I caught up to Tex and followed him to the crime scene. The deputy guarding the scene got out of his car and started swatting mosquitoes. He informed Tex he'd had no visitors and left. Tex had me walk the perimeter of the crime scene with him. "Did you see them siphoning the propane?"

"Nope. Heard them saying there wasn't enough pressure in the big tank to fill the last twenty-pounder." I pointed to the empty small tank.

"Guess I should check the other camps around here, too," Tex said in a weary voice.

My stomach clenched. He'd find the ATV Niki had used the previous night. "Can I do it for you while you process the scene?"

He pointed to the tubing and tools the guys had used to create the siphon. "Thought I'd dust those for prints. If these two aren't the only ones stealing propane, we might get lucky. Yeah, you could save me time and check those camps. Don't touch anything, okay? Leave anything that looks suspicious for me."

I felt like I had won the lottery. Not only did it get me away from Tex's questions, I had a police-sanctioned reason to run over the ATV tracks I had left last night while hiding the other four-wheeler.

I confirmed no break-ins had occurred at those camps. My cellphone rang while I was returning to report to Tex. Colleen Carpetti on the display. I checked my watch. She wasn't supposed to get into Iron Mountain for another hour-plus. I answered with, "Something happen?"

"We're in Detroit, ready to board our flight. Someone wants to talk to you. Just a sec."

I was too tired for games. She must have run into someone who knew us both. A voice I'd known all my life said, "Surprise."

Forty-One

"CAT GOT YOUR TONGUE?" MY mother asked at my lack of response.

Then, I figured it out. At 83, my mother no longer took part in darts tournaments, but she was still a star at charity events, entertaining folks with the story of her life and taking on all comers at darts. She often traveled and must have run into Colleen in Detroit. "What charity are you helping this time? And are you coming or going?"

She released a hurricane of air. "I'm coming to see you, Seamus. How many times have you wanted me to see this place? Colleen told me she was helping you with an audit, and I figured it was the perfect opportunity."

And Colleen didn't talk you out of it? "What did Colleen tell you?"

"Nothing. She's as surprised as you are. I was talking with Elisabeth—you know, your ex-wife—and she was saying you were looking for help caring for my one and only great grandchild, and that Colleen had mentioned she was taking the first flight in the morning. I booked myself on the same one. When you picked up Colleen, *ta-da*, I'd be a surprise bonus. Colleen got on the plane later than me and was closer to the front. She didn't even know until she saw me at the gate here in Detroit. She insisted I call you. Apparently I didn't bring you up right, and you weren't planning on meeting her."

I did a quick count to ten, not that I couldn't have used more time to get control of myself, but if I didn't say something, she'd fill the silence—and to my detriment. Sometimes I wished my mother would return to her self-imposed muteness that had kept her institutionalized for decades. Not really. I loved this feisty mom, but sometimes I could throttle her.

"Here's the thing, Mom. We're not at home and Colleen wasn't coming to the lake. It's complicated." I waited out a boarding announcement before continuing. "Book a room for tonight in the same motel Colleen is staying at. You'll have to pretend you just met her. Colleen will fill you in."

"I see." Her disappointment dripped down the line. "I have an open ticket. I can go back today if it's too much of a bother."

My Jewish friends have claimed that no one can lay on guilt better than a Jewish mother. I'd be willing to enter Mom into that competition. "Mom, get a room. We'll make it work. And even though it doesn't sound like it, I'm pleased that you wanted to surprise me." A thought tried to surface, but I couldn't grasp it. "Could you give me back to Colleen, please?"

I expected some sort of acknowledgment from my mother, but the next I heard was Colleen chuckling into the phone. "It was on speaker. I got to see a side of our mother I had not experienced. I'll make it look like she was expecting someone to meet her at the airport—no acting necessary there—and offer to give her a lift in my rental. Maybe you and I should get together sooner rather than later. I leave that up to you. I'll call once we're in the motel. I got to say, being part of the McCree clan ain't dull."

McCree—that's what had been bothering me. "Mom needs to pay cash and not use her real name. We don't want anyone named McCree appearing on their guest register."

"Good you thought of that. I'll hit an ATM in town."

I verbally gave Colleen my thanks and silently extended her my prayers.

Forty-Two

WITH MOM'S SHENANIGANS, I ABANDONED any thoughts I'd had of catching a few Zs. After reporting to Tex that all was well at the neighboring camps, he gave me permission to leave. They'd write up their notes and ask me to sign them or make corrections in the next couple of days. I drove the ATV to Lake Tranquility. Breakfast dishes were drying on damp dishtowels.

Megan heard me arrive and came squealing up from the lake. "Grampa Seamus. We're training an eagle."

I must not have heard that right. I killed the engine and asked her to slow down and enunciate her words. Wrong again, I had heard it correctly. She grabbed my hand and leaned her entire weight, pulling me toward the pier. Megan had devoured the *How to Train Your Dragon* boxed set I had given her. I figured she and Valeria had combined their imaginations.

I should have known better.

As we approached, I heard the high chirping calls from a pair of eagles who had a nest across the lake. They had fledged a single bird but were still at the stage where they were its primary providers. We often saw one, two, or all three fishing the nearby lakes.

"I got one," Valeria called from the lake.

Megan ran ahead of me, helped Valeria unhook the fish. Megan grabbed the perch by the tail, gave her hand a quick flip, and whapped its head against the cedar planking of the pier. Okay, that wasn't how I stunned them, but it worked. Megan helped Valeria stand and settle on her crutches. Megan laid the fish near the end of the pier, grabbed the fishing pole, and followed Valeria onto land.

"We hide there," Megan pointed to a massive hemlock that had blown down decades earlier and was well on its way to becoming a nurse tree. Hiding was not accurate. They used the downed log to lean against. "Watch."

I asked what I was watching for.

Her shush would wake the dead. "It doesn't work if you aren't quiet."

I sat down and jerked awake from falling asleep. I forced my eyes wide and, to stay awake, kept track of all the animals I could hear or see. Megan's bald eagles, chickadees, a nuthatch—not sure if red-breasted or white-breasted—robins, a least chipmunk exploring my boot, purple finch, goldfinch, two chattering red squirrels in a chase, the plink of a downy woodpecker, a white-throated sparrow scratching in last year's moldering leaves.

Valeria tensed. I followed her gaze and watched an adult eagle at least five years old, its head and tail pure white, glide on bomber wings from across the lake toward us. It banked, wings and tail feathers flaring to brake its flight, and dropped onto the edge of the pier. It hopped like a crow, grabbed the fish with its talons, and jumped into the air. Its wings pressed against the air in audible whooshes, wingtips touched the water once, leaving expanding circles in its wake. Two more struggling beats, and it was up and cruising away from us.

I did not move a millimeter, not wanting to spoil whatever was keeping the kids statue still. They waited to clap and cheer until the eagle landed in a massive white pine. Megan stuck two fingers in her mouth and produced a major league whistle.

I hugged the girls, making sure I didn't bump Valeria's ankle. "How did you guys figure that out?"

"Yesterday," Megan said, "Nana called for us to come eat. We accidentally left a fish on the dock and saw the eagle grab it." She slid me a look. "Pier. You told me. Piers stay in the water, docks come out for winter. We did a science experiment and left one on purpose. The fish have to be keepers. They won't come for the little ones."

The eagle is training the kids. "Now *that's* a science experiment. How many fish has it taken?"

They traded looks. Valeria answered. "That was five. It was the fastest ever. Let's do it again."

"That is extra special." I ruffled their heads. They spun away from my hug, and I steadied Valeria. "I'd love to get a video of that. Right now, I want to peek at Valeria's ankle. How's it feeling, hon?"

I boosted her onto the hemlock log, rolled her pant leg up past her knee, and removed her sock. The purple was fading to putrid yellow-green. The swelling was lower, and when I squeezed her ankle, she said it hurt only a little.

While putting her sock on, I noticed a red rash on her calf. It was warm to the touch, and on closer inspection, she had the classic bullseye suggesting Lyme's disease caused by a deer-tick bite. I asked her if she had recently pulled off a tick.

"Momma found a baby one before she—" Valeria stifled a sob.

"Can you describe its back or the color of its legs?"

She shook her head. No reason to question her further. Given the bullseye and that it was a "baby" tick—meaning smaller than a typical wood tick—I figured it was a good bet she did have Lyme's.

If so, Valeria needed to undertake a multiple-week course of antibiotics to prevent the disease from getting into her joints, heart muscle, and nervous system where, like chicken pox, it could hide for decades and return with debilitating effects. I helped her put her sock on. "We need to show this to Nana." The kids objected—they had to catch another fish for the eagle before it flew away.

"Tell you what, how about Megan catches fish while Valeria and I talk with Nana? It won't take long. She can join you for the next eagle flight. You'll record it, right?" I handed Megan my cellphone. "Be careful with that."

I suspected the compromise worked only because it was Megan's turn to catch the fish. Valeria didn't want me to carry her even if it meant she could play with eagles sooner and insisted on crutching to the fire ring area. My kind of kid. I called for Niki and Nana.

Niki saw us and hopped off the swing she'd been pushing back and forth with her feet. "Neat trick the girls have, isn't it? You look like something the cat barfed up. Did you get any sleep?"

I hooked her arm, and we walked a few paces away from Valeria. "Did Nana agree we could report Kat missing?"

"Kat hasn't ever been away this long. Nana's heart tells her she has lost her daughter. Even though she might be right, I told her someone could be holding Kat, and if Kat had any chance, we had to find her soon. I know she understood me, but her fear of losing Valeria is too great. I pressed her just a little to ask what she would do if Kat were dead. She thinks she'll have to take Valeria to a place she knows where the meat-packing plants help people get fake documents. But she's not there yet. Maybe we should talk to the people at the motel again."

"There are two complications. My mother surprised me with a spur-of-the-moment visit." I related what had happened.

Niki snickered. "Yep, that's a complication. What else?"

I informed her of Valeria's bullseye tick bite. "I can't let that go. There must be somewhere that will treat her without reporting Nana, right?"

Confusion painted Niki's face. "Why would they even care?"

"Because she's a minor and they have forms, and they need payment. The issue isn't the money, it's the paper trail. In a tight community, the wrong people could hear." I pointed to Nana's approach. "Wish me luck that Valeria's tick bite is enough to change Nana's mind."

Forty-Three

I USED VALERIA'S LEG FOR show and tell, then sent her to play with Megan. I explained, cajoled, pleaded. Niki translated and added her own pleas. Nana would not budge.

Despite my frustration and lack of sleep, a little voice of reason told me I had no right to judge or feel put upon or anything else. I had not walked a single step in Nana's shoes. Being a white male citizen with money gave me privileges that made it impossible for me to appreciate her position.

I was out of my element and overwhelmed with uncertainty. Nana's fearful expressions and handwringing showed the situation also stressed her. If they had been Christian Scientists who rely on prayer for healing, what right would I have to impose my beliefs on them? Unlike smallpox or polio, where vaccinations are required for the wider community to be safe, no one would catch Lyme's disease from Valeria. She alone would suffer the consequences of Nana's decision to avoid the medical community.

Yet the consequences of doing nothing for the kid could be severe and long-lasting. I would not impose my values, but the only way I could live with myself was if I removed every obstacle I could to Nana changing her mind.

"Niki, don't over-promise, but tell Nana that I will do everything in my power to make sure Valeria stays with her. I'll hire the country's best immigration lawyers. Faith communities exist that provide sanctuary for illegal immigrants. If that's what she wants, I will find her sanctuary. Valeria's rights as a US citizen will help with this."

I released a long breath before verbalizing my thoughts. "I know Nana believes she can not have any dealings with the police or with health officials. I will take that on for her. Whenever Megan stays with me, her parents give me a signed document giving me parental rights in their absence. I'll create one for Valeria that models Megan's. I can say the mother left her with me while she was gone."

Niki shook her head, but I bulled over her potential objections. "I know it's totally illegal. I can not live with myself if I don't do everything I can, legal or not, to get Valeria the medical attention she needs."

Niki scowled. "We're not talking a little misdemeanor, Seamus. These are felonies that could put you in prison for years, decades."

"Tell her what I said." My voice came out rock hard. I softened it. "Please."

In the end, whatever Niki told Nana partially won the day. Nana would not leave, but I could take Valeria to a clinic. A mixture of elation and dread filled me. I had won, but at what cost?

Forty-Four

THE EARLIEST APPOINTMENT I COULD get at the urgent care clinic in Crystal Falls was 1:30 that afternoon. I left everyone else at Lake Tranquility and used back ways to return to my house, where I constructed a document to give me temporary parental rights. Not knowing Kat's signature, I scrawled Katrina Serrano and an illegible date at the bottom.

I enjoyed a quick shower, put on town clothes, and patted my pack to confirm I had my phone. I couldn't feel it. I dumped the pack's contents onto the table, confirmed the phone wasn't there. Then shit-for-brains remembered he had given it to Megan to record her eagle training.

I threw everything in the pack, raced the ATV to Lake Tranquility, retrieved my phone from Megan—first she had to show me her eagle-fish-snatching video. Niki and I transported the kids to the house. I piled them into the F-150 and prayed I didn't get stuck behind a logging truck on the way in because if I did, I'd be late.

"Okay girls. It is really, really, really important we have our story straight. Valeria, why are you staying with Megan and me?"

"My Nana broke her hip, and my Mama had to take care of her."

"And . . ."

"Mama asked you to keep me because I was already spending the weekend with Megan."

"Have you talked with her since she left?"

She shook her head.

"Because . . ."

"I don't know her telephone number."

"Right, and I didn't think to trade numbers with her." Or ask Kim for it, or take the girls to the Amasa Summer Arts Academy where they'd met, or done a thousand other things a reasonable person would do in a similar situation. Fingers crossed, no one would think to ask those questions.

FORTY-FIVE

AT THE CLINIC, THE RECEPTIONIST gave us surgical masks to replace our cloth ones and handed me several forms to complete before we could see the nurse practitioner. Valeria wasn't a lot of help. She didn't know what allergies she had—I scrawled none known. I used my address, put down my name as the responsible party, considered adding something about Valeria's mom coming in next week with insurance information, and caught myself. This family had no insurance other than whatever Medicaid provided—and maybe not even that.

I turned in the clipboard and played paper, scissors, rock with the girls while we waited. The longer we waited, the more nervous I became about what would happen next. I'd had to leave so many lines on the form incomplete. Would they even see her? The kids had a blast beating the stuffing out of me because I couldn't concentrate.

"Valery Sea-ran-io?"

The receptionist mangled the name, and I didn't realize she had called Valeria until my charge snagged my hand and pulled me out of the chair. Rules being rules, Megan had to stay in the waiting room with a wailing baby while I accompanied Valeria as she crutched into the examination room. The nurse practitioner knocked on the door and entered. "Didn't they tell you the X-ray tech isn't in on Wednesday afternoons?"

"That's not what we're here for. Valeria has a tick-bite bullseye on her left calf. She has no other symptoms of Lyme's disease." I boosted Valeria onto the examining table and pulled off her sock.

The nurse unwrapped the ace bandage. "How did this happen Valeria?"

"I was running away and fell."

"What were you running away from?"

Ice froze my heart. We had not discussed the ankle because I had been thinking only of the Lyme's disease, not the whole of Valeria as a medical professional would do.

Tears filled her eyes. No doubt she was reliving the attack at her trailer, her missing mother, our escape. I had better come up with something fast. "No one's mad at you for jumping with Megan when you weren't supposed to. I'm not, and your mom won't be either."

Valeria nodded and blessedly said nothing.

The nurse gave me a side glance I couldn't interpret. "The ankle looks okay, although I can't be sure without an x-ray. You wrapped it?"

"I had experience from playing soccer years ago." That sounded lame to my ear. "I was a professional until an ankle injury ended my career."

"Huh." She turned her attention to Valeria's calf. "Yep, classic bullseye. You're the third one this week. Did you pull off a little tick?"

"Mama did." A sheen filled her eyes. She snuggled her nose into the bear attached to her wrist. The dread of impending disaster filled my core.

The nurse rewrapped the ace bandage. "When was this, Valeria?"

I cleared my throat to invent something plausible. The nurse ignored me and handed Valeria a tissue. "What's wrong, sweetie?"

"I miss my mama."

The nurse pulled a cellphone from her pocket. "Let's call her and see if she remembers exactly when the tick bit you."

Valeria stared at her feet. "I can't," she blubbered.

I wanted to feed her our practiced line and hoped against hope she would think of it on her own.

"Why not?" The nurse's voice sounded sharper.

She looked up at me, her mouth a grim line. "Because she's missing. Grampa Seamus says—"

Her cutoff left the nurse giving me the stink eye. "You're her grandfather? What is this girl's mother's name and number?" Her cellphone came alive with the press of her finger.

"Grampa Seamus isn't my grampa."

I talked over Valeria. "I'm the grandfather of Valeria's friend, who is sitting outside. Valeria's grandmother fell and broke her hip. We'd planned for Valeria to spend the weekend with my granddaughter, Megan. Kat asked if I could take care of Valeria until she returned. I said sure."

I rushed on, keeping the nurse's attention on me, not Valeria, who was shaking her head. "My own kids give me *in loco parentis* for Megan. I made up one for Kat to sign. But in the rush, I neglected to get her telephone number and Valeria doesn't remember it."

The nurse positioned herself between Valeria and me. "Do you feel safe?"

In a cracked voice, Valeria said, "No."

The nurse dialed 9-1-1 and asked for an officer to investigate a "situation with a man and a young unrelated girl that does not sit right."

For Valeria's sake, defuse the situation. I settled on the chair farthest from Valeria and crossed my legs. "Can I ask my granddaughter to join us? This is taking longer than expected, and I suspect the girls will both feel better if they're together."

While that was true, I also hoped the kids' demonstrating their friendship would de-escalate the situation.

The nurse jumped at the chance to separate me from Valeria. "I'll put the girls in another room while we wait."

"Great." I pulled a coloring book from my backpack. "Valeria, do you want to color? I have books and pencils, or would you rather Megan read more of the Harry Potter?"

She preferred to color, and I watched the nurse lead her into the room across the hall and wait until Megan joined her. The nurse propped the door open and positioned herself to watch both the kids and me.

Keep acting like nothing is a problem. "Could you call in the script to the local pharmacy? I appreciate your caution, but given the delay, I'd prefer not to have the kids wait a long time for us to collect the prescription." Mr. Cool Calm Collected on the outside presenting the air of imperturbability had acid burning a hole in his stomach.

To have any chance of keeping Valeria with us and away from Child Services, or whatever they called it here, I had to stick to my story and hope Megan's presence would buck up Valeria so she could get her part straight. With any luck, the deputy who answered the call would know me, which would give me a leg up in escaping this mess.

Forty-Six

A Crystal Falls City police officer who didn't know me from Adam arrived with a professionally dressed woman—late twenties, early thirties. They talked in hushed tones with the nurse before the three split up. The nurse bustled into another patient room. The woman entered the room with the kids, gave me a hard stare, and shut the door with an ominous click. The officer adjusted his service belt—another inauspicious sign—and joined me.

I handed the guy my ID and the forged document that "gave" me permission to handle Valeria's medical issues. He asked if I had the same for Megan, and I provided it to him. He weaved between three questions: how Valeria came to stay with me, why I had no way to contact her mother, and whether anyone could verify my story.

Then he posed a question I had not anticipated. "Would it be okay if I called one of Megan's parents and verified that they gave you permission to have her with you?"

"I'm fine with that, but they're rafting down the Colorado River, and I believe incommunicado. I can give you the name of the outfitters. Maybe they have a way to reach their guide. If nothing else, they should be able to confirm my son and daughter-in-law are on the trip."

I pulled up the outfitter's website on my phone. The officer copied their main number and made the call without bothering to step outside. From his side of the conversation, it was clear he had no luck contacting Megan's parents. The officer said, "And I am to understand that you require a court order to verify Patrick McCree and Cynthia Nelson are on one of your rafting tours?"

"I know I'm their emergency contact," I said. "Tell them it's an emergency and you need to get in touch with that contact."

The officer gave me a thumbs up, repeated the request, and wrote the information in his pocket notebook. He disconnected, dialed a number, and the phone in my hand rang. "That, at least, checks out. Please wait here. I'll be back, Mr. McCree."

Those words did not reassure me. Twenty minutes that felt like twenty hours passed before the officer returned. "I have a few additional questions. Where did the girls meet?"

"The Amasa Summer Creative Arts Academy. I signed Megan up to let her spend time with kids her age and not be stuck with her grandpa twenty-four/seven." Please, please, don't ask for Kim Belanger's name and call her because she'll tell you Valeria's mother is missing.

"Where have you been staying with the kids?"

Given he asked that question, I assumed the kids had mentioned they were camping. "Most recently, we've been camping on land I own. The kids have enjoyed sleeping in a tent and fishing." An idea struck me. I opened the video storage on my phone. "And they're training an eagle to retrieve fish they leave for it. Have you ever heard of such a thing?"

He watched the video and watched it again. The great distraction would work for only so long. "I know you must be vigilant about kids. I've worked with the Iron County Sheriff's department several times. Talk with Lon, Sheriff Bartelle. He's met my son and can vouch for me."

He stepped from the room. On his return, he seemed more relaxed. "Sorry to take up your time, Mr. McCree. Have a good day."

I got up.

"Oh, and Sheriff Bartelle asked you to please stop by his office. I don't think it's a request you want to ignore."

Forty-Seven

PRESCRIPTION FILLED AND STARTED, ICE cream bribe delivered and consumed, I took the kids into the library. The head librarian knew both girls and assured me it was fine to leave them. She didn't care if they browsed the books and borrowed an armful or Megan read the Harry Potter to Valeria. The first unmitigated good news all day.

I left my truck in the rear courthouse parking area and walked to the sheriff's complex. I secured my mask and entered the outer lobby. The door buzzed open, and the receptionist motioned toward Bartelle's office. "You know the way."

I gave his door a polite double tap, walked in, and plunked down on the chair.

"Shut the door, why don't you?"

I closed the door, took two pumps of his antibacterial gel, and rubbed my hands. The office filled with the biting scent of ethanol. "You wanted to see me?"

"Had a pleasant chat about you with my city colleagues. They were afraid you were molesting young children. Where are they? The children, not my colleagues."

"Library, which won't hold them forever. You have my statement ready to review?"

He leaned back, laced his hands behind his head, and stared down his nose. "Only you could construct a statement that's totally true and a crock of shit. How do I know this?"

My gut spasmed like he'd punched me in the solar plexus. *Here it comes.*

He leaned forward, placing both hands on the desk. "You hate guns. Someone who didn't know that would read your statement and think you single-handedly took down those two boys. A careful reading never says you were by yourself. I need the truth, the whole truth, and nothing but the truth before I get the prosecutor to sign off on charges."

He paused. Most people would start talking, but I can do silence like a Trappist monk when I choose.

Lon knew that and gave up that tactic. "Not only would you not use a gun, you wouldn't even *think* to pick up a gun—of which, last I knew, you had none. Plus," he held up a finger, "it is extremely uncharacteristic of you to leave two eight-year-old girls alone at your house or camping, if that's what you were really doing. Which means, not only was someone else at the crime scene, another someone else was watching the kids."

His face wrinkled into a frown. "This smells like skunk fart. It has all the makings of something your undercover agent, Niki—I looked in the files and couldn't turn up her name—would do. Why are you covering for her? So help me God, Seamus, you don't come clean, I'll tell that wet-behind-the-ears City officer I didn't believe your story, and you'll be in a world of hurt."

Busted. "You're right that I didn't lie. And you're also correct that Niki and her guns were there." I leaned toward him and lowered my voice. "I'm sorry I wasn't entirely forthcoming about her. Whatever undercover assignment she's on means her name cannot appear in any paperwork. I could either let those guys get away or live with her conditions. She hopes to catch you later this afternoon to explain. I don't know the whole story, but my guess is someone she's looking at is a law enforcement officer. Rather than speculate, I'll leave it to her to fill you in."

He stiffened at my mention of law enforcement officers. "That's your story? If both of you were there, it still doesn't explain who was taking care of the kids. And you didn't give me her name."

And that investigative expertise, combined with caring about the men and women working for him, is why Bartelle is one of the better cops I know. "Above my pay grade, Lon. Those two talking yet?"

"Nope, and not likely to. They're bailed out. One's mother paid for both."

"You didn't tell me?"

"How's it feel to be kept in the dark?"

A cheap shot, but I was in no position to call him on it. "The side-by-side and trailer?"

"The skinny one paid cash for them a couple of months ago. We have them dead to rights on possession of stolen property, and that's all we have since no one saw them filling the tanks. Prosecutor dangled a plea bargain for information and got nothing."

"Who are they? Any known associates?"

Bartelle rose, telling me the interview was finished. "I look forward to seeing Niki and learning her name. If she can't get here before six, have her call." He handed me a card.

I had bought a little time. Given this conversation with the sheriff, I knew how I was spending the next few hours.

FORTY-EIGHT

MY PLANS DID NOT LAST the drive to camp. The girls were using the bathroom at Tall Pines while I pumped gas. My phone dinged a notification that the Shank Lake Road trail camera had downloaded pictures.

The first two shots of the triptych captured the front and rear end of a jacked-up blue Silverado. The third caught the tailgate of a gray Tundra. Mud obscured the license plates on both trucks.

I texted Niki a warning that the two vehicles were in the area and requested she call me once she had a good signal. My phone buzzed seconds later.

"Well, isn't that special?" Niki said.

"To avoid running into them, I'll use Lukes Road coming in west from the highway to get to Lake Tranquility. Remember the sketchy area where that timber bridge rotted out?" She knew the place. "If I get stuck there, I'll text you and you can come on the two-up and transport us in. They can't get their trucks through those rocks. No four-wheeler in the Tundra, but with the Silverado jacked up, my camera didn't see into its bed. They might have one there."

"Then keep the kids out until they leave. I'll make sure Nana's safe."

Well, that was the obvious answer, and the fact I had not come up with it proved how diminished my brain functions were. "You're right. We'll go meet Mom and Colleen somewhere near Iron Mountain. If it weren't for Nana, I could keep the kids in Iron Mountain at another motel. Better yet, go to Marquette, where no one is looking for them. Ah shit, I'm babbling."

"I'll let you know if they come this way, and your camera will alert you when they leave. Give your mom a hug for me."

Colleen answered my call with, "What's the scoop?"

"The scoop is I have two eight-year-olds bored out of their tree, and the guys we think are searching for Valeria and Nana are sniffing around my woods. Niki is staying to protect Nana. We can't come to your motel because Megan and I have been there—in fact, we shouldn't be together anywhere around Iron Mountain. Let's meet at a walking trail that runs along the river on the Wisconsin side. We can talk while the kids burn off some energy. Let me look it up on my map app."

I found the parking lot for the Menominee River Walking/Cross-Country Skiing trails and gave her directions. "We're an hour away. Your bodies are on Eastern time. Why don't I stop and get food for an early picnic? If we don't find a place to eat there, I know a rest area south of town."

The kids helped me buy supplies for a cold-food picnic and snacks to maintain them until then. I considered buying energy drinks to help me stay awake, decided that was asking for trouble. A six-pack of diet Dr Pepper would keep me sufficiently buzzed to stay on the road.

The map app offered multiple driving routes. I chose one that used county roads and avoided Iron Mountain all together.

Mom and Colleen pulled in three minutes after our arrival. Megan swarmed them and waved Valeria over to make introductions to her Geema, as she had called her great-grandmother since she was two. Valeria turned shy until Mom asked her about her crutches and sprained ankle. Then, in no time, Valeria was showing off her rash and asking my mother if she knew I had a metal plate in my ankle.

While the youngest and oldest were making nice, I edged Colleen aside. "Everything go okay?"

"Not bad, considering our mother does not like anyone to tell her what to do. I'm thinking I may have gotten the best of this whole adoption deal."

I had no clue what that meant and said so.

"Well, my adoptive parents raised me, and they were great. Trudy was in no position to look after me."

True. Back then, Mom couldn't even care for herself.

"But I get her genes. I want to be that active at her age. Look at her. Eighty-three and walks two and a half, three miles a day, lifts weights, does an exercise routine. Sharp mind. Hands steady enough to do darts exhibitions. And feisty enough to tell the world to go—" she glanced at the kids "—tell the world to pound sand if it thinks it can stop her."

"Remember, she had a heart attack five years ago."

"Yep, a wake-up call. Did you remember to contact the seller?"

I tapped the sides of my head with the heels of my hands. "Never crossed my mind. That's how crazy things have been. Let me do that right now."

I used my contacts list to dial Mike Crenshaw's number and put it on speaker. A woman's voice answered. I introduced myself and asked if Mike was around.

"Nope. This is Bunny. He said you were interested in buying some land."

I had not recognized Bunny's voice. "Mrs. Crenshaw? Yes, I am, but I hoped to talk to him about the motel. In Iron Mountain?" I let my voice rise in question. Had he talked with his wife about that, too?

"He'll be pleased to hear that. He's always back from golf in time for his five o'clock cocktail. Let me jot down your number."

I disconnected and said to Colleen, "Let's pry Mom away from the kids, and I'll give you both the scoop on the deep hole I've dug."

Colleen bribed the kids with a movie she streamed on her phone. It had them in stitches, laughing so loud we couldn't talk until we walked further away. I told Mom and Colleen everything: the propane thieves who were out on bail and knew I had instigated their capture, the little we knew of Kat's disappearance and the Crenshaw business practices, Nana's illegal status and her fears for herself and Valeria, along with her unwillingness to engage the police, and her intransigence about remaining until she knew Kat's fate. I closed with the threat by the guys in the Tundra and jacked-up blue Silverado.

The more I talked, the more still my mother became. Her response surprised me. "No one knows how far a mother will go to protect her children."

Did she mean Kat or herself?

"I have to take your word for it," Colleen said. "I assume you have a plan, Seamus. How can we help?"

"The more we flail around, the more dangerous it seems to get. The guys in those two trucks will figure out we haven't left the area. They're hunters. Given time, they'll track us to Lake Tranquility. I feel obligated to keep my charges safe, even if I can't convince them to leave for a sanctuary situation. That means I'm stuck guarding Nana. But I can't do that with Megan around. Mom, will you take Megan with you to Boston? Lizzie can help once you're there."

Mom gave me a skeptical look. "While you do what?"

"Move Valeria and Nana to a safer property I own until I understand Kat's disappearance. While I do that, Colleen and Niki can work the Crenshaw angle. I'll take Megan away if I have to, but—"

"But," Mom said. "You think the new place is safe?"

"If no one sees us going there. That buys time until I have to resupply them. Each trip to the site increases the risk."

A smile lit Mom's face. "That settles it. Move them with enough supplies to last several days. Megan and I will stay with them. You know I can use a gun. That way, you can concentrate on solving the Kat mystery. Maybe as a grandmother and great-grandmother myself, I'll have more luck convincing Nana to listen to your concerns.

Shit, I stepped into that cow pie. "It's rough camping, Mom. Have you ever been camping?"

"Are you suggesting I can't do it?"

I threw up my hands. "Far be it from me to suggest—"

"Then that settles it."

From behind Mom, Colleen rolled her eyes and mouthed, "You are so screwed."

Forty-Nine

WE WERE FINISHING OUR PICNIC dinner when Niki's text arrived: *Trucks found the rocks. Rogers and Korpi looked around and left.*

Ten minutes later, the trail camera sent pictures of both trucks heading out Shank Lake Road. I conferred with Niki by phone. She chortled when I told her how my mother outfoxed me. We agreed Lake Tranquility was safe for one more night, provided I avoided any risk of running into the guys in the trucks. I'd drive north through Republic to M-28, take that to Covington, and drive south on US 141 to catch the western end of Lukes Road.

Colleen took Mom back to the motel to grab her clothes and check out. The trip to Lake Tranquility was uneventful, although I required four-wheel traction to drive across the area on Lukes Road where the wood bridge lay rotting in a stream bed.

The kids were asleep when we arrived. Niki and I carried them to their tent and made sure Valeria took her next dose of antibiotics. We left them to pretend to brush their teeth before crawling into their sleeping bags and letting the frogs lull them to sleep.

We returned to the fire ring to find Nana stoking the fire. Mom rubbed her hands over it while they chatted. Niki joined in their conversation. How much in life had I missed because I'd learned French, not Spanish, in school? Well, Seamus, it's not like you couldn't have fixed that over the last forty years.

The heat relaxed me, and I startled myself awake. "I hate to interrupt," I recognized the irony of my statement. "I am falling asleep on my feet. We need to make plans. Mom, I'll give you my sleeping bag. It's warm enough I can sleep without it. We don't have an extra tent. You can sleep with the kids—they won't mind that you snore like a chainsaw. Or you can inflict your sonorous torture on me, and Niki will share Megan's and Valeria's tent."

Niki was translating for Nana, who interrupted her. "No." She pointed to Mom and herself and rattled off something in Spanish. Niki said, "You're safe. Nana insists the grandmothers will sleep together."

Thank you, Nana. "Now for tomorrow. We have several problems to solve. The rocks stopped Rogers, Korpi, and friends today, but they'll be back tomorrow with a way to move the rocks or drive something around them. Plus, I'll bet Sheriff Bartelle is steamed that Niki didn't show at his office today. He's sure I haven't told him everything, but he knows we're camping on my land. I wouldn't put it past him to systematically check our properties. We need to relocate."

Niki's translation elicited questions from Nana. Her face grew worried at Niki's answers. I waited for a pause and added, "Borders are magic because people don't look across them. The Iron County Sheriff's department's jurisdiction ends at the county line. I have several hundred acres in Baraga that I only recently purchased. Even if Bartelle thought to consult the Baraga County plat book, he'd find the prior owner, not me. He'd have to go to the Baraga County records to find the sale, and he won't do that. A river runs through that property. No bridge. The only way to get to the land on the other side of the river is by boat or wading."

To Mom, I said, "Not too late to make me happy and take Megan to Boston." I could hear porcupine bristles rising. "This is luxury compared to where we're going. You're eighty-three years—"

"Seamus Anslem McCree. I'm well aware of how old I am. I know I'm a city mouse, not a country mouse. But something told me it was time to visit you, and now we know why. I have my medicine and my rosary. If I become a burden, I will take Megan and leave. Until then, you're stuck with me."

Exactly so.

FIFTY

IN MY DREAM, IT WAS the last day of college. One course had a term paper I had forgotten about, and I had to turn it in before midnight or I wouldn't graduate. I struggled to wake from the semiconscious state of knowing I was experiencing a stress dream. Couldn't do it, and now I sweltered in a prison cell with loud noises piped in to torture me.

I blinked my eyes open to light baking the tent and the sounds of kids squealing. My phone claimed it was past ten. With a gazillion things to do today, why had Niki let me waste five hours of daylight sleeping? I pulled on clothes and stumbled out of the tent to discover the camp was packed in the truck or stacked next to it.

Niki stepped from behind my truck. "Rip Van Winkle has arisen from his twenty-year nap. I was considering requesting the coroner."

"Comedy Central is not calling. Where are the others?"

"The kids are playing with their pet eagles. I told them it was their last chance for now because we'll soon have a new adventure. Nana and Trudy are watching them while I finish striking camp."

The two of us confirmed our plan for the day and made quick work of cramming the remaining stuff into the truck. While I drove everyone else to the new spot, Niki would cut through the rocks on the ATV and stop at the house to launder the dirty clothes we had strapped to the four-wheeler. We'd meet back up at my house for the last part of the trip.

Plans in place, truck packed, we allowed the girls to catch a final fish. Megan held the perch up for the eagles to see. The immature eagle launched from its perch, no longer waiting for the kids to hide. The kids had to hustle away before the bird swooped in for its meal.

Niki and I herded the kids toward the truck with the women following behind.

Megan tugged my arm. "Grampa Seamus, I'm going to miss George and Martha."

"And Gonzo," Valeria added.

At my obvious confusion, Megan explained. "George and Martha are the parent eagles, like George and Martha Washington, see? And Gonzo is like the Muppet, trying to get attention but not doing things right. We don't know if Gonzo is a boy or girl, so we can't give it a real name."

"And you can tell the adults apart?"

"Don't you remember? The girl eagles are bigger than the boy eagles."

I remembered and should have realized my granddaughter, the knowledge sponge, would not forget. "You guys are too smart for me. It's forty miles by truck to our new spot because I don't have the Bobcat to move those boulders. It's only four miles as the eagles fly. Maybe we'll see them there. Valeria, how's the ankle feel?"

She handed Megan the crutches and walked with shuffling steps.

"Super," I said. "Don't overdo it." I waited for the kids to go ahead and my mother to catch up. "You sleep okay?"

"Like a newborn baby."

"Meaning you woke up several times during the night and cried for someone to feed you and change your diaper?"

Mom looked up at the cloudless sky and released a dramatic sigh. "I thought I raised you better. Speaking of, what were you thinking, giving Valeria that rock and telling her you'd find her mother?"

Pointing out that Niki had given Valeria the rock, not me, avoided the main issue, which I needed to address. "I promised *to try*, Mom. A big difference from promising *to find*. I remembered how badly I wanted answers after Dad died. I simply knew I had to help Valeria learn what happened to her mother. At first, I hoped it was an accident or something."

Mom squeezed my hand. "It's been nearly fifty years and I still miss him."

FIFTY-ONE

MOM RODE SHOTGUN WITH NANA, Valeria, and Megan in the back seat. With supplies crammed everywhere, everyone had their knees tucked to their chins. The truck bed contained the generator, propane tanks, and everything else that didn't fit inside the cab. We weren't as overloaded as the Dust Bowl refugees arriving in California from their parched, foreclosed farms, but I took care to avoid bumps and make gentle turns.

My phone dinged while I was praying us past a muddy section of Lukes Road. Four-wheel drive pulled us through. I stopped and checked the notification. The trail camera had new pictures of the gray Tundra with a driver, a passenger, and an ATV in the cargo bed. I called Niki.

"That puts a crimp in my plans," she said. "I can't exactly pass them unnoticed with a rifle strapped to the ATV on top of a pile of dirty clothes."

We agreed she would wait to see if they arrived at the rocks. If they offloaded their ATV, she'd retreat and take a twenty-five-mile detour to get behind them. Then she could provide a rear guard for us. I would risk driving part way, stopping where I had multiple ways to avoid them.

It didn't take long before Niki reported Rogers and Korpi were at the rocks and unloading the ATV. "No sign of the blue monster. You should hang loose."

"If we don't do this now, we'll have to set up in the dark. Instead of you taking the long way around, I vote you hide and allow them to drive past. Then drive through the rocks and deflate a tire to slow them down."

"Pro tip, Seamus. Vehicles have spare tires. If you choose to declare war, let the air out of at least two. I'll see what happens. From now on, only text. I'm silencing my ringer."

Mom waited until I had disconnected. "Where did you pack the other guns?"

"No way. We're not bringing loaded weapons into the cab where we have no room to use them."

"They don't do any good if we don't have them."

"Then we'd better not need them, right?"

FIFTY-TWO

NIKI'S TEXTS KEPT ME INFORMED of what the Tundra guys were doing.

ATV unloaded

Testing drone

Loading drone on ATV

One staying with truck - I gotta go around

Wait until I catch up to you

I responded with check emojis. No reason to tell Mom and Nana I was ignoring Niki's advice—well, she probably considered them orders—to wait for her. The two guys and the Tundra were looking in the wrong area. Nothing suggested the Blue Monster or the other two people were around. I couldn't do anything to figure out where Kat was until I got people set up at the new site. And the window for Niki to help before she had to return to Minnesota was closing fast. Now was the time for a quick dash.

If I ran into the jacked-up Silverado, I'd have to rely on my knowledge of the local roads, two-tracks, and connected skidder trails to lose it. My aching hands alerted me to my death grip on the steering wheel. I shook out my fingers and told myself to relax. Who the hell was I kidding?

More than an hour later, I triggered the camera on Shank Lake Road driving by, saw no one on the road to my house. The chain was still up at the driveway, garage doors closed, meaning Niki wasn't yet there. No way I was putting off setting up the new camp until we had clean clothes. Niki would have to do the laundry on her own and bring it later.

At the turn toward the river, I stopped at a gate. Megan did the honors of unlocking and relocking it once I had driven through. A quarter mile farther on, we did the same thing with the gate that marked the boundary of my Baraga property. With the two gates locked behind us, tension melted off my neck and shoulders. When we reached the river, I adopted a jovial voice. "Oh oh. The bridge is missing. I guess we'll have to swim across."

"Grampa Seamus, Valeria can't swim with her ankle."

Mom looked back at the kids. "Megan, he's pulling your leg. I'll bet there's one right around the bend."

"I told you, Mom, no bridge. That's the whole reason we're crossing. I have a canoe and the river is shallow enough I can wade it. A quarter mile from here is a rise with a lovely growth of hardwoods where we'll set up camp. It's surrounded by swamps with no back roads in. You'll have excellent cellphone coverage up on the hill. For extra safety, I'll move the trail camera between those two gates to alert us if anyone is snooping."

"I see," Mom said. "And if we had to, we could defend it against someone trying to cross the river. Can you transport everything across? The generator? Propane tanks?"

"I'll leave them in the truck until Niki can help. We can handle the rest. Let's go see the spot I have in mind."

With two canoe crossings, I transported the girls, Nana, my mother, and sufficient supplies for everyone, other than Valeria with her crutches, to carry. I expected more pushback, but the kids were up for finding a perfect tent site, and Nana proved to be a packhorse. I kept forgetting that although she looked like she was in her sixties, she was only in her mid-forties with arms made of ironwood. Valeria and Mom set our pace, and we arrived in half an hour.

"Seamus," my mother said, "this is lovely. It's so open. I thought we were going to have to—I don't know—pull brush or something to make a spot for the tents."

The grove included twenty acres of mature sugar maple, cherry, a few white and yellow birch, and a smattering of evergreens. "I suggest y'all choose tent sites on the old logging road. Fewer stones sticking in your back. Find a flat spot or a gentle slope and point your feet down. Mom, why don't you and Valeria collect loose rocks for a firepit while Nana, Megan, and I bring the remaining gear?"

In three trips we humped everything up. While Nana set up her "kitchen" supplies and inventoried the food, I helped the kids pitch their tent and move their stuff.

Valeria rooted through her bag. "Grampa Seamus, have you seen my bear? I can't find it." She tapped her wrist where she wore her stuffed animal.

We double checked the tent. "Maybe it's still in the truck? I'll check later." Valeria's lip quivered. "Let me set up the tent for Nana and my mother, then I'll cross back over the river and check." Valeria agreed that was fair.

With Mom's help, we erected that tent. I motioned Mom inside. "Lie down and check for poke-y things. Maybe take a rest."

Her face became stone. "We still have lots to do."

"And if you get overtired and trip and break your hip, where are we? You have nothing to prove. You're already doing better than ninety-nine point nine percent of your peers."

Her tongue worked her way around her mouth like she was checking for missing teeth. "Well, I should make sure it's comfortable." She lay down on the bedroll, rocked back and forth. "You did a good job, Seamus. No rocks or sticks. Do I have to worry about snakes?"

"No poisonous snakes in the U.P. and the others will stay away. The breeze is keeping the bugs down now, but if you let them into your tent, they'll keep you up all night. The kids will collect you for dinner. Anything you're missing?"

"You have a dartboard and darts in the guest cabin, right? Can you bring them? We could hang the board on a tree?"

Funny what each of us needs to make a place a home. Darts had been the one constant for Mom wherever she had lived. It had facilitated her return from mental illness. Only in the last two years had she stopped treating as a permanent accessory a fanny pack that contained a set of darts my father had given her shortly before his death. Setting up a dartboard and measuring the distance to draw an oche on the forest floor was the least I could do. "Next trip," I said. "And thanks, Mom. You're a trooper."

I created a list on my phone of things to collect from home: clean clothes, food, a splitting maul, chainsaw with gas and bar oil to construct seats and work up some of the larger limbs into firewood, the first-aid kit from my truck. The list grew with dartboard, darts, sharpener—sure as rain, Mom would get the kids playing and that meant darts missing the board and hitting a tree or the ground or a rock. I'd need a hammer, nails, tape measure to place the board at the exact height—Mom would know if I was a quarter inch off—and to draw the oche the correct distance from the board.

I set the kids to gather kindling and downed branches for Nana to burn while I looked for Valeria's bear in my truck. No luck. I texted Niki to ask her status and if, by any chance, she had the bear. Her reply was immediate.

Folding laundry

No bear

Waiting for gray Tundra to leave area

Come here

Which meant we did not know where they were. With an involuntary shudder, my body reacted to the thought of meeting them. I asked if she thought I should wait until we were sure they were gone.

Nope.

If they kill you, I'll get them on 1st deg murder.

She followed with a laughing emoji.

Fifty-Three

NIKI MET ME ON THE screened porch with a glass of wine in one hand and a semiautomatic rifle in the other. Alcohol and guns did not make me happy. I shook my head.

"This is for you, asshole. I'm not drinking." She thrust the wineglass at me, slopping a little over the edge. "You're tense and you're not gonna like what I have to say. Drink some wine, grab a shower, get into clean clothes. No arguments, or I won't tell you what I learned."

That tone brooked no discussion. I enjoyed a refreshing shower and found Niki rocking on the porch. She pointed me toward a chair. "The Tundra just passed your camera."

"Excellent. Now I can move that trail camera."

She waved off my enthusiasm with a whatever hand flip. "They used their drone to survey a lot of ground. I'll bet they would have found you at Lake Tranquility. Your binocs are nice. I used them to watch the drone fly over the lake and past your house several times. It's a fancy model that allows the operator to swivel the cameras and zoom in."

I'd already figured out that using a drone extended their reach and allowed them to check out my house. I would if I were them. "Did they spot you? Is that what I won't like?"

"How long can your mother pretend she's not eighty?"

I chose not to call Niki on sidestepping my question. "Mom's like a child, except in reverse. Tell a kid they're too young to do something, and they'll kill themselves to prove you're wrong. Mom will never admit that coming here was a lousy idea. Her body won't hold up long, and I can force the issue. If you keep delaying telling me the bad news, you'll lose any positive effect of the shower and the wine."

She pointed to my F-150 in the driveway. "I can't help you get the generator and propane tanks across the river this evening. Colleen and I agreed to a girls' night out. We're having drinks and dinner before we wander into the Silver Fox. After a few more drinks, we'll see if we can audition for a pole position, maybe even an impromptu lap dance or two."

I pushed down my anger that they would subject themselves to hands pawing their bodies and perverted hard-ons poking them, even if they stayed in the guys' pants. In a voice that sounded hard to me, I asked, "What do you hope to accomplish?"

"You thought there might be a connection between the Silver Fox and Kat's disappearance, right? As Megan knows, you don't catch fish without bait. And you—" She punched my chest with a strong finger. "—aren't the right lure."

She rose, ran her hands down her sides, and shimmied. "Whereas I surely am. And dressed right, Colleen looks even hotter than me. We'll meet for dinner in Norway, make our plans, and visit the Silver Fox together. The place doesn't close until two, two-thirty. Rather than drive back here, I'll stay the night with Colleen in Iron Mountain."

During my work on Wall Street, I found excuses to miss the strip-club outings where the bigwigs entertained clients and hauled some of us analysts along to justify deducting the expense. My feelings became well enough known that the bosses had stopped inviting me years before I quit the business in disgust.

I would make an exception to keep Niki and Colleen away from that place, especially since they were attractive bait.

"This is such a bad idea. Colleen doesn't know what she's getting herself into. She doesn't even like guys. What if someone recognizes you? That could screw up the whole deal with Crenshaw. I'll go."

"And do what? Ask the girls while they're doing a lap dance if they know what happened to Kat? You couldn't hide your feelings. Just because Colleen is gay doesn't mean she can't be looking for a side gig. Who said all dancers were straight?"

She nudged the wine glass toward me. "Relax. Nothing will happen while I'm there. And no one will recognize me in my disguise. I'll make sure Colleen's safe. To make you feel better, I'll text you when we're done for the night. Let's talk about tomorrow. You still jog?" I did. "Let's meet in Iron River. There's a high school with a track, right?"

"West Iron," I said. "I'd rather run in the woods."

She released a dramatic sigh. "For a really smart guy, sometimes you are dumber than a musk ox. If we kick something up at the Silver Fox, we'll change plans. Otherwise, we should check out Randy Crenshaw's and Glenn Korpi's places. If they drive away, we might discover they forgot to lock their doors. You have a better idea?"

"Maybe try talking to the motel maids again?"

"And if Crenshaw hears of that, where are you?"

I finished the wine. "You win. I don't want to drive into town with the generator in the bed. Can you help me store it and the propane in the cab? I'll put up the back seat. What time do you want to meet?"

"Ten, unless you hear from me otherwise. I'll stop on the way for my long overdue personal chat with Sheriff Bartelle. Having a time to meet you gives me an excuse to escape his third degree." She checked her phone. "I have to leave soon. While you were showering, I took the liberty of folding down the bedspread to save time for more interesting things. Let's get that generator moved, so I have your *full* attention."

FIFTY-FOUR

MY PHONE'S WHOOSH ANNOUNCED PICTURES from the trail camera now set up between the two gates guarding our new hiding place. I fumbled on my glasses. The phone said 1:07 a.m. and new images continued to arrive. A light breeze had stirred a thin weed that triggered the camera's sensor. I checked if I had missed any messages from Niki or Colleen—I hadn't—and put the phone in airplane mode to kill the notifications. I was awake and needed to pee. A squadron of blood-thirsty mosquitoes accompanied me. I killed most of those that followed me into the tent. The survivors tortured me with their hypodermic proboscises and incessant buzzing throughout the night. The first pink etched the eastern sky and further sleep was hopeless.

I chased down the living remnants from the night's aerial battle and completed my pyrrhic victory. Red splotches and squished carcasses marked the nooks and crannies where they had hidden until I dispatched them. At least these gals wouldn't lay a gazillion eggs to populate the next generation.

I released the phone from airplane mode and notification whooshes ran for a full five minutes. I ignored the obnoxious sound and opened my messenger app to learn if Niki and I were still on for ten o'clock. No new messages. Her last message, sent at 10:30 p.m., had shown Niki outfitted in a Dolly Parton blond wig and a sheer blouse—more unbuttoned than not—revealing a lacy black bra. Colleen leaned in, her patterned blouse opened to show lots of cleavage. Niki had captioned the selfie "two hot girls on a hot summer night."

Where the hell was the message telling me they had returned safely? Was the trail camera hogging the phone's capabilities and not letting Niki's messages through? Or had she not sent a text after they returned to the motel? Assuming they had returned. I'd drive myself nuts worrying about everything that could have gone wrong. I silenced the phone.

Nothing to do but pluck the weed triggering the trail camera.

Fifty-Five

THE LONGEST PART OF ELIMINATING the offending weed was getting there and back. I zipped through the trail camera's pictures. At 3:47 a.m., the camera captured a handsome male wolf in mid lope. Wait until Megan saw that. On the return walk to the camp, I kept my eyes on the ground, finding several wolf tracks. It had crossed the river the same place we had.

With the brighter light, and knowing what I was looking for, I followed the wolf tracks on the far side of the river to within fifty yards of where we had camped. Curious, but not bold—a good way to know what was going on and not get in trouble. I entered our compound quietly, not wanting to wake up the sleepers.

Last night's dishes left to air dry glistened with a light morning dew. Once people woke up, I'd use the chainsaw I brought to make portable seats for around the firepit, freeing up the camp chairs to be used elsewhere. And I wanted to create drying racks for the dishes. I added twine to my list of stuff to buy.

Nana's and my mother's tent was nearest the firepit, its lines taut, rain tarp in place. An occasional snort told me Mom was still alive. The kids' tent was forty yards away from the snoring. Their tarp was also taut, but in front of it lay soggy coloring books. Nature had provided a better lesson than I could about what happens to stuff you leave out when the air temperature drops below the dew point.

From inside I heard Megan whisper, "You awake? Something's out there." In a louder voice, she said, "You awake?"

I shook a guy line and snorted through my nose, sounding like a wild boar—not that I had ever seen evidence of feral pigs in the U.P., although I had read there were some in a neighboring county. Both girls screamed.

I wanted to kick myself and said in a stage whisper, "And I'll huff, and I'll puff, and I'll blow your tent down." I gave the dripping guy line another shake.

"Grampa Seamus," Megan said, "you didn't fool me."

You betcha, Pumpkin. "Never know," I said. "Trail cam has a wolf, and I found lots of tracks." That got her attention. "Since you're awake, you want to come with me while I get a couple of pails of water from the river? I can show you a spot where I've seen fish."

"Can Valeria come, too?"

"Good by me, if she can manage her crutches."

Valeria used only one crutch. Although she could put most of her weight on her ankle, she'd have to guard against twisting it again before it healed.

The spot I showed them was downriver from the campsite and not visible from where the road met the river. "Bring down camp chairs and mosquito repellent and you can fish all day."

Megan peered into the clear water. "Perch? Bass?"

"Suckers, for sure. I'm told the river has brook trout. I haven't seen them here, though."

Valeria, who had been quiet, piped up, "Nana will want to know if she can cook them."

"Suckers? For sure. Filet and fry them like perch. And if you catch a trout—yum!"

By the time we returned, me carrying the water, Valeria carrying her crutch, and Megan carrying a renewed enthusiasm for outdoor life, Nana had breakfast cooking. I closed my eyes and inhaled the combined smells of woodsmoke, boiling coffee, and frying bacon.

Perfect, if only it weren't closing in on seven-thirty and still no message from Niki. I had to steady my hand to type. *You okay?* I hesitated before hitting send. The question presupposed she was not, and that was not what I wanted to suggest. I erased it and tried, " *We still meeting at 10?*"

Not wanting the kids to pick up on my nerves, I told them to replace the firewood Nana had used. I wandered to my tent, which I had erected under several towering hemlocks. *Come on, Niki. Don't do this to me.*

I planned to count three hundred seconds before switching to Plan B. As the moments ticked by, my stomach knotted tighter and tighter until it felt like a hockey puck.

At three hundred, I texted Colleen. *Niki with you?*

No response.

Now I wished I hadn't texted them. During the walk back to the fire, I extinguished the molten lava burning in my stomach to project a positive posture and voice. Megan was scrambling eggs with a fork while Nana looked on. "I'll be gone for a while. You do what Geema says, Pumpkin, and help her and Nana and Valeria, okay?"

Her mouth formed a pout. "Why do *you* have to leave?"

The lava in my stomach threatened to erupt. "You hired me to do a job. I couldn't get back to it until I made sure Valeria and her nana are safe. Do you agree it's safe to hide here?" She thought so. "Good, that means I can work real hard to find Valeria's mom and not worry about you." *But first, I need to learn what happened to Niki and Colleen.*

FIFTY-SIX

AFTER CROSSING THE RIVER, I hauled the canoe into the woods several hundred yards distant from the river, the road, and any of the paths I maintained. It would take a miracle for someone to find it. Even if they did, nothing would suggest that I was using it to supply people hidden across the way.

I cursed everything that slowed me down, starting with the seventy-two-point turn to do a 180 with the truck on the narrow trail. At each gate guarding the property, I had to stop, get out, fumble open the locks, prop the gate open, get back into the truck and drive through the gate, hop out to close the gate, and return to the truck. With the engine running, the mosquitoes had their way with me. Slapping at the buzzing bastards who had joined me in the truck, I cursed the rational speed dictated by dodging protruding rocks and sprawling holes on Shank Lake Road.

I released my frustration and hit the accelerator when I got to my smooth driveway. And slammed on the brakes to avoid hitting a deer. With wide eyes and fearful snorts, it bounded away, its white tail flashing a danger signal. I closed my eyes, let my heart settle. Thank goodness the deer had been alert. It was a timely reminder that whatever had happened to Colleen and Niki, I couldn't help them if I didn't make it to them.

Inside the house, I changed into running clothes, grabbed breakfast to go and a couple of bottles of diet Dr Pepper from the refrigerator. Couldn't think of anything else I needed and locked the door behind me.

I used my phone to get directions to the track and saw the icon showing I had a text message. I fumbled through the phone's security to open the message app and read from Colleen:

sleeping

do I need to wake her

???

Bam—instant headache. I pulled my head down until my chin pressed into my chest and counseled myself to be happy they were okay, not angry because they couldn't find thirty seconds to let me know they were fine.

Telling myself what to feel and feeling it are two different things. Keeping my chin pinned, I pulled my elbows behind my back. The iron bonds of tension gradually released.

I texted, *Don't wake Niki. I'll see her at 10:00 unless I hear otherwise.*

Colleen replied with a thumbs-up emoji. As if that made everything okay.

FIFTY-SEVEN

I PARKED CLOSE TO THE West Iron County High School football stadium and used its oval to warm up. From there, I followed a route I'd plotted on my phone that brought me past the house Glenn Korpi rented, on to Randy Crenshaw's home, which was less than a half mile away, and looped back to the track.

Korpi's driveway held no vehicles, nor were any parked nearby on the street. My disappointment vanished when I spotted the blue jacked-up Silverado parked on the grass next to a sad one-car garage several doors down. It faced out, preventing me from capturing a plate number without being obvious. The likelihood of there being two such trucks in town seemed minuscule. Had Korpi moved and the records Niki tapped were old? Or was Korpi so lazy he'd driven his truck to visit someone that close? I noted the address. With a reverse white pages search, I could learn who lived there.

On the half-mile to Crenshaw's house, I rolled the possibilities around in my mind and came up with more questions than answers. How could a working guy like Korpi spend so many daylight hours wandering the woods? Where did Aaron Rogers stay, and was the gray Tundra his?

No sooner had I thought of the gray Tundra than it steamed out of Randy Crenshaw's driveway with tires squealing and headed toward me. I wanted to know who was in that truck, but I did not want them to get a good look at me. I moved to the side of the street and kept running, hiding my face by using both hands to swipe away streaming sweat.

At Crenshaw's driveway, I faked checking my shoelaces. No vehicles or people around. What an enormous piece of luck. It's not like Earth only contained one gray Tundra, but odds were I had linked Rogers with Crenshaw. Crenshaw was not the blurry picture guy Niki's camera had caught, but he might be the fourth person.

I continued my planned route, which in eight minutes brought me back to Korpi's street in time to see the Tundra driving away with the jacked blue Silverado following. Each had a passenger. The gang of four were together and moving fast, and I was on foot.

I returned to my truck at a brisk clip. To get my phone to recognize my fingers, I had to towel-dry the sweat. I wrapped the towel around my head to keep my eyes clear and texted Niki to the effect that when she finished her beauty sleep, I had info, and we needed to talk. Call.

The phone buzzed. Niki's caller ID. "I am so sorry, Seamus. I was so exhausted last night, I didn't hit send for the message I typed after we returned to the motel. I hope you weren't worried. We've got news. What's yours?"

Rather than admit her mistake had caused me massive angst, I suppressed my feelings and detailed what I had witnessed and asked what she had learned.

"As luck has it, Aaron Rogers picked us up. He admitted he spelled his name differently than *the* Aaron Rodgers of Packers fame. His pal, the fuzzy picture guy, was with him. Went by the name of Bobby last night. I pickpocketed his wallet and took it to the ladies for a little look-see. The Indiana driver's license had him as Drew Dombey, address in Gary, age thirty-one, brown and brown, six even, one sixty, wears contacts, not an organ donor. Sources tell me that Mr. Dombey has led a charmed life for someone who has been pimping since he was a teenager. Also has several battery charges. Zero convictions. I'll bet there are a lot of frustrated prosecutors because his girls recanted or disappeared."

"Disappeared?" A realization struck me like a gut punch. "As in he killed them?" *As in he killed Kat?*

"Or sold them. Or they ran away to another city, changed their name, and found a new pimp to supply them with drugs. More likely, he scared them so thoroughly they wouldn't testify. His knuckles had the scars you get from hitting teeth. Last night, he got the manager—woman named Felicity St. Agnes—to agree to interview Colleen this afternoon. Felicity is a Florence, Wisconsin local with one DWI, one leaving the scene of an accident, both a decade in her rearview mirror."

My gut tightened to a walnut at the thought of Colleen interviewing at a place like that. I could fight that battle with more information. "Given Dombey, do you think the place is legit or a front for prostitution?"

"Parts are legit. It's a nude bar, but they still have to keep their liquor license. The girls work the pole, encourage patrons to buy them drinks. I'm sure the bartender has a special watered-down bottle for them. Nothing illegal with that, provided they don't sell it to customers. Some, not all, girls went into rooms screened by heavy curtains. Colleen will learn tomorrow what goes on there. I did not see any drug deals, but we did nothing to suggest we were interested. The parking lot smelled like a herd of skunks had passed by."

"Why smoke weed there if it's legal across the border in Michigan?"

"Seamus, in Michigan you can buy and carry a certain amount for personal consumption, but you can't smoke it in public places or in the great outdoors. For a Thursday night, the place was hopping. I assume it'll be packed tonight."

"You know I think this whole thing with Colleen is a terrible idea, even worse now that we know this guy Dombey's involved. I understand that the interview might give us insight about the operation." It was all I could do to not say something stupid like, "But I forbid it." That line rarely worked on my granddaughter. It didn't stand a chance with my thirty-seven-year-old sister. "I can't stomach the thought of her going through with it. You'll be there?"

"I'm on my way to talk with Sheriff Bartelle. I thought you and I should pay another visit to The Menominee Rapids Resort. Try a couple of different meals for lunch, maybe take a peek into the private area."

"You can't do that and go to the Silver Fox afterward. That begs people to ask questions."

"Yep, it does, which is one reason Colleen should go alone. It's been more than a week since anyone has heard from Kat. We have to shake things up, which is why you and I are going to the resort, and she's interviewing at the Silver Fox."

"I suppose nothing much can happen at an interview. But to visit the resort, I need to shower and change clothes."

"For Pete's sakes, Seamus, shower in Colleen's room. She can sneak you in so no one sees you. Buy new clothes in Iron Mountain. You can afford it."

Such a thought would never have occurred to me.

"Donate them to St. Vincent de Paul," she said, "and get a tax deduction. Do I have to teach you everything?"

Fifty-Eight

I FINISHED CLOTHES SHOPPING AND texted Colleen. She met me at the motel's back door. We trooped up the stairway to the fire door on the third floor. While I remained hidden, she made sure the cleaning ladies were not around to see me enter her room and held her door open. I executed a mad dash down the hallway, my backpack slapping against my shoulders.

The shower's steaming water massaged away the tension in my neck. I dressed in the bathroom and emerged, looking like someone ready to go to the resort.

"Don't you clean up nice," Colleen said. "Have you scheduled an appointment for me to examine the motel's books yet?"

"I'll call right now."

Mike Crenshaw picked up on the first ring. The holdup was because he had been waiting for his son to arrange a time for our accountants to get together to look at the financials. Since it was already midday on Friday, I asked if Monday morning, say, eight o'clock might work.

"I'm tired of waiting on that little pissant. I'll call our accountant and make sure it happens. Do you have children, Seamus? I wanted the twerp to take responsibility for this."

"One son. He's doing okay on his own, and we don't share any business responsibilities." I remembered his daughters had children. "The best part is I get to spoil my granddaughter. You have grandkids?"

We shared pleasant recollections of our next generational progeny. He was looking forward to seeing his in Florida. I thought it was a good idea to mention that I planned to have lunch with my fiancée at his resort. He sounded glad to hear the news and wondered if my investor might want to buy the resort, too. Regardless, he'd meet us there and treat us to a meal. His offer provided Niki and me excellent cover and might yield information regarding how hands-on daddy still was and the extent of his son's involvement with the resort.

I claimed I didn't know when we'd get there. My betrothed was shopping for something—I wasn't sure what, but it would cost me a pretty penny. His brayed laugh hurt my ears.

"Bunny's shopping, too," he said. "Maybe the two of them are plotting behind our backs."

Oh yeah. For sure. "That's a scary thought. Shall I call you before we head over?"

"No reason to. I'll putter around, stick my nose into everyone's business until you get there." His laugh made it seem like he was joking, which I doubted. We disconnected.

Despite the fact that the guy might be involved in multiple illegal activities, I kind of liked him—until I remembered the look in his eyes. I sat at the desk while Colleen reclined on a bed. I asked her to tell me about her appointment with Felicity what's her name.

"St. Agnes. She gets in at four o'clock. I know you're not happy, but I won't do anything stupid. Trust me on this, Seamus."

I said all the right things about trust and that she was a big girl and that I appreciated everything she was doing to help. To avoid allowing my true feelings to surface, I shifted the conversation to how our mother, who Colleen called Trudy, was doing as a new camper.

"So what you're saying," Colleen said, "is that you may have to carry Trudy out on a backboard because she'll never admit she was wrong not to take Megan to Boston?"

"Oh, she'll admit it was a mistake, but only after I summon the medivac. You don't have to tell me, but did you ever ask who your biological father was?"

She cocked her head. "Is there someone you're rooting for?"

"The two people I thought were potential candidates are both dead now. I can't see any resemblance between you and either of them. Rooting? No. Curious? Yes. I'm not like my sister—my older sister—who thinks Mom betrayed dad. He'd been dead for years. Mom didn't owe him anything other than raising the two of us well. I have no complaints. I take it she's said nothing to you."

"Haven't asked. The Carpettis will always be my parents—I've told you that. Fingers crossed, the guy had good genes. I want to live a long, healthy life. I'm happy Trudy's still going strong. If she wants to tell me, I'll listen. If she doesn't, that's okay, too."

"That's a fine attitude."

A key tapped on the door. "Housekeeping."

It sounded like Juanita. I considered using Colleen to translate and ask if Juanita had any news of Kat. The risk of my presence here getting back to someone was too high. I ducked into the bathroom and waved for Colleen to send her away, which she did.

We listened to the key tap on the next door and the squeak as that door opened. Colleen played lookout, and I escaped without being seen. I texted Niki and asked if I should wait for her in Iron Mountain or we should meet somewhere along the way. She responded that her meeting with Sheriff Bartelle had gone splendidly—whatever that meant—and she'd meet me at the first gas station on the Wisconsin side of the border.

I arrived and found her parked at a far corner of the parking lot. She hopped into my truck, blessed me with a million-watt smile. "Things are going to get very interesting. Soon."

FIFTY-NINE

I WAITED TO SPEAK UNTIL I had the truck cruising along the highway. "Explain interesting."

"Bartelle was pissed because I hadn't given him a heads-up I was working in the area. So I built on your suggestion that it related to militia and police officers were involved and served up a whopper. I said my investigation focused on how the militia was getting its funding. They had tasked me to look into certain relationships to determine if those individuals and their illegal activities were the militia's money source."

I asked how he had taken that.

"He was all kinds of bothered until I assured him I was unaware of any officers in his department being under investigation. To make him feel better, I gave him a few names I was checking out."

I risked a glance to gauge her expression. She looked like a little kid who had just entered a candy shop with a five-dollar bill in her hand. "Whose names did you give him?"

"Aaron Rogers or Aaron Robinson or Aaron Riddle, Glenn Korpi, and that new guy we just kicked up, Drew Dombey. He had never heard of Rogers or Dombey. He had run across Glenn Korpi at a minor altercation at the logging outfit he used to work at. By the time officers got there, they had settled the dispute. Other than that, Bartelle was of little help. But now those guys are on his radar."

"Meaning what?"

"I gave him the recognizance photographs, but I did *not* tell him where I took them. I also provided him with Rogers' and Dombey's records. He saw the geographical connection—Rogers from Chicago and Dombey from Gary. He had heard rumors of an out-of-state criminal element moving into the county, but these were the first names attached to that intelligence. Let's say I wouldn't want to be speeding, or have a taillight out, if I were driving the Tundra or that jacked Silverado."

Now I understood why she reminded me of the lucky kid in the candy store. "Did you happen to mention that these guys might be funding the militia?"

"Bartelle made that connection all on his own and concluded it was likely drugs. He asked to share this information with UPSET, the joint drug task force that covers the entire Upper Peninsula. I said it was too early, but if we came up with evidence of drug-related offenses, we'd turn that intel over to him and UPSET. I enquired about prostitution or sex-trade rings in Iron County."

She paused, rubbing her eyes with both of her fists. I asked her what was the matter.

"He was adamant that he would have heard of any prostitution rings operating in his county, and he had not. Hell, it's here. It's everywhere. He's overwhelmed with drug crimes and people ODing. Anyway, it means he's unlikely to hear about us looking into the Silver Fox."

"Speaking of, let's drive by it and check if we spot any known cars there."

"You think Randy Crenshaw is the fourth guy?" she asked.

"If we see that orange Caddy Blackwing and it's not with either truck, then no. Otherwise?" I shrugged. "How do you see our meeting at the resort playing out?"

She patted my arm and laughed. "Hey, this is your play. I'm just the hot-babe fiancée, remember?" She hooted at the concept. "You two business tycoons should talk about how the resort works and what kinds of changes Randy has instituted. Find out if Mike thinks they're good ideas. I can disappear to the ladies' if you want to ask more man-to-man questions regarding what goes on in that private room."

SIXTY

The Silver Fox parking lot had a smattering of vehicles, but none owned by my targets. The resort's parking lot was half full and didn't include any of the target vehicles either.

Mike Crenshaw must have seen us drive into the parking lot, because he was waiting at the reception desk. "Seamus, and Niki was it? Your timing's perfect. My stomach was just grumbling." He led us into the dining room and the server ushered us to the table farthest from the kitchen doors.

"Good afternoon, Mindy," Mike said to the waitress. "Please put this on my account. And add a twenty-five percent tip for yourself."

"Thank you, Mr. Crenshaw. Can I get you folks something to drink while you look at the menus?" She handed them around and took our beverage orders. Mike had his favorite beer. Niki went for a glass of Chardonnay. I stuck with water and asked whether he had reached his son.

Crenshaw shook his head. "Someone from the accountant's office will meet your accountant at the motel Monday morning at eight. Our guy will have access to the electronic accounting records. Plus, your guy can look at our reservation book for two fiscal years, and anything else he'd like to see on site."

I effused about how much I appreciated his making it happen. "My accountant is a she, by the way. Name's Colleen Carpetti. She's been staying at your motel for the last couple of days to get a feel for the place. I hope you don't mind."

He looked amazed. "It makes it seem like your buyer is anxious."

"It's me that's anxious. The opportunity to purchase some or all of your landholdings has me excited. The guy I know who might be interested in the motel and resort is a savvy investor. You two will either agree on a price or you won't. That has nothing to do with me. Although I'd like to think my enthusiasm for your property could influence him, I know it won't."

Mindy brought the drinks, took our orders, and the conversation shifted to his landholdings. I asked if there were any particular pieces of property he was unwilling to sell. His belly laugh caused the other diners to stare at us. "Everything is for sale for the right price." He was reluctant to lose a favorite forty acres nestled within thousands of acres of state land. He had bought it decades ago and built a small camp, off grid, where he and a few of his friends could get away and leave civilization behind. The hunting was terrific because no one else had access to that land except by walking in. "Hunters these days," he said, "are too damn lazy to walk a couple miles. They want to drive up to their deer stand, park, and shoot the deer. Not my kind of hunting."

He gave me the coordinates for those forty acres to eliminate them from my places to visit. He had no issue with my checking any of the other land he owned. We could come to his house, and he'd lend us a set of keys to the gates that block several of his holdings. I claimed we had another appointment that afternoon. I'd have to take a rain check on his most generous offer. If nothing else, this gave me an opportunity to follow up with him if I wanted to see him.

Over an excellent lunch, I steered the conversation to resort operations, and even recorded notes on my phone to demonstrate my interest. He was circumspect about changes his son had made, but I got the notion he did not approve them all but was giving his son rein to make the business work. Mindy cleared away the dishes, and Niki excused herself to "powder her nose," leaving me alone with Mike.

I waited until Niki was out of hearing range before mentioning that Randy had said they often used the private room for bachelor parties. I pointed across the dining area to the room. "He gave me the impression that he could bring in women to entertain my friends. I forgot to ask how those services would appear on my credit card. I don't want the little lady to see any—let's say extraordinary entertainment charges—if she looked at my statement."

His eyes glinted, and his mouth pinched before broadening into a smile. "Well," he said. "I don't know how Randy does it, but in my day, we had some outlandishly expensive bottles of champagne that we sold at a considerable markup. No one ever drank them, you understand."

Sixty-One

I ARRIVED HOME WITH FRESH produce for the campers and an uneasy feeling I was running on borrowed time. My trail cameras had shown no traffic past my house since I'd left that morning, but for all I knew Aaron Rogers and friends had drones surveilling it.

Given that uncertainty, I should minimize the number of trips we took to the Baraga camping spot, which meant I'd wait until Niki and I could go together. I stored the groceries in my refrigerator and the ice in its freezer.

The forbidden fruit is always the most interesting one, and the forty acres Crenshaw wouldn't sell roused my curiosity. With Google Earth software, I zoomed in and explored the image. He had downplayed the size of the compound. It included a two-story house that had to run at least 3,000 square feet, a pole barn building spacious enough for three or four vehicles, and a smaller building that I guessed was a sauna. He'd cleared an acre around the buildings.

Crenshaw had to be spending a lot of money to maintain a place he claimed to use only a couple times a year with friends. It shouldn't have surprised me. The rich are different from the rest of us. Now that I saw its size, I was more eager than ever to explore the one area he didn't want me to see. Round trip from my place was three hours. Too far for today, and I had no reason to think it related to Kat's disappearance.

Better I should find out who owned the property and trailer that the Serrano family stayed in and ask them questions. Iron County records showed a limited liability company owned the land. I tracked its registration to Delaware. My heart sunk. Delaware does not require the true owner's name to show on the filing documents. The Registered Agent was a lawyer whose entire practice was setting up LLCs. Another dead end.

With time before Niki's arrival, I called Lizzie to provide her an overdue update.

"Colleen's been filling me in," she said. "With your mother surprising you, I figured you'd be too busy to call. You caught me heading out the door for a registration drive. Gotta go. Stay safe."

Niki showed up at 5:30, bursting with news. While we packed my truck with the groceries, she filled me in: Colleen had gotten the job. Besides Felicity St. Agnes, she saw Randy Crenshaw, but not Rogers or Dombey. Colleen would start Saturday night.

"You can't keep going with her," I said. "She—"

"I didn't this time, remember? The only way Colleen can learn what's going on is if they accept her as what she presented herself to be: a woman scratching for a few extra bucks. She won't ask questions about Kat—because *that* could be dangerous. It's only two nights. She'll blow her cover on Monday if Randy Crenshaw shows up with the motel's accountant."

She was missing my concern. "Maybe earlier if his daddy tells him her name. We can't send her in there with no backup."

"Let's go, Seamus. We can discuss this later."

Good, I thought, I'll enlist Mom's help. In some ways, my mother was a feminist before the term became popular; in other ways, she was more conservative than the Pope. I figured she would not be in favor of her daughter working in a strip joint.

Sixty-Two

NIKI AND I MOVED THE generator, propane tanks, and all the other stuff to the other bank of the river. Schlepping them the quarter mile to the campsite was another issue. It took us several trips to cart everything up the hill. Task completed, we moved camp chairs out of the fire's smoke and relaxed onto them. A rich smelling stew bubbled on the stove. Nana and Mom were working together in the "kitchen," chopping veggies for a garden salad to go with the dozen suckers the kids had caught.

Niki closed her eyes and dropped her chin to her chest. If I followed suit, I'd be asleep in a second. I asked where the kids were.

"Resting before dinner," Mom said and called their names. The kids boiled out of their tent. Megan in a mad, squealing dash, followed by Valeria, who was walking without crutches.

"Grandpa Seamus! Niki! You'll never guess what!"

Megan was right. I would never guess what, but that is not how we play the game. "You caught twelve suckers," I said.

"Geema told you that. That's not what I want you to guess. Niki, you guess."

Niki opened her eyes and rubbed her chin like she was thinking hard on the subject. "You found a secret fairy village."

Valeria caught up with us. "The eagles found us. We left them a fish, and they came and took it. How did they know we were here?"

I said I didn't know for sure. "They have excellent eyesight, you know." The eagles were just the thing to help lessen the kids' trauma of having to move from Lake Tranquility. I sent the birds a silent thanks. If only I could enlist them to find Kat.

Dinner was uneventful. Rather than go back home, we stayed the night to allow time to talk to Mom after the kids and Nana went to bed. Mom reported that Nana remained firm about not contacting the police. Mom thought if Nana believed she had a safe place to take Valeria, they might persuade her to do it.

Given the fantastic progress I had made on determining Kat's whereabouts, maybe I should concentrate on finding that safe place so we could get the police involved. Who was I kidding? If someone had taken Kat, the chances of her still being alive were minuscule. The only reasonable chance she had of remaining safe was if she had left of her own accord. Being resigned to bad news did not mean I could stop searching for the truth. Which brought me to Colleen and the Silver Fox.

I was correct that Mom would blow her stack about Colleen wanting to work at the Silver Fox. I was wrong about who she targeted with her anger. "First, Seamus, it's your own damn fault she's doing this. Second, she's a big girl. It's not like the first time she's ever been to a bar with strange men around. Third, what makes you think she wants you, or anyone she knows, to watch her dance?"

Just because the women were all against me didn't mean my concerns weren't legit. "Niki, you told Bartelle you were looking into possible prostitution. Maybe you could talk him into having a deputy at the Silver Fox while Colleen's there? I know it's not his jurisdiction, but that might make it more effective."

"No way," Niki said. "Jurisdiction is everything. And don't try the drug angle with UPSET. Wrong state."

So Colleen was on her own. Crap. I hated that. Maybe I could sit in the parking lot. I asked Niki if we had a game plan for tomorrow.

"We do, but it involves breaking a few laws."

Mom let out an exasperated sigh. "I do not need to hear this. I'm heading to bed."

We said our goodnights. Once Mom couldn't hear us, Niki told me her plan. "First thing, we go to your house and pack a full day's worth of supplies. Your job is to follow Randy Crenshaw wherever he goes. Fingers crossed he sleeps in his own bed tonight."

"How can I do that without him seeing me? It's not like we're in Boston, and I can hide in traffic."

"I don't care if he sees the car, Seamus. But I don't want him to see you driving the car. I'll give you a wig and you'll take my SUV. Bring your Kindle. You're gonna have lots of waiting. Bring snacks and water and something to pee in."

"And while I am having a blast, what are you doing?"

"Knocking on doors to learn who lives where and with whom."

"And they'll tell you because you're such a pretty face?"

"No, they'll tell me because I am a US Marshal looking for information on a dangerous fugitive."

I had forgotten that as part of her undercover work, they had made her a US Marshal with an official badge and everything. "And that's the illegal part of our day?"

"The first part."

Sixty-Three

I PARKED DOWN THE STREET from Randy Crenshaw's house, where I had a good view of his porch and driveway. After finishing the William Kent Krueger, I started a new-to-me Michael Connelly thriller featuring Renée Ballard. What would happen if Renée and Niki met? They'd be best friends or two cats in a burlap sack. That visual put a smile on my face.

Crenshaw's appearance interrupted my reading. He walked from his front door to the garage. His engine roared to life, and a puff of white exhaust wafted past the opened door. I followed Crenshaw's orange Caddy Blackwing to a local restaurant. I had no sooner found my place in the thriller, when he exited carrying a brown paper cup. His next stop was gas in Crystal Falls. From there, he drove to the Menominee Rapids Resort.

Although Niki didn't care if Crenshaw saw her SUV, I couldn't remain hidden if I followed him into the resort parking lot. Unless I put down a huge deposit on a bachelor's weekend, I had run out of excuses to visit the resort. I performed a U-turn and pulled under the shade of a massive pine. After losing my place several times while reading, I decided to explore on foot.

I found a spot screened by thick bushes that afforded a view of the parking lot. Crenshaw was loading supplies into an eight-person passenger van. Five guys, all white, all in their mid-30s or early 40s, stood around chatting in a way that suggested they knew each other. This outing wasn't to hunt, nothing interesting was in season. No fishing poles or tackle in sight. They weren't birdwatchers. I knew those folks. They'd be peering into the treetops and underneath bushes to see what birds were around. Whitewater rafting?

I didn't want to lose them, which was likely if they left while I was just standing there. I gave up spying and returned to the SUV. Several minutes later, the van passed. I gave them a thirty-second head start and followed.

My whitewater-rafting theory unraveled after we crossed into Wisconsin and left the river behind. We passed the Silver Fox, reentered Michigan, and I ran through the various events happening in Iron County this weekend but couldn't come up with anything to justify this trip. Earlier in the month we'd had Bass Fest—I'd run in the "Run Your Bass Off" race. Next month was the Humongous Fungus Festival celebrating the largest plant by size, not weight, in the US—a thirty-eight-acre fungus. My next idea was they were traveling to Alpha, Michigan, known as the smallest village in America with a brewery.

They passed the cutoff to Alpha and drove through Crystal Falls. On our way toward Iron River, I let two trucks get between me and the van and immediately the pinch in my shoulders disappeared. If I had Niki's job, I think I would die from stress within six months. I texted her to ask if she was still in Iron River, got an affirmative, and asked her to call if she could. Seconds later, my phone rang.

I explained the situation. Did she want to join me in a tag-team to decrease the possibility of being spotted?

"I'm not done here. Use common sense, like you did at the resort. We want to know where they're going, but not let on that you're following. Got it?"

You betcha boss. Easy peasy. The pain between my shoulders returned at double strength.

They left US 2 to take a narrow road that soon became what I realized was the forest road leading to Mike Crenshaw's remote forty acres. I'd wanted to learn more about this place and Crenshaw was providing me that opportunity. With only one way in, I chose a good hiding spot to determine what other vehicles traveled to the compound or left. Bonus—I could pee in the woods, not in a bottle, and I could stretch away the stress.

Sixty-Four

I SPENT THE AFTERNOON IN the car, alternately sweating and freezing. I didn't dare open the windows to catch what little breeze there was because when I had stopped, the car's exhaust had attracted a horde of mosquitoes. Each time it got so hot my head ached, I turned the car on and left it on until I shivered. Each boil-freeze cycle lasted about forty minutes.

At 1:30, a delivery van drove past, going too fast for me to capture its registration or the lettering on its side. It returned two hours later with Crenshaw, driving the passenger van, following on its heels. No sign of the five guys.

Niki finished sleuthing and joined me at 4:00. To give ourselves more flexibility to have one person drive while the other took pictures or whatever, we decided it made sense to ride together. That required a strategic retreat to park the F-150 on the paved road. We returned with Niki's SUV. She used her phone's map to direct us to a closer observation point, where we waited, and waited, and waited. I asked how she had gotten people to talk to her.

"Told them the US Marshals service had gotten a tip about a man wanted for jumping bail while appealing his conviction on breaking and entering and aggravated assault. We believed he was hiding with an unknown associate someplace in the Upper Peninsula, and sources had him in town. I showed them a picture of a guy who's deceased and described him as medium height and weight. He might have grown a beard and dyed his hair brown and might disguise himself with glasses. Basically, he could look like almost anyone. We didn't know whether the person he was staying with was also new to the area or had been a longtime resident.

"I had to calm down some folks who worried they weren't safe. I told them that his crimes had all been out-of-state."

"And people opened up to you? I've found most people are fairly reserved with folks they don't know."

"I had some of that, but most people talk to badges. Aaron Rogers has been in town for only three months. He and Glenn Korpi seem to be best buds, although no one could say how they'd gotten together. The big scuttlebutt was that Korpi's wife caught him screwing around and threw him out last week. He's staying a few doors down with a friend. Seems the wife found a map to the other woman's trailer in the woods. Made me wonder if Mrs. Korpi drove the blue Silverado up to Kat's trailer and went apeshit not finding anyone there."

"Which would explain the screaming woman," I said. "But was Korpi having an affair with Kat, or was he putting the screws on her because of her immigration status?"

Niki sighed. "Or both. Until we find Kat or can question these guys, I don't think we'll know the answer. Seems another guy sometimes lives with Aaron Rogers. No name. Descriptions varied, but it could be Drew Dombey. Or maybe the fourth guy? More work to do there. I saved Mrs. Korpi for last and asked the same questions. She was not in a sharing mood. She became flustered when I asked if her husband was home. Told me the asshole didn't live there anymore and slammed the door in my face. Interesting, right?"

It struck me as odd and unenlightening. Niki figured the wife had to know something about her husband's illegal activities. No one mentioned anything suspicious concerning Randy Crenshaw. Most thought he was a nice guy because he let neighborhood kids use the swing-set. Disappointing. I wondered out loud what we would do with that information.

"It's all part of the stew, Seamus. All part of the stew."

My stomach growled and I laughed. "Can't eat that stew. How long do we hang here? They could stay for the entire weekend."

Niki handed me an apple. "It's not like you have anything better to do. Besides, what are they doing there? No place to fish. No nearby ATV trails. This looks to me like a place you come to screw your brains out where no one can see you. If the women aren't already there, my guess is they won't arrive until evening. If someone shows up after dark, I have night goggles." Niki waggled her eyebrows at me.

"What the hell don't you have in this car?"

"Answers."

Sixty-Five

DUSK ARRIVED WITH NO ADDITIONAL traffic. Time to reconnoiter. It took us the better part of an hour to find a safe spot to observe the compound. Long before we got there, we saw light shining above the trees.

A generator ran at full tilt, providing an underlying burr to the thumping bass from a sound system that pounded the air. At least we didn't need to worry about being quiet.

We stationed ourselves in the woods several feet from the mown area. The house was lit like a torch, and several exterior lights attached to the buildings illuminated the front of the house and the surrounding grounds. Light bounced off windshields of two vehicles in the driveway. The garage doors were down, and that building blocked our view of the sauna. A faint hint of woodsmoke perfumed the air.

From our distance, my binocs picked up only glare from the house windows. We watched for outside movement. A half hour showed no exterior guards or roaming dogs.

"Looks like party time to me," Niki said. "Guess I'd better see what I'm missing. You stay here. I don't want you to have to make a fast retreat through an open field with your ankle."

She couldn't see me shaking my head. "My ankle's fine. It's been fine. The plate they put in makes the odds of me re-injuring it way less than of you breaking your skull. Let's consider what happens if I go. You can observe with your night goggles, and you can cover me with your rifle. If you see anything, you have that incredible whistle to alert me of the danger."

She grabbed my shoulder. I kept making my case. "Whereas, if you go, we both know I'm more likely to shoot you than someone else. And I can't whistle for shit. Well, I have a pleasant whistle, but it carries only about three feet. So, it's my job to sneak."

I shook off her hand and trotted down the tree line until I could use the garage to shield my approach from the house. Closer in, the country-western music blaring from external speakers was so loud I couldn't hear anything else. The only reason to have outdoor speakers is if people were outside. Just because we hadn't seen them didn't mean they weren't there, and it was unlikely I could hear a warning whistle from Niki should she try to alert me of danger. I was on my own.

The wolf had been curious enough to scout out our camping spot and smart enough to keep his distance. I was not as smart and sprinted from the woods to the corner of the garage without incident. I knelt, my heart a thumping tympani in my chest. I brought the binocs to my eyes, used my elbows to steady myself, and scanned the area.

The two vehicles were between me and the house. One was a passenger van larger than the one Randy Crenshaw had used to transport the five guys. That fit with Niki's guess that women were already here. The other was a well-used Dodge Ram.

A paver walk led from the driveway to a centered front entrance two steps above ground level. Light poured from the first story's floor to ceiling windows. When I focused on the windows, all I saw were shadows of movement behind some kind of material that reflected the outside lights. The same floodlights that didn't allow me to see in made it easy for someone inside to spot me if I got careless.

I pushed away that negative thought. The only way I could see inside was to be close enough to shield a bit of window from the glare, which meant being right next to the window. With no ability to know if someone was looking out, I could not approach the house from the front. Before I tried a different side, I used the vehicles as cover and crawled across the gravel and copied the license plate numbers. I retreated, circled around the garage, discovering it had no windows, and explored the sauna. Its external firebox was warm, not hot, and the inside was dark and quiet. They had used it earlier in the day. Parked behind the sauna was a five-by-eight trailer stacked with split maple. A fenced area occupied 10,000 square feet between the sauna and the woods. Rows of vegetables filled the garden except for a recently tilled rectangular plot in the far corner.

I used an oblique angle to reach the back corner of the house with little chance of anyone inside spotting me. From there I eased to a position that allowed me to peer into the nearest rear window, which, I was pleased to discover, did not have the reflective film. A middle-aged couple worked in a massive kitchen. The woman was up to her elbows in a soapy sink. The man dried dishes, storing them into open cupboards well supplied with dinnerware, glasses of all sorts, and paper products. This was not a facility used by Mike Crenshaw to entertain a few friends only a few days each year. No wonder he wanted me to stay away. Fine, Seamus. So what are you going to do about it?

Sixty-Six

AFTER CONFIRMING MY CELLPHONE'S CAMERA was in no-flash mode, I positioned its lens just above the windowsill and snapped their pictures. Between the truck tag and Rembrandt, Niki had a good chance to ID them. Maybe I should leave while my luck held. But if Kat was in the house and I chickened out, I'd feel like I had let everyone down.

I crawled along the foundation to the next window, which was dark. When I poked my head up at the remaining two, I was disappointed to see they had the frosted panes people use for bathrooms.

I reached the corner and scanned the open area on that side of the house. With the corner of my eye, I caught movement inside the tree line but beyond the reach of the house lights. My heart seized, then kicked into a high gear as I willed my eyes to find whatever it was. I dared not move and staring didn't help. I very slowly turned my head and my peripheral vision again caught movement. Was he/she/it trying the same thing with me? Neither of us could hear over the music. I sipped in air and eased it out, hoping my chest didn't move.

A white flag rose and the ghost of a deer trotted away, it's tail waving a warning to any who would pay attention. I remained frozen, concerned a guard had frightened the deer. The deer soon reappeared, closer in and chowing down on the grass.

I told myself to trust the deer's instincts and moved around the corner to the first window, which looked into an L-shaped dining room that ran the entire width of the house. A wooden table polished a warm gold remained piled with the detritus of a feast. Saliva flooded my mouth as I surveyed the remains of a carved roast, tossed salad, fresh vegetables, and what I'd bet was cherry pie. I counted fourteen place settings, complete with linen napkins.

Given the five guys I had seen get into the van at the Menominee Rapids Resort, even if the help ate with the guests—unlikely—that left seven people I hadn't identified. With no lights on upstairs, everyone needed to be in the room off the front of the dining room. Unless the door was closed, I should be able to see in from the last window on this side.

After elbow-crawling to stay below the windows, I reached the final window and slowly raised my head enough to see in. Separated by open pocket doors, the dining room flowed into a parlor. Light from a wood-burning fireplace danced on the ceiling. A setting of two stuffed love seats at right angles blocked my view farther into the house. The tops of two heads close together rose above one sofa. One had long blonde hair. Not Kat.

Movement from the other love seat drew my attention. A tiger-striped six-inch stiletto heel bounced at the end of a long, bare leg. The foot stopped tapping, and a head, covered by Irish red tresses, rose. Green eyes stared into mine.

She winked.

I sprinted toward Niki and the safety of the woods. Arms pumping, thighs burning, I didn't stop until I was five yards into the foliage. I squatted next to a downed tree to catch my breath. A dozen or more people poured from the house, wandering around, lights from their flashlights looking like spotlights at a fairground.

Niki stepped next to me. "What the hell happened?"

I waved a finger to signal I needed a minute. Once I could speak, I explained.

"How much is truth and how much is fantasy? No way you could see that lady's eyes were green."

Well, yeah. "Educated guess. Anyone with that hair either has green eyes or wears green contacts. How do Peeping Toms do it? I'd die of a heart attack worrying about getting busted. What if they had shot through the windows at me?"

Niki gave me her what-the-hell-am-I-going-to-do-with-you look. "Well, they didn't. And since Rembrandt requires sharp pictures, not educated guesses, we'll wait and try to get them. And we need your good cameras."

Sixty-Seven

I OFFERED TO LET NIKI call the coin toss to determine who had to drive to my place and retrieve my camera gear to get the sharp pictures for Rembrandt. With the quarter doing lazy loops, she said, "Not edge."

I snagged the coin midair. "You're supposed to choose heads or tails."

"You're sore because I found the winning call. Off you go."

Someday I'll learn. When I returned, the outside lights and most of the inside lights were dark. Niki had scouted a better spot for our surveillance, this one providing an unobstructed view of the front door from an angle that avoided having the morning sun reflect off my telephoto lens. I set two cameras on tripods, one fitted with infrared equipment, the other with a standard lens.

As consolation to my "losing" the coin flip, Niki took the first watch. She woke me at 4:30 and reported nothing had happened. Two hours later, the kitchen crew dumped a dozen garbage bags into the bed of the Dodge Ram. I captured sharp pictures of both of them.

My next picture opportunity came after another three hours. The five guys Randy had brought from the Resort and nine women, all wearing flip-flops and bathrobes or dressing gowns, paraded to the sauna. I zoomed in on individual faces and kept my finger on the camera trigger. The rapid-fire shutter woke Niki.

Photo opportunity complete, I said, "I wonder what happened to the other woman."

Niki's look told me I needed to explain. "You know: two girls for every boy. Golden oldie. Jan and Dean. Surf City." I sang the refrain and got the don't-be-an-ass look. She was right. She hadn't yet been born, and the only reason I knew the song was because, as a kid, I had found it in my mother's collection of 45 rpm records.

"Ignoring your prehistoric references, you have a valid point. I wonder if Kat was supposed to be the other woman. If that's the case, it puts another nail in her coffin. It's been—"

The synth-pop beat from the Wonder Woman 1984 trailer stopped her dead. She answered her phone, listened, then said, "Yeah. Here he is, Sheriff Bartelle."

I had been finishing Niki's sentence with "nine days since Kat disappeared" and accepted the phone like it was a rattlesnake. "Hey Lon, this is Seamus. What's up?"

"You avoiding me? Why didn't you answer your phone?"

"It's turned off. You got me now."

"Where are you?"

I didn't lie, but I didn't choose to tell the truth, either. "A ways outside Iron River. Your tone of voice is getting me worried. What happened?"

"Is your granddaughter with you?"

My heart clogged my throat. Something had happened to Megan. "No. I sent her away with my mother. You're scaring the shit out of me. What the hell happened?"

"Better see for yourself. Make sure Niki is with you. I expect answers from both of you."

Sixty-Eight

As **N**iki **packed the gear** in our vehicles, I found several messages from Bartelle on my phone, each more curt than the previous one. None from Colleen. I dialed Mom, got no answer, and left a message. Unlike me, she didn't forget to charge her phone. One more worry burning an acid hole in my gut.

Niki led, and I followed in my truck. She carved the ninety-minute trip down to an hour. That probably saved me going even faster and winding up in a ditch. A county patrol car blocked the road at my property line. The deputy contacted Bartelle, who said we should walk down to my guest cabin.

I ran with Niki in my wake.

We found Bartelle and Tex pacing the cabin's screened porch. Bartelle asked if I would give them permission to search my property, vehicles, and look at my trail camera pictures. I tossed Tex the keys to the house. "Garage is unlocked. You need a card reader?"

Tex caught the keys with a "Thanks, we're good."

Bartelle ordered Tex to take Niki to the scene; he'd talk with me here. Tex and Niki left at a jog.

I sounded calm, although I had to choke down the spew burning my throat. "Now that you've separated us, will you stop dicking around and tell me what the hell happened?"

"In time. Your granddaughter and mother aren't here?"

Sure hope not. I walked around the picnic table to put Bartelle between me and the porch door in part to see if anyone was coming, but equally to assure Bartelle I wasn't a threat. It took both my hands to support me as I sat down, making it shortly before my shaking legs collapsed. I crossed my arms. "Why don't you believe my mother took Megan?"

"Tell me where you and Niki have been since I saw Niki yesterday morning."

"Niki speaks for herself. I've been following a lead on the prostitution that doesn't happen in Iron County. I refuse to answer another question until you tell me what's going on."

"When and where did you last see the two guys you made that citizen's arrest on?"

My conscience was clear about them. My stomach unwound a quarter turn. I gave him a little head shake. "Not since then. Why?" He leaned over me. I countered his power move by folding my arms, putting a blank look on my face, and staring past his shoulder.

His eyes became resigned. "You can be such an asshole sometimes. Fine. Follow me." He spun on his heel and marched out the door, not looking to see if I was coming.

I scrambled past the picnic table, caught the screen door before it slammed, and followed him on the path from the guest cabin to my house. He would have delivered any bad news concerning Megan or my mother while I was alone and sitting down. Right? My stomach flipped, then settled. This was something else.

The hill between the guest cabin and my house provided my first opportunity to see vehicles filled my driveway. My lungs stopped working while I scanned the collection for Colleen's rental. Two state vehicles, the state's portable evidence trailer, another Iron County cruiser, and one unknown truck. I couldn't see the area blocked by the garage. The last time I saw this many police resources, dead bodies were involved.

Sixty-Nine

I asked Bartelle's back, "Who called this in?" Whether he didn't hear or pretended not to, it had the same effect of adding to my angst. He led me past my 1,000-gallon propane tank, which had the same siphoning equipment attached as the bear and the beanpole thieves we caught had used. Stolen propane did not explain this many cops. He strode around the garage corner and pointed to tarps covering two bodies sprawled next to my Subaru Outback, still up on its jack, waiting for its replacement tire.

My feet forgot how to move. "The same two? Who killed them?"

"I was hoping you would tell me. I'll ask again, when and where did you last see them?"

"When your officers drove them away in separate patrol cars. How did they get here? Who called it in?"

"Text message supposedly from your neighbors across the lake."

"They're not around."

"Yep, plus it was a spoofed number. Someone wanted to stick this on you—unless it's you trying to make it look like someone wanted to frame you."

The smell of excrement, and piss, and blood reached me. I sucked on my cheeks to generate enough saliva to swallow and tamp down my desire to puke. "I assume they didn't walk."

"Truck with a bunch of propane tanks and a wheelbarrow is parked at the end of your driveway. We removed the lock on your chain. Sorry about that."

I positioned myself to see the rest of my driveway. Colleen's rental was not there. "It happened after 11:30 last night. I might not have seen the bodies because my car is blocking them from the house, but I couldn't have missed the truck."

He stepped into my space. "I thought you said you were gone since yesterday morning?"

I retreated a step and waved away the implication I was lying. "I returned briefly to pick up camera equipment for our stakeout." Past Bartelle's shoulder, I saw Tex and Niki walking down the driveway, their heads together in conversation. What had Niki said we were doing?

Bartelle motioned toward the tarps. "Want to see them?"

My stomach flipped. "Hell would I want to do that?"

"You're right. Gunshot victims are never pretty." He raised his voice to address Tex. "Anything from the trail cams?"

"All missing," came the reply.

"Well," Bartelle dragged out the word. "Isn't that convenient, Seamus?"

<h1 style="text-align:center">Seventy</h1>

NIKI WANTED TO VIEW THE bodies. Now that I was over the shock of knowing two people had been killed on my property, I wanted everyone to finish up so I could find out what was going on with my mother not answering the phone. I swallowed the acid of my saliva and held my counsel.

Bartelle performed the unveiling while Tex checked with the officers searching my house. Both bodies lay face down. The big guy had a shotgun blast in his back. The shorter fellow had taken one in the shoulder. Someone had dispatched them with small-caliber shots to the head. The muzzle held close enough to burn the skin.

Niki pointed to a pellet under my car next to an evidence flag. "Looks like zero-zero buckshot, but it's a bogus clue. The blast caught the bear from behind—best way to deal with someone that size. The beanpole was probably second and was running, which is why the blast caught his shoulder. Didn't happen here. Someone moved the bodies."

With Niki's words I looked more closely and couldn't find the bits of skin and blood I should have seen if the murders had occurred there.

Bartelle said it didn't prove anything. "Seamus here is smart enough to frame himself to throw off the scent. Any idea how much propane you should have in your tank?"

"Around six-fifty."

Tex rejoined us, holding something behind his back. "House is clear. You're still at six-fifty, so no theft. Tell us about that package you left under your passenger seat?" Seeing my confused expression, he added, "Your Subaru?"

I couldn't imagine what Megan had left under the seat and said so. Tex displayed an evidence bag holding another clear bag filled with a white substance with a yellow tinge. "Never seen it. My Subaru's been sitting like that for days waiting for a new tire. Doors are unlocked. I assume whoever did this," I waved at the murdered men, "planted it."

Bartelle jabbed his crooked finger at me. "Because murder isn't enough?"

Niki stepped between us. "Give it a rest, Bartelle. We all know Seamus didn't do this, and he's not running around with drugs under his car seat. His granddaughter's only eight. She didn't accidentally leave her stash of meth or whatever lying around. I gave you some names. You do anything with them? I'm pretty sure one of them flew a drone over Seamus's property two days ago."

My phone rang and displayed Colleen's name. I pressed the do not answer button and muttered, "Possible Spam."

"That's news you should have told me," Bartelle said. "They are on my list for a little chat, but we've been busy."

"I won't tell you how to do your business," Niki said, "but the State's got the crime scene. You and Tex should talk with those guys, and I wouldn't mind tagging along." She flashed him a flirty smile. "I'll drive myself, if that's okay?"

Bartelle squinted at her. "Is this the Feds way of sticking their nose into our tent? You plan on commandeering this investigation?"

"Absolutely not. Three heads are better than two."

Tex gave Bartelle a slight head bob. Bartelle crooked his arm around his head, massaged his neck with his hand. "Okay, but while we're together, you will tell me everything about this alleged prostitution ring and what you and Seamus were doing. Deal?"

"Deal" Given the way Niki faced, only I could see her give me a wink.

Whatever the hell that meant. I had bigger worries: learning why Colleen had called and running to the river to find out why my mother hadn't returned my phone call. "How much longer before I can use my house?" By which I meant, how long until everyone finishes, and what can I accomplish before they leave?

Bartelle addressed the larger question. "We'll check with the State boys, but I'm guessing your house is fine. The outside may take a while yet. Stay available. We may have more questions."

I gave him my most sincere smile. "Of course."

SEVENTY-ONE

MY FIRST QUESTION TO COLLEEN was whether she was okay.

"Bored. I have the day to myself until I dance tonight. I thought maybe I could visit your camp. Love to see it. I learned a couple of things. Nothing major. Did I mention I'm bored?"

For a woman who enjoyed living in Boston, I could see how Iron Mountain might get a little confining. Especially with no one to do stuff with. I tried to scare her away by telling her what had happened here. She reminded me she was a cop's daughter and did she tell me she's bored? "Problem is," I said, "I need to check on the campers. Mom's not answering her phone. I don't even know if I'll be here."

"No problem. At least I'll enjoy a pleasant drive in the country. Hopefully, I'll see you soon."

I gave her directions from the motel and explained where I hid a key if she found the house locked.

The State police confirmed they didn't need me around. I installed a spare trail camera on the road near my home, then armed with a pair of old binoculars to back up my story about going birdwatching, I hiked through the woods and rejoined Shank Lake Road a half mile north. From there, I ran to the river, crossed, and arrived at the camp to find Mom and Nana throwing darts at the board I had set up.

"Mom," I called once I was in hailing range, "is everything okay? You never called me back."

Mom's wave acknowledged she had heard me. She waited until I was closer to tell me her electronics had died, and none of them had figured out how to start the generator. She handed Nana the darts and fisted her hands. "The line for the oche isn't square to the board, and you set the board three-eights of an inch too high."

"I triple measured it, Mom. It is exactly five feet eight inches to the bullseye. I drew the line in the dirt with a stick. Give me a break."

She shook her head at me like I was ten-years-old. "Not possible. It looks too high and my darts are landing low. Maybe your measuring tape is wrong."

Mom had thrown a bazillion darts over the years. If she said the board was too high, it was too high. But not because the measuring tape was wrong. This wasn't my first rodeo. I had picked that tree because the ground surrounding it was level. I stood next to the tree and compared the bullseye to the height of my eye. It was not too high.

I turned to look at Mom and laughed when I realized the problem. "I hung it the right height, Mom. The ground slopes down from the tree to the oche. My fault. I should have thought of that. When I get a moment, I'll drop it for you."

"Soon as you fix the generator. You should get one of those laser-level thingies and do it right the first time."

You betcha, Mom. A lot of call to install dartboards to tournament specifications outside in the woods. I checked the generator set up and found they had somehow flicked the switch that changed the fuel source from propane to gasoline. I showed them the solution, and the generator roared to life. Megan came running from her tent, electronics and charging cables in hand. Valeria, crutchless, walked at a slower pace.

Once we plugged everything in, a snake's nest of cables running everywhere, the kids wanted to drag me down to show me how well they had trained their eagles. I sent them to catch fish and promised to join them in a few minutes.

With the kids gone, I asked my mother how things were going.

"You saw how well Valeria's ankle is doing. She puts on a good face, but she cries a lot in her tent. No news on her mother?"

I figured that meant Nana had not yet agreed to leave. Now was the wrong time to spring my newest idea to get Megan and Mom onto a plane to Boston. I'd have two McCree females, three generations apart, digging in their heels. I chose not to mention the murders at my house. Not knowing how much English Nana understood made me reluctant to go into any detail in her presence about the Crenshaw compound. That left subterfuge as my weapon of choice.

I told Mom that Colleen was coming to visit me and wondered if she'd like to take Megan to my house. They could get a decent shower—or run a bath if she wanted—and spend time with Colleen. It would also give Valeria and Nana space from McCrees.

"Might not be a bad idea, but you'd better go check on the kids. I was with them yesterday, and we got an eagle to catch a fish in the air. The girls don't have strong enough arms to throw the fish high enough. I barely could. You could do a good job. I'll make sure Nana is okay with us leaving."

SEVENTY-TWO

WITH THE POLICE AT MY house, I was not in a hurry to depart. And I feared Megan's reaction to leaving Valeria. I figured to let them have a long final play time. "And ask Nana what she wants for extra supplies. While I'm here, do we need more drinking water?"

"There's plenty. The kids take turns running water through the filter. Nana is a real workhorse. Have you seen her woodcarvings? They are *gorgeous.* She could sell them for good money."

The girls had beaten a trail to the river. I arrived to find they had caught two suckers. The eagles called from downriver.

Valeria hauled in another fish. Megan removed the hook and stunned it on a rock. "Grandpa Seamus, watch. The eagles come when I call."

This I had to see. Megan grabbed a fish and walked to a hummock of grass that stuck into the river. She waved the fish above her head and yelled, drawing out each word, "George. Martha. Gonzo. I've got fish." To my amazement, two of the birds called back. Seconds later, Megan identified the one that landed in a nearby dead tree as George. Martha, who I agreed was the larger of the two adults, did lazy loops overhead.

"Grandpa Seamus, can you toss the fish?"

"Geema told me about your new trick." I accepted the fish from Megan. "Anything special before I toss it?"

She instructed me to hold the fish high above my head to let the eagle see it. When it flew near, I was to throw it as high as I could over the water to allow the eagle to retrieve it if it didn't catch it on the fly. I channeled throwing-in a soccer ball and used both hands whipping past my head to chuck it. Martha swooped down but missed; the fish plopped into the river and started flowing downstream. Martha circled, swooped down, and grabbed the sucker from the surface without missing a wingbeat, carrying its meal to a high exposed limb of the tree in which George perched.

Gonzo flew in and tried to swipe the fish. The adults' rebukes were loud and shrill. Eagles aren't like herons that swallow fish whole. They use their hooked beaks to tear the fish apart. It did not take it long to consume the offering.

Megan brought me another fish and told me to wait to throw it until an eagle was closer. I waved the fish by the tail. Nothing happened. "Not working, Pumpkin."

Megan let loose with her George and Gonzo calls, and George launched from the tree heading toward us. The thought of a bird with a five-foot wingspan and talons that could rip me apart flying toward me had my heart thumping against my ribcage. I bent down and flung the fish high into the air. Whether it was the higher throw, or George had better talon-eye coordination, I don't know, but this time the eagle snatched the fish from the air. It gave a kri-kri-kri call and, instead of returning to the tree with the other eagles, flew upriver. Gonzo saw a potential meal flying away and pursued. Martha stayed on her perch, her piercing stare directed at us. Did she hope for another fish?

I asked Megan if she thought she could video the action. She wanted to be in the video with me and suggested Valeria do it. Sounded like a great idea. I let Valeria take a couple of selfies with Megan to get the feel for using my phone before showing her how to record a video.

At Valeria's okay, Megan called in Martha. I reared back and launched the fish into the air. In my enthusiasm, I released the sucker early and lofted it overhead. I watched Martha swoop toward the fish, the fish drop, and realized the trajectory of the two met at my head. I took Megan with me to the ground. We slid across the grass hummock and into the cool embrace of the river. Megan was on top of me and only got a little wet. I came up sputtering and laughing. Neither Megan nor I had seen what happened with Martha and the fish. Valeria laughed so hard she dropped my phone into the water. She retrieved it, and I yelled at her to dry it on her shirt.

Megan grabbed my arm with both hands and told me not to be mad at Valeria for dropping my phone. I assured her all was good. It was my fault we fell into the river. I was glad I hadn't hurt her and that the eagle had avoided both of us. The phone was okay, and we played the video. Martha caught the fish right where I had been standing. It was a terrific video, even if I did look the fool.

A motor's high whine interrupted our second viewing of the video. Megan agreed it was coming from downstream. Valeria spotted a drone flying above the distant tree line, working its way up the river toward us. Aaron Rogers had to be close enough to control the drone.

Crap on a stick. I hustled the kids into the woods.

SEVENTY-THREE

MY INITIAL REACTION WAS TO call Sheriff Bartelle, but I had promised Nana I wouldn't contact the police. I stomped on that temptation and did the next best thing, texting Niki that Rogers' drone was getting close to the hidden camp. She replied with a check mark and "working on it."

I sent the kids to the campsite and stayed hidden behind a screen of cedars, watching the drone scan both banks of the river. I could hide, which meant the first thing Rogers would find interesting would be the road we followed to the river. After that, it would soon discover the canoe on this side of the river—evidence someone was over here. I'd have to risk drawing Rogers' attention to my movement to haul the canoe into the woods. If his lens wasn't too wide . . .

Damn. The kids' fishing poles and bait box remained at the river's edge—a dead giveaway that we were here. I parted the cedar's branches and spotted the drone 100 yards downriver. *Screwed.* I had no safe way to grab them. When Rogers saw them, he would broaden the drone's search area and find the tent compound.

My phone buzzed with a text. I looked down, expecting to see something from Niki. Instead, Colleen informed me she had reached my house. *Police say they're nearly done.* I sent a thumbs up.

Across the river, Martha ruffled her wings and called, her head focused on the drone. Had it ever seen one? The eagle launched into the air, flapped several wing beats headed upriver, did a lazy U-turn and spiraled up, gathering height. Soon it was high above me, circling and calling. The drone continued its search pattern. Martha circled several hundred feet behind the drone and glided down on flat wings to match the drone's elevation over the water. With powerful wingbeats, Martha caught up to the drone and rose above the spinning blades.

The eagle hovered above the machine and slammed its talons into the metal contraption. My stomach flipped at the loud crack. I feared what the drone's blades had done to the eagle's feet. The two split apart. The drone's bent blades dead, the contraption plummeted to the ground on the far side of the river. Martha circled the wreckage twice before flying upriver. Man, I wished I had videotaped that.

Okay, now what? Niki had mentioned Rogers could watch the drone's live video stream. He'd know it was down, but since Martha nailed it from behind, Rogers wouldn't know what happened. Rules state you're supposed to have your drone in sight. I doubted he felt constrained by rules. Regardless, he couldn't be far away.

A new text hit my phone from Niki. *Sorry ur on your own.* I had guessed that, but confirmation was still a letdown.

The mix of tag alders and wet marshes covering much of the river's edge would make it hard for Rogers to follow the riverbank to his downed drone. He might waste more time looking for nonexistent roads or trails leading to the river near where the drone crashed.

Okay, Seamus, you have time before he gets here. Use it wisely.

I collected the poles and bait bucket and ran them up the hill to the camp, where I gathered everyone together. "Nana and Valeria have proved they can hide well in the woods. Mom, that's not your superpower. I need to move you and Megan to the house. Get your walking shoes on. It's our only way to get there."

Mom looked like she was going to argue, but after a moment's hesitation, she gave me a nod.

I continued with instructions. "Valeria, you and Nana must be quiet. No noise. No fire. Very, very quiet. If you hear anyone coming toward the camp, hide in the woods like you did at the trailer. Mom, make sure Nana understands that."

While my mother translated, I told Megan to grab her and her grandmother's electronic stuff. Nana and Mom engaged in some back-and-forth discussion. Mom asked me if I planned to leave the rifle with Nana. "No. It will only slow her down. The only thing that will keep her and Valeria safe is not being found."

Nana nodded agreement with Mom's translation.

"Tell her I will return once it's safe. I will not leave them here by themselves."

The look in Valeria's eyes was enough to make me cry. No child should be that scared. Yet it was their prior experience that gave me confidence they would be okay. "Remember to take your medicine, Valeria. Promise me you won't forget."

She pulled the piece of granite from her pocket and held it up to me. "I promise, Grampa Seamus. Hurry back."

That tore my heart.

Seventy-Four

ONCE WE WERE ACROSS THE river, I gave Mom the rifle and told her to walk far enough up the road to ensure no one could see them from the water and wait for me. To hide the canoe to prevent it from giving Rogers ideas that Nana and Valeria were on the other side, I paddled several bends upstream and hauled it into the woods.

I found Mom and Megan fretting under a hemlock. I texted Colleen to learn whether the police had left and she could drive down and pick us up. Not yet. We'd start walking, and she would meet us on the way. Mom made me lug the gun. Wandering around with a loaded rifle when the police were in the area didn't strike me as my best plan. But if we ran into Rogers, maybe I did want it. I relented and brought it along.

We soon lost cellphone coverage. I wouldn't know if Colleen was coming until she arrived, but as Mom said, it was only two and a half miles and the day was mild, with enough breeze to keep away the biting bugs. The longer we walked, the more I wondered what was preventing Colleen from picking us up.

A couple hundred yards before my driveway, phone coverage returned and brought several messages from Colleen.

They towed the truck and trailer. I parked your F-150 down by the house.

Cops pulling out now.

I'll give it five minutes and leave.

Nope. Company.

I propped the rifle against the shady side of a broad maple and told Mom I didn't know what to expect. I'd never spoken truer words. From the head of the driveway, I saw the jacked-up blue Silverado by my house, facing out, blocking in my vehicles and Colleen's rental. Leaning against the hood were Glenn Korpi and a guy I had never seen. The fourth guy?

"Okay, Megan. Take Geema to the dock, and not a peep from either of you. They can't see you on the road. You'll be safe if you stay quiet. Mom, wait until you get there and call 9-1-1. Leave a message for Sheriff Bartelle. Tell him Glenn Korpi—two Ns in the first name. Last is spelled K-O-R-P-I—is at my house. You got that?"

She repeated it. I told Megan that she was to lead Geema to our safe spot from before. I waited until they were a ways down the road, then strode down the driveway like I owned the place, which I did. "Hey guys," I said in a friendly voice. "What's up?" I was relieved Colleen was not with them.

I took the measure of the guy who was not Korpi. We looked to be the same weight, but he carried his weight on a squattier frame. At my approach, he flipped out a badge holder and flashed a shield. "Agent Carpenter with ICE." He tucked his badge holder into his pocket. "We're responding to information regarding an illegal immigrant. Young girl named Valeria, and the illegal is her grandmother. Family goes by the name of Serrano. Might have adopted false names. They often do."

These two were no more ICE agents than I was the man in the moon. Interesting that they didn't mention Valeria's mother. I saw no reason to let them know I didn't believe them and said, "My granddaughter went to a day camp in Amasa with a girl named Valeria. Good friends, but my granddaughter hasn't been there for more than a week."

"You know where they live?"

"I can give you directions. One time Valeria's mother was late picking her up from camp, and Kim—Kim Belanger, the proprietor of the day camp? Anyway, she and I took Valeria to a trailer far back in the woods. To get there, you—"

"Abandoned," Agent Carpenter said. "Our sources think you are hiding the girl."

Time to fake aggravation. "You need more reliable sources. Why someone fed you that bullshit is beyond me. Was it somebody I fired because they came to work drunk? I hire lots of people to help manage my forest land, but every single one is a US citizen or has a legitimate green card. You want to check my records? My accountant will be delighted to show you proof. I don't have to hire illegal immigrants because I pay higher wages than almost everyone around here." Academy award time for the heat I added to my voice.

They shared a look. I spotted Colleen watching us from an upstairs window. Good, she was safe.

Agent Carpenter broke the silence. "You mind if we have a little look around? Talk with your granddaughter. Maybe she heard something from her friend about their plans?"

"Yes I mind. You come waltzing in, accusing me of I don't know what. This is private property. You want to search it, show me a warrant. You've wasted enough of my time. Please leave my property now and don't come back until you have that search warrant."

Korpi stiffened and reached behind his back. Going for a gun? "Sounds like you got something to hide."

I stepped toward him, forcing him backwards. "Maybe you need a refresher on the Constitution. Specifically, the fourth amendment prohibiting illegal search and seizure." I held out my hand to Agent Carpenter. "Got a card? I hear anything about this Valeria or her grandmother, I'll be sure to call."

To my absolute shock, Agent Carpenter pulled a card from his badge holder. "I appreciate that. Let's go," he said to Korpi. "We're done here."

Korpi gave me a long stare. "You sure you shouldn't bring him in for questioning?"

Agent Carpenter said, "Not yet. We know where he lives, though."

Seventy-Five

I RACED INTO THE HOUSE, past Colleen, who asked what was happening, and to the upstairs bathroom window to confirm Agent Carpenter and Korpi had indeed driven up the road. "Tell you as soon as I retrieve Megan and Mom."

I found them on the log bench watching a pair of trumpeter swans feeding in the waters off the grass island. I accompanied them to the house and told Mom to pack all Megan's things. They were leaving today.

"Grandpa Seamus," Megan whined, "I don't want to leave Valeria. You—"

"Megan Nelson McCree, this is not a negotiation. You will help Geema pack your stuff. If you don't, I will tie you to a chair, and Geema will do it for you. Mom, everything is in the upstairs bedroom."

Mom bent down and took Megan's hand. "There is no reasoning with him when he's like this. If I could, I'd put him across my knee and spank him. I'd let you help. But he's bigger than us both, so let's do what he says."

Megan tried to stifle a giggle and let Geema lead her upstairs. I asked Colleen if she had her computer. She did, and I gave her the password to my Wi-Fi. "Go online and find the earliest flight to Boston. Check Marquette, Iron Mountain, Green Bay, even Milwaukee. It's an hour and a half to Marquette and Iron Mountain, three hours to Green Bay, five to Milwaukee."

I wanted to determine if Carpenter was an ICE agent. Calling the phone number on his card was like clicking on a link in an email. You never knew what was real or fake. My online search for ICE offices in the Upper Peninsula came up blank. Homeland Security Investigations had an office at Sault Ste. Marie, but no information on employees. I texted Niki and asked how to verify someone worked for ICE. Her return text said, *Contact ADNI Park. Tell him I told you to get the information.*

Brilliant. Averell Harrington Park, an Assistant Director of National Intelligence, was one of her two bosses, and I served as a cutout to shield their relationship from prying eyes. I thundered upstairs two at a time and retrieved the secure cellphone from a desk drawer. I logged into the messaging app and requested him to confirm whether ICE employed an agent named Carpenter who met the description I provided.

Nothing more I could do with that. I called downstairs, "How we doing on those flights?"

"Found a United flight leaving Green Bay at five-thirty this evening. One stop in Chicago, but doesn't arrive in Boston until almost one a.m."

"Perfect." I pulled up the United site and booked tickets for my mother and Megan and asked Colleen for her information to get her a ticket too.

"No, Seamus. Don't you remember? I have an appointment to review the motel's books tomorrow."

"This has become way too dangerous. I'm not risking any family with whatever's going on."

Her hoot echoed off the cathedral ceiling. "Don't waste your money. Even if you buy a ticket, you can't force me on the plane. I'll accompany you to Green Bay. Gives us time to strategize. Come with me to look at the motel's books if it makes you feel better. But I'm not backing down, Seamus. Give it up."

I shouted into the bedroom, "How's it going in there?"

Mom responded they were almost ready. "Megan and I both have clothes at the campsite."

Megan stormed over to me and stamped her foot. "If you're deporting me, I want Atalanta and Cheech and Chong with me."

I had almost laughed at her stamped foot. Her words sobered me. She and Valeria must have been talking about deportation, even if Megan didn't use the word precisely. "Pumpkin, you know I don't want to do this, but I have to. Your hound and your cats are at their own sleep-away camps. Besides, they hate to fly, and Geema has no room for them. Do a last check to make sure you found everything." She stomped back to the bedroom.

Mom came out and motioned me to follow her downstairs. In a low voice, she said, "You know I can't keep Megan at my place. A day or two, I could do, but her parents don't return for another week, right?"

"Lizzie has plenty of room and even if she's not around, I'm sure she'd be happy to let you both stay there. I'll express mail your stuff that's at the campsite. This will work."

The app on my secure phone notified me I had a message. I entered my password to the messaging system. ADNI Park had responded much faster than I expected. A Matthew Carpenter, who fit my description, was employed as an ICE agent assigned to the Chicago area. Another Chicago connection.

Whatever his game, I didn't wish to meet him until I had moved Mom and Megan to safety. Instead of driving the normal way into town, I followed an obscure track through the neighbor's property and onto the A Grade. From there, I used the Cut Across Road and continued up to Michigamme. It added an extra forty-five minutes to the trip but avoided any possibility Carpenter would spot us.

SEVENTY-SIX

MOM AND MEGAN MADE IT through Homeland security's screening around 4:30 p.m. My ex-wife, Lizzie, agreed to meet them at Logan Airport. Mom thought it was unnecessary. She knew how to take a taxi; she'd been doing it since before I was born. I ignored her. Mom might be capable, but I was uncomfortable with an eighty-three-year-old woman and an eight-year-old child unaccompanied at Logan at one o'clock in the morning.

On the way back north, I asked Colleen to take the wheel to allow me to have my hands and mind free to work. I had deferred talking to Niki to avoid further worrying Megan. I waited until Colleen made it to the highway and put Niki on speaker. Niki, being Niki, interrogated me about what had happened at my house and gave me an attaboy for shipping Mom and Megan to Boston.

I steered the conversation to learn about her excursion to Iron River with Bartelle and Tex.

"Total bust. First problem, I couldn't tell Sheriff Bartelle about Aaron Rogers and the drone without giving away your location. Then dispatch called with your message that Glenn Korpi was at your house. Bartelle and I did a one-eighty and drove all the way to your place. Never saw hide nor hair of the blue Silverado nor the gray Tundra—not that Bartelle knew we were looking for it. You were gone—I let Bartelle in to do a wellness check. Meantime, Tex struck out finding anyone in Iron River. They'll turn up. You've had time to concoct a plan. What are you thinking?"

Colleen snorted. "You're giving him too much credit."

"Thank you, sis. Colleen still thinks she should dance tonight at the Silver Fox." My voice carried all the enthusiasm of opening my mouth to accept a tablespoon of castor oil.

"Wait, you guys," Colleen said. "I haven't told you what happened last night at the club."

She described the atmosphere among the girls as friendly. She had worried about catty women, claws extended, competing for tips or special services. They split general tips among the dancers. The house took fifty percent of whatever a dancer earned behind the curtains. They allowed zero hanky-panky in the pole-dance room. Catcall requests for provocative behavior were fine, but no touching. A guy touches a girl in that room, he's escorted out the door.

I wasn't sure I wanted to know the answer, but I asked anyway. "What goes on in the curtained rooms?"

"Can't tell you from experience. It's optional, although only one other girl opted out. I felt zero pressure from management or the other women. Maybe that comes later. One thing that surprised me was they'd fire me on the spot if they caught me buying, selling, or using drugs on the premises."

I asked Niki if that was unusual from what she understood. "What? You think I have a vast knowledge of pole dancing and nude bars and private curtained rooms?"

Her phrasing it that way told me I was in danger of digging my grave. "I thought maybe you covered stuff like this in your FBI training."

Niki chortled. "Good try. Maybe they had past problems?"

Colleen said, "It's not like the place is totally clean. One girl told me she could get me anything I wanted. I got the feeling something hinky was going on. Is it possible they don't want drugs there because they're using the place for something worse?"

I asked if there was any place they wouldn't let her see.

Colleen read my mind. "You mean where they could keep Kat prisoner? The place is built on a slab, so no basement. I've been in the office area, and they showed me around the detached storage area because it also has a small space where the girls can lock their purses. Sorry, no. Anyway, I see no reason I shouldn't dance tonight, and I might learn some more from the girls."

Niki asked, "Did you see Aaron Rogers or any of the other people we've been targeting?"

"No, but I forgot to mention that the manager who hired me wasn't there last night. Another woman—Bonnie, maybe?—was in charge. Not tall, well put together, thin as a pipe cleaner."

Niki and I said together, "Bunny?"

"Possible. It was noisy. Yeah, could be Bunny."

Colleen gave us a detailed description. Yep, Bunny Crenshaw. Wasn't that interesting?

Niki volunteered to do a background check on her, which reminded me that she had intended to run my photographs from the Crenshaw compound through Rembrandt. I asked if she had.

"The five guys are from the Chicago area. One's getting married in two weeks. The other four are his groomsmen. The women are an interesting group. One is a Yooper. The rest are also from the greater Chicago area."

"Chicago," I said, "seems to come up a lot. Rogers is from there, and Dombey comes from Gary, which isn't all that far away. But we have nothing to link the Crenshaws to the Windy City. We're missing the bigger picture."

Niki agreed and mentioned the Chicago women had various arrest records, drugs and soliciting, but none of them had ever done time. Some traffic violation stuff on the guys, and one had a sealed juvie record. The married couple in the kitchen were born and raised in the Iron River area, had four kids in school, and the woman's mother lived at the same address. He had a couple of old DWIs; she'd been arrested a decade earlier for shoplifting, but the charges were dismissed.

Niki would forward the pictures to Colleen's phone to look at before her shift started in case any were dancing tonight. I used that opening to argue Colleen should skip the Silver Fox. Niki pooh-poohed my fears. Colleen dances, keeps her eyes open and her mouth shut, and we learn if any of the guys or gals showed up.

Was I the only one who saw danger? "If she's going, I'm going. I had planned to take supplies to Valeria and Nana. Make sure they're doing okay and try once more to convince them to let me take them away from the area. That will have to wait."

Niki said, "Already did that, Seamus. They're fine and have everything they need for now. Valeria is taking her medicine and has no symptoms other than the rash. And Nana has not changed her mind. Seamus, you or me showing up at the Silver Fox will endanger Colleen more than her going alone."

I pointed Colleen toward the left fork in the highway.

"People are looking for you. That's why you took that circuitous route down to Green Bay. Nothing links Colleen to you until she shows up tomorrow morning to review the motel's accounting records. It was fine for me to accompany her to support her when she was there to ask about a job, but it would draw unwanted attention for me to show up by myself while she dances."

Niki's logic had no holes, and I had no argument to keep Colleen from her appointed pole at the Silver Fox. "Fine. Then we should research the hell out of everybody we've come in contact with and find the damn linkages. We use those to drive some sense into Nana so we can get her the hell out and give the information to Sheriff Bartelle."

Colleen gave me a thumbs up. Niki told me she'd have more info when I got home. I dropped Colleen at her motel and, again to minimize the chances of running into anyone who was looking for me, took the long way back to my place. That gave me time to reconsider every piece of evidence we had uncovered.

The more I thought, the glummer I became. I put the odds at twenty to one that Kat was dead, and we were no closer to knowing what happened than we were a week ago.

Seventy-Seven

NIKI AND I WORKED LATE into the night. She tapped into various databases to pull up prior addresses, social media posts, arrest details, etc. Every quarter hour, she'd dump her most recent findings onto my desk. I took the data and looked for connections.

The U.P. woman lived in Norway, grew up in Bark River, had been a cheerleader, and did not have an arrest record. She danced at the Silver Fox.

The Chicago folks helped paint the picture. The groom-to-be was a heavy hitter on Chicago's commodity exchange, worth a billion dollars. His groomsmen were guys I'd expect in a wedding party: the groom's brother, two high school best buds, and the guy's college roommate. Nothing more than speeding tickets on any of them. I guessed they had their bachelor party so far away from home because they knew the area from fishing or hunting and had learned of the Menominee Rapids Resort.

The first thing I found that linked any of the eight Chicago women was three of them, and—surprise, Drew Dombey—were witnesses at a stabbing in a northern suburb of Chicago. Two drunks at a party in Lake Forest had gotten into a fight. One stabbed the other with a cocktail fork.

I brought that intel to Niki. "Lake Forest is a pretty ritzy neighborhood, and the cocktail fork is telling. With the groom's money and this tidbit, I bet these women are high-class hookers, and Dombey is their pimp or manager or whatever."

"Bingo." Niki pointed to her computer screen. "They're high-end escorts. This website quotes their weekend services as ranging between twenty-five and forty thousand. Each."

I whistled at the rates. "I guess if you're a billionaire, spending that much on a bachelor weekend is chump change. Do they work for an agency, or what?"

Niki backed her browser to show one woman's website. "That's my assumption. Their websites are similar. If your son were here, he could apply his computer expertise to determine where the links go. All I can tell is that they're dummy addresses and forwarded to an offshore server. These girls are not just pretty faces either. One is a PhD candidate at the University of Chicago. Two are minor actresses. One was Miss Nebraska, another an Olympic downhill skier hopeful who blew out her knee at the most recent trials."

She clicked on the contact form and used her finger to highlight her points. "This takes you to a secure server—at least that's what they claim—on the dark web. You select your level of service, check their calendar for availability, and upload a copy of your driver's license. And look at this: you have to tell them who referred you to the client."

I did some quick arithmetic. If the average weekend cost thirty grand and each girl worked once a month, that grossed $360,000 a year. Split 50-50, each girl grossed $180,000. The nine women working one weekend a month grossed management $1.6 million a year.

Niki rubbed her eyes. "They don't have this set up for just these nine women. This is a multi-million-dollar operation."

I blurted out the thought before I considered it. "Kat sure didn't have that kind of money. I guess that could have been the motivation, huh?"

"Or," Niki said, "they were forcing her into it if she was indeed the missing tenth woman. My badge and I could pay a visit to the one who lives in Norway."

We concentrated on trying to connect either Mike or Randy Crenshaw to Chicago. Not a whiff. Anita "Bunny" Crenshaw, nee Palumbo, was born in Rockford and had grown up in Libertyville, a Lake County village north of Chicago. No arrest record on her.

I gathered the notes into a pile and squared them. "We've got bupkes. It's Mike's property, Randy brought out the guys, and Bunny has a hand in at the Silver Fox. We know they're involved, and now we know they're talented at hiding their tracks. The local woman is the one outsider who could tie it all together for us. She might even know Kat. Let's double-team her tomorrow before she leaves to dance at the Silver Fox."

"Remember, after tomorrow, I have to go back to St. Paul. Is that the best use of my time?"

I pulled my elbows back to stretch. Everything was taking longer than we wanted, and no lead had produced enough data to give us direction. Without Niki, Colleen and I were left with trying to find something actionable with Crenshaw's businesses.

"I'm all ears if you have a better idea."

Niki shook her head. "I don't even have enough energy to drag you to bed. But I have a feeling things are going to break tomorrow."

Seventy-Eight

"COMPANY'S COMING," **I** YELLED UPSTAIRS to Niki. "I don't recognize the Jeep. I'll meet them outside. Why don't you keep watch from the window up there?"

With our late night working on the case, we'd slept in and woken up a half-hour ago with plans to visit the local dancer early afternoon. Nine in the morning was a weird time for an unknown visitor. I threw on a wool shirt and walked into the cool of the morning of what should be a spectacular day with enough wind to keep the bugs down and temps hitting the mid-70s. The air smelled clear and dry, although wispy clouds in the west suggested rain might arrive within forty-eight hours.

The dark green Jeep pulled into my turnaround and backed down the driveway, giving me a view of the driver.

I greeted Agent Carpenter after he got out of the car. "What brings you here early on a Monday morning?"

He stretched his hands high above his head, then reached into the car and pulled out a sheet of paper.

"Mr. McCree." He handed me the document. "A judge agrees with us that you have been less than forthcoming. Here's the search warrant you wanted."

That he hadn't believed me wasn't a surprise—I had not been entirely forthcoming. His convincing a judge to issue a search warrant was a shock. That required probable cause, and I didn't think he had that. I bought time to think by telling him I wanted to see what it said.

The search warrant allowed ICE agents to seize all electronic equipment, including cellphones, laptops, desktop computers, and any audio recordings. I asked what audio recordings meant.

"Answering machines, dictation devices, cassette players, that sort of stuff. A judge signed this. It's legal."

While scanning the warrant, I replayed my last conversation with Carpenter. I didn't think I had lied, even if I hadn't told the entire truth. The document allowed them to search my house, garage, generator building, unattached cabin, woodshed, and personal vehicles. I had three woodsheds and wondered whether he had to choose one—not that I had anything other than wood and tools in any of them.

They could seize *any* property belonging to Katrina Serrano—so this time, they mentioned the mother—her minor child, Valeria Serrano, and any family members. They didn't know Nana's name? I was confident neither Valeria nor Nana had left anything in my house. However, he couldn't help but notice the neat pile of last night's research notes on my desk. Those were off limits to him, but he'd find plenty on my computer and know what to look for.

Oh boy, explaining that would be—my stomach did a back flip—*nothing compared to what was on my phone.* Its location history would show everywhere I had been. Sure, they could eventually get that information from the carrier, but the selfies Valeria took were damning.

A judge's scrawled signature on the bottom made it seem legit. "I always comply with legal requests, but I don't know jack about search warrants. I need to call my lawyer."

"You can call your lawyer. But this search warrant is legal. If you obstruct me, I will arrest you. You'll stay handcuffed in my vehicle while I proceed with the search. Let's start with the house. Things will go faster if you show me where everything is."

I pointed the papers at the house. "That's my house. And there," I waved the papers toward the pole barn building, "is my garage. The generator shed is behind it. Feel free." I headed toward the screen porch.

"Not so fast," he said. "You got your cellphone or any electronics on you?"

"Nope. You gonna strip search me?"

He scowled. "If you won't cooperate, you stay outside."

To prevent me from destroying evidence. "It's a beautiful day for it. May I sit on the screened porch?"

He followed me onto the porch and checked behind the wood rack, underneath the chairs and tables, peered at the ceiling. He pursed his lips and shook his head. "Two entrances into the house. You'll have to wait outside. When did you say you last saw Valeria?"

"You can lock the doors to keep me on the porch."

"You last saw Valeria when?"

"I insist that my lawyer be present before you question me."

He invaded my space, standing inches from me. "I've never heard an innocent person say that. Never."

I wanted to avoid a conversation in which he could later use my words against me. "May I get something to read?"

He tilted his head, squinted an eye, straightened. "Sure," he said with a chipper note, "we can do that."

He followed me inside. *Where's Niki?* Nothing stirred upstairs or in the kitchen. I retrieved my Kindle from the drum table, and he said, "Electronic device. I'll take that."

Well, you fell into that, dummy. All he'd find was my eclectic bookshelf. I never use it to browse the internet. "Whoops, my bad. I have some books down in the basement. Shall we?"

He followed me down and looked around while I chose an essay collection from Outdoor magazine. I had enjoyed reading them several years earlier. "This will do." I marched upstairs with him scurrying behind me. Didn't want me alone upstairs. Still no evidence of Niki. Interesting.

"You got your book, now get." He pointed to the door as though I didn't know the way. "And if you want to use the facilities, find a spot in the woods."

I gave the asshole a jaunty salute that may have included an extended middle finger. I walked to the Wildlife Viewing Platform at the lakeshore, plopped onto one of the swivel chairs, and checked the water for ducks. None in view. I opened the book to the first essay.

And couldn't concentrate on a single word. Where the hell was Niki?

Seventy-Nine

Fifteen minutes later, Agent Carpenter came grumbling down the path, holding the secure cellphone I used for Niki's undercover work. "Unlock this for me."

I considered saying something snarky to the effect that his mother hadn't taught him to use the magic words: please and thank you. No reason to antagonize him any more than I already had; I didn't want him trashing my house. "Before that happens, my lawyer will have to agree."

He thrust the phone at me. "So, call him."

I waved it away. "Nice try. You finished?"

He stomped off, and it was all I could do not to laugh.

Niki appeared soon after Carpenter left and copped the other chair. I asked where she'd been.

"Let me read the search warrant first."

I waited in silence for her to finish, wondering what she thought humorous. She returned it to me. "When I saw him hand this to you, I guessed what it was. While you kept him occupied outside, I put your laptop, your cellphone, and our work from last night in a large garbage bag and hid everything in the outhouse."

I leaned over and bussed her cheek.

She waited until I had settled in my chair before continuing. "I hoped he wouldn't think to look down into the shitter. Turned out even better because his search warrant doesn't include the outhouse. Once he realizes his mistake, he'll correct it. The thing is, he can't do that over the phone."

"Which means," I said, "if he's working by himself, he'll have to leave. That's great for last night's workpapers, but my computer and phone records automatically back up in the cloud. All he has to do is subpoena them. Is your stuff with mine?"

"Nope. In the rental's backseat. You're right about your cloud backup. To gain access, he has to figure out who your cell provider is and where you back up your computer. Then dealing with Microsoft or Amazon or Verizon or any of those guys means jumping through more hoops."

"Which means we have a little time before he can use my cellphone to learn where we've hidden Nana and Valeria. My truck can rat me out, though."

She ducked her head in agreement. "Again, it takes time. After Carpenter leaves, we need to check the vehicles for trackers—legal or otherwise. If I were crawling up your ass, I'd stick one on anything that moves."

The net enclosing Nana and Valeria was closing fast. "He can't legally tag your rental, right?"

Her smile flattened. "Not legally. Yet. Look, Seamus, if they're doing the full Monty on you, they'll be monitoring your credit cards, your bank records, when you change your underwear."

Meaning they'd know everything I did as soon as I did it. I'd have to find another way. "And they'll soon know who you are. Colleen is our only source of a clean vehicle."

Niki nodded. "Unless you borrow or steal wheels. Speaking of Colleen, I called her after I hid the stuff. She said the only people of interest to us at the Silver Fox last night were Bunny and Randy Crenshaw. Those two got into a heated discussion, and Colleen chatted with some of the other girls about it. They said that happened often, but either didn't know or wouldn't say what the disagreements were about. I wonder what Colleen's finding in the motel's records."

"Time will tell. Besides fretting about where you were, I've been down here wondering what makes the Serrano family so important to justify this level of attention. First from Rogers, Korpi, Dombey, and friends. Now from ICE Agent Carpenter? Nana's illegal immigrant status nominally justifies Carpenter, but don't you agree Kat triggered this? Did she steal something? I don't mean their drugs, incriminating evidence. And the reason they want Valeria and Nana is they think one of them has it?"

"Another fine theory," Niki said, "with nothing to back it up."

EIGHTY

Agent Carpenter's next appearance came with him holding a power adapter for my laptop. He saw Niki and asked, "Who the hell are you? I didn't hear anybody drive up."

"That's because I walked."

"Let me see some identification." He held out his hand.

"No." She waved the search warrant at him. "I'm not entering your search zone, and therefore you do not need to know who I am. You're a little understaffed, aren't you? I've never seen a search conducted by only one person. At the Bureau, we'd assign a ton of people to swarm a place like this."

The flash of his eyes widening before drawing into slits told me Niki had surprised him. He recovered and arranged his mouth into a gash. "I will not have you interfere with this legal search."

Niki offered him a contrite smile. "Never crossed my mind. Make sure you leave a detailed inventory of anything you take. Seamus may not know a search warrant from a hole in the ground, but I do."

Carpenter stabbed his finger at me. "I'll find your laptop even if I have to bring a backhoe and dig up your eighty acres or drain the whole damn lake."

I sent him back to the house with a comment that before he could disturb the soil, he needed a soil erosion permit, and draining the lake would require a DNR permit. He did not appear to appreciate my sense of humor.

As noon became one o'clock, my stomach started grumbling. Niki and I returned to the house. I stuck my head inside and called to Agent Carpenter. "Can you take a break long enough to watch us grab lunch from the fridge? I'll be happy to get you a yogurt or something."

He clumped down from the upstairs bedroom. "Make it quick."

I opened the refrigerator, gulped when I spotted Megan's juice boxes on the top shelf, and grabbed four Greek yogurts.

Carpenter threw out a hand to prevent me from closing the door. "How long were the kids here?"

I gave him my best puzzled look. "Huh?"

Carpenter pointed. "The juice boxes are for the kids, right?"

"Granddaughter loves them, but they're perfect for a quick pick me up while hiking. Lots of sucrose and they wet your whistle."

He shook his head in disgust. "You're only digging your grave deeper."

"Nope," I said. "No soil conservation permit."

An hour later, Agent Carpenter left the house, told us we could go inside. He entered the garage. If Korpi had related the Bobcat incident, he'd now know for sure that it belonged to me. I counted the days since that confrontation. A week. Carpenter spent a brief time in the garage, then visited the generator shed and trooped up to the cabin. After a half hour, he joined us on the house's screened porch.

"I've compiled a list of items on my phone. Give me your number and I'll text them to you."

Hoping I'd cough up the number? "Email me, but I want to see the list before you leave."

"Sorry, doesn't work that way."

I gave Niki a side glance. She nodded an affirmative. I guess I didn't have the right to an immediate list. In which case, who was to say he had listed everything he confiscated? Not a perfect system, for sure. I provided him the email address I used for junk mail. He could troll through that to his heart's desire.

Carpenter left with a sealed box containing my things. I'd seen him take my Kindle, desktop computer, the secure phone—good luck with that— and a digital recorder I hadn't used in a decade. I wouldn't know what else he had taken until I received the complete list or realized something was missing.

Niki and I watched him roll up the driveway and down Shank Lake Road. "So what—"

"Don't say a thing, Seamus, until I check this whole place for bugs."

EIGHTY-ONE

THE HOUSE CONTAINED NO AUDIO bugs, but Niki found trackers on my truck, Subaru, and the ATVs. She saw the gears clicking in my head. "With one, you could leave it lying on a rough stretch of road and argue that it must've fallen off. They could still arrest you and make you go through the hassle of getting bail. If they all disappeared, they would charge and convict you with obstructing an investigation."

I held my hands in surrender position. "They provide us an opportunity to leave false trails. You're sure your vehicle is clean?"

"I think so, and it convinces me that he had a legal warrant for those trackers. No judge would allow him to stick a tracker on any old vehicle that he found parked at a particular address."

"We need to gather as much intel as we can and decide how to play this. Before we can get to the local call girl's place in Norway, she'll probably be at the Silver Fox, and we couldn't talk to her there. I'll call Colleen and find out what she learned from her review of the motel's books. Why don't you squeeze Bartelle and Tex for an update on Aaron Rogers and Glenn Korpi?"

Niki reminded me I should retrieve my phone, computer, and papers from the outhouse. I used a rake to snag the garbage bag and haul it into the light. No one had used the outhouse in years, so the bag was almost clean.

I washed my hands in the lake and called Colleen from the dock. She'd found shortages in the motel's reported revenue. For example, the records did not reflect the cash my mother paid for her one-night stay. Colleen couldn't know if the cash had vanished at the time Mom checked in or whether the night clerk was blameless and the money evaporated later.

I asked if she had any idea how much was involved.

She cleared her throat. "Normally, cash payments are rare, and you wouldn't expect it to amount to squat. Running a prostitution ring that uses the motel could create some serious bucks. Unless we get our hands on a second set of true financials, we won't discover the answer from the accounting. Not much gets by the motel's housekeepers, though. Maybe that's what precipitated Kat's disappearance?"

Given what was going on at the Crenshaw compound, a prostitution ring could work several ways. The girls could pay off someone with cash to allow them to use rooms. Or if management ran the hookers, they could provide the rooms for free. With enough time, the accounting records should show discrepancies. They'd use more cleaning supplies than justified by the bookings. Same for the quantity of breakfast-buffet food. An analysis to uncover those inconsistencies would take more resources and time than we had.

While I had gone into my silent considerations, Colleen had continued talking. I asked her to repeat what she'd said.

"Crenshaw's accountant also brought information for the Menominee Rapids Resort. I guess he hopes your buyer might be interested in that, too. The hotel part of the resort breaks even, maybe makes a few bucks. The restaurant does much better than I thought most restaurants did. Referral fees for arranging outings are their big money-makers. River rafting, fishing, hunting, even birdwatching. Who knew birdwatching was lucrative?"

I mentioned my suspicions that some of the "entertainment" was being run through the restaurant's books. "Was Randy Crenshaw there?"

"Just me and Mike Crenshaw's 180-year-old accountant who asked me to dine with him. What's our next step?"

I explained our recent situation with Agent Carpenter, his search warrant, and the bugs on the car and truck. She offered to drive to camp and swap her rental for my truck. "I like your thinking. We might be able to fool them once. Let's reserve that trick until we need it."

"I have nothing on my dance card, so to speak, until the Silver Fox tomorrow night. Since Randy wasn't at the meeting, I guess I can still do that. Maybe I can strike up a conversation with that woman from Norway."

Not the time to refight that battle. "I have something more important than that and it requires a phone ICE could not have tapped." I told her what I wanted.

She said she was on it. "One question, Seamus. What if they've already tapped your phone?"

"Then you'd better buy a burner."

Eighty-Two

NIKI HAD LEARNED VERY LITTLE. Iron County deputies had not set eyes on Aaron Rogers or Glenn Korpi. Sheriff Bartelle was unaware of any ICE activity in the area. I mused whether it was time to approach Mike Crenshaw and see his reaction to Colleen's suspicions about the motel's books and my belief his son was involved in a high-end prostitution operation using his compound.

Niki chewed on her upper lip. "It's hard to fathom he would agree for you to look at the books if he knew they had issues. And what do we have on the prostitution ring other than that his son drove the five guys to the compound? The rich husband-to-be could have arranged bringing the girls up from Chicago on his own. And even if Randy Crenshaw is involved—well, he probably is, given the one local woman was there—what do you accomplish if you convince the old man?"

"Whacking hornet nests? Okay, Kat worked at the motel, danced at the Silver Fox, maybe worked parties at the Resort, and maybe hooked at the compound—explaining the occasional weekends she was gone. We could try talking to the motel housekeepers again, but if something *is* going on and they think Kat got in trouble, they aren't likely to talk, are they?"

"Nope."

"And Colleen has seen nothing in the Silver Fox that would justify making Kat disappear. Not that Kat couldn't have stumbled over something."

Niki filled in my thoughts. "Given the time, we—meaning you—can't talk to the woman until tomorrow at the earliest. And we've poked around at the resort as much as we can."

I blew out a long sigh. "Which leaves Crenshaw's compound for tonight."

Niki slapped me on the leg. "I wondered how long it would take a bright boy like you to figure out our next step. Then, like it or not, I have to take off tomorrow for my St. Paul commitments."

I hadn't forgotten, but a piece of me had hoped Niki would blow them off and see this through. "Understood. Right now, I'm going bear hunting and take Carpenter on a wild goose chase."

She shook her head. "You are nothing if not a mixed metaphor."

I LEFT NIKI AT HOME to pack and then follow more leads from Rembrandt and took the two-up ATV on a meandering route starting in the opposite direction from where Valeria and Nana camped. After a couple of hours of leading Agent Carpenter's tracker hither and yon, I reached Lake Tranquility where I searched the tent area for Valeria's missing bear. No luck.

The flat calm lake attracted me, and I kicked off my shoes and dangled my feet off the end of the pier in the cool water. The eagles called from across the lake, and soon one adult was flapping hard toward me. As it came near, I yelled, "No fish. Sorry. Next time I'll catch some before I visit. By the way, thanks for downing that drone. If it wasn't you, thank your partner. I hope you didn't get hurt."

It was like the eagle understood. It circled once above my head, wings audibly compressing the air, then flew to the far shoreline. While staring into the lake, my subconscious brought up a memory of Valeria. To gather rocks at her trailer, she had wrapped her bear around a slender tree. Had she done something similar while fishing? I laced my shoes, walked to the spot I'd last seen the girls fishing and found it strapped to a sapling looking as though it was shimming up the tree.

The bear's weight surprised me. The magnets that held its paws weren't that heavy. I poked the critter and found a small rectangular solid inside it. A capital U of tiny stitches marred its stomach. To focus on the threads, I pushed my glasses on top of my head and brought the bear to my nose. The thread's color didn't match the bear's fur.

I snipped the stitches using the Swiss army knife scissors, dug my finger into the stuffing, and found a USB flash drive.

EIGHTY-THREE

NOT WANTING TO LEAVE ANY trace on my computer of whatever was on the thumb drive, we plugged it into Niki's laptop. Pictures. We scrolled through selfies of Kat in a party dress taken on the Saturday before she vanished. She was an attractive young woman with a quizzical smile. Next came a loaded buffet table and one of a tuxedoed waiter handing a drink to another woman attired in a dress identical to Kat's.

I tapped the screen. "That's the private room at the Menominee Rapids Resort, right?"

Niki moved my finger. "That's the painting above the door." She quickly scrolled through many pictures of people enjoying themselves at the party.

"Wait," I shouted. "Go back. I think I recognize that guy."

Niki scrolled back two pictures, and Vincent Otto stared at me. "You remember my daughter-in-law, Cindy Nelson, is an investigative reporter in Chicago?" She did. "A year, maybe two years ago, she did an exposé on this guy's law firm. Not only are they the go-to defense counselors for the mob, Cindy found proof they were a major conduit for bribing Chicago and Illinois politicians. Several of the junior partners pleaded out or were convicted. Otto ended up with a hung jury. Everyone believed he'd paid off somebody. What the hell is a Chicago mover and shaker doing at a private party in Iron Mountain, Michigan?"

We scrolled through Kat's party photos. The only other people we recognized were Randy Crenshaw and Mindy, the waitress who had served Niki and me during our lunch with Mike Crenshaw.

The next picture had me dry-swallowing to keep from throwing up. Lying face up in a motel room bed was a young woman. Nude, her eyes stared at nothing. Tongue protruded through foam leaking from her mouth. Ligature marks around her neck. Kat had a picture of a murder victim.

Niki scrolled to an earlier picture at the party. "It's the woman who was dressed like Kat."

She was right, and a scenario formed in my mind. Somebody at that party had taken this young woman and strangled her in one of the motel rooms that Kat cleaned. It could have been a sex act gone wrong or something else. This photograph could explain why people wanted to find Valeria and Nana. What had Kat done after she found the dead woman? I urged Niki to let me see the remaining pictures.

The next one showed a room number. The last was a blurry shot of the printed bill for that room, naming Vincent Otto as the responsible party.

A heavy weight settled on my shoulders. "Kat, what did you do after you took those pictures? The date stamps say these were Sunday morning. As far as we know, nothing changed in her routine until Thursday. Someone calls her into the motel's office. Then, she comes home early, leaves again, and vanishes. Sometime between Sunday and Thursday before she left home, she downloaded photos from her phone onto this thumb drive and hid it in Valeria's bear."

"Wait," Niki said, "did she have a computer?"

"Nope, which means someone did it for her. Friend? Office supply place? One of her workplaces?"

"Good questions." Niki brought up a browser, made several searches, and announced, "No stories featuring a dead woman found in the motel. Kat didn't report this to the police. Neither did whoever Kat told. Or if Kat didn't tell anyone, whoever later found the body didn't report it either."

"Look at the time stamps. She snaps the body at 10:06 a.m. Was she cleaning rooms or was she checking in on one of her party friends? She doesn't take the picture of the room number until 11:25 a.m. The printed bill picture occurred fifteen minutes later. Something happened that made her take those last two pictures. Do an internet search for 'missing woman from the Upper Peninsula.' And if you don't come up with anything, try Northern Wisconsin."

Northern Wisconsin hit pay dirt. A two-inch article said Peggy Dowson's sister reported the Pembine, Wisconsin woman missing. Police discovered Peggy's car in a nearby park-and-ride and were looking for any information, blah, blah, blah. It was dated the day after Kat disappeared.

This changed everything. I said, "We have to take this to the police. Which means we inform them Kat's gone missing. And that requires moving Valeria and Nana to a safe place unknown to me. I have Colleen working on a plan, but we must convince Nana to leave now. I assume Carpenter could have received a judge's approval to tap into your rental's GPS?"

"Unlikely, but not impossible."

I pointed out the windows to gathering thunderheads. "Storm's coming. We'll get wet walking, but I don't think we should wait."

EIGHTY-FOUR

THE HEAVENS OPENED WITH A blowing rain that soaked us even with rain gear. I was a little nervous in a metal canoe on water with thunder and lightning in the distance, but no harm came to us.

We found Nana and Valeria hunkered down under a tarp, eating a cold dinner. I placed myself between them to distract Valeria while Niki worked to convince Nana to leave. "I found your bear down by where you were fishing at Lake Tranquility."

Valeria sprang to her feet, knocking over her cup of water.

I handed her the soggy bear. "I'll bet you didn't realize your critter is a fantastically special animal. He's a panserbjørn, an armored bear whose hands can clasp, who keeps great secrets, and who never lies. His name is Iorek Byrnison. When you're a little older, you and Megan can read all about him."

I hugged Valeria. "I'm sorry I hurt its tummy. Your mother hid something super important inside. We have to give it to the police and tell them she's missing."

Valeria examined the bear and my sloppy stitching. "Thank you, Grandpa Seamus. Iorek is a funny name, but I like it." She slapped it around her wrist. "You're not gonna find my mama, are you?"

"I haven't given up, honey. I promised to try, and I promise I will keep trying. Once we tell the police, they'll start looking, too."

She pulled the granite stone from her pocket and rubbed it between her hands. Tears leaked from her eyes. I felt awful that this little girl would probably never see her mother again. The uninterrupted sound of rain on the tarp made me realize Niki and Nana had stopped talking. I switched my focus to them.

Niki said, "I told Nana about the murder, that we had to tell the police, and that I have to leave tomorrow. She's petrified she'll lose Valeria, but she agreed to let us send them away."

I half rose.

Niki stilled me with a finger. "First thing tomorrow morning. That's the best I could do."

That changed the order of things. I thanked Nana for trusting us and told her that since we were not leaving immediately, my plans required Niki and me to return to my house. Our walk home was miserable. Even though temperatures were in the high sixties, Niki and I were bone-chilled on arrival.

I waited until I'd warmed up with a hot shower and a change of clothes to call Sheriff Bartelle's cellphone. I informed him I had information concerning a probable murder and a missing woman. The woman lived in Iron County; the crimes had likely occurred in Dickinson County. Could he please contact the Michigan State Police and have them send a detective to talk to me at Bartelle's office? I'd be there in forty-five minutes.

He cleared his throat. "You won't tell me what this is about, will you? Why am I your intermediary?"

"Because if I'm thrown in jail, I want it to be yours."

"Won't that be special?"

Niki arrived from her shower in time to hear the last bit of my conversation with Bartelle. She blocked my way to the door. "I understand you wanted to get them away before you told Bartelle about the murder. And given it is murder, I agree with your decision to tell them tonight. But since you might not make it home, you'd better tell me your plan for Valeria and Nana."

"I already set Colleen looking for a UU congregation that belongs to the sanctuary movement and will take them in. Can you work with her and lock that down tonight?"

"That I can do, but I need to know how you're intending to get them past ICE and Rogers."

"Whatever time I get back tonight, I'll walk to the river, cross over, and sleep there. In the morning, we'll paddle downriver. At eight o'clock you'll drive my truck to the river and lead ICE to them, except, by that time, we'll be long gone. I'll give you keys to open and lock the gates behind you—we don't want to make this look easy. Wait an hour and return. If Agent Carpenter shows earlier, no problem. Either way, your part is done, and you can bring my truck back here and drive your rental to St. Paul."

"Fine, and while I act as decoy, what are you doing?"

"Two or three miles downriver, the river flows under Lukes Road. No one is tracking Colleen's car, so she can meet us there and take Nana and

Valeria to whatever sanctuary you find. Make sure that on her way out, she drives north to Covington to avoid all but two miles of Iron County. I'll walk home—it's only six miles—and deal with the fallout."

"And if they throw you in jail?"

"You and Colleen will have to create a new plan."

She smacked me on the arm and wished me success.

EIGHTY-FIVE

I MADE IT THROUGH THE Michigan state police interview following the advice a lawyer had given me about testifying at a deposition. If I did not absolutely, positively know something, I should say so. No guesses. No suppositions. Do not respond to speculative questions. If I once knew an answer but no longer did, I must say, "I do not recall." Great advice. That was the same lawyer who had told me under no circumstances should I speak to the police without having a criminal defense lawyer present—a luxury I had no time for.

The central fact I could attest to was how I had discovered the thumb drive. I gave them precise details covering who, what, where, when, and how. To that, I added hearsay evidence that Valeria said her mother gave her the bear, and that Nana claimed she had last seen Kat leaving the trailer that Thursday afternoon.

I maintained I had not reported Kat's disappearance or the trashing of the trailer because Nana did not want me to. No, I did not know why (who knows why anyone else does something?) and refused to speculate about her reasons.

I was on safe ground until they asked where Valeria and Nana were. I admitted they had stayed with me. My statements that they had stayed in my guest cabin and camped with me at Lake Tranquility might not sway a judge of my veracity. I stated truthfully that I did not know where Valeria and Nana *currently* were. I'm sure I was supposed to tell them they had also camped on my Baraga County property, and I had last seen them there a few hours earlier.

The state trooper went into bluster mode at that point. I let his threats wash over me. Sheriff Bartelle interrupted the trooper's tirade. "Seamus McCree can do silence like Charlie Chaplin. He won't tell you, even if you jail him as a material witness. If the grandmother or the kid was involved with the mother's disappearance, you can arrest him later for impeding the investigation. Seems to me, you have a missing woman to find and a murder to investigate, and they both revolve around the motel in Iron

Mountain." Turning to me, he said, "Anything else you can tell us that will help find the murderer or Katrina Serrano, assuming they're not the same person?"

That thought had never occurred to me. I told them Mike Crenshaw owned the motel and provided them the name of his accountant. "They have a records management system that should verify who booked that room where the woman was killed." That led to more questions about why I knew that. I related my interest in buying Crenshaw's forest property and that my sister, Colleen Carpetti, had reviewed the motel's books on Monday.

The state trooper gave me the bullshit line, "Don't leave the area without telling us." I said I understood what he was saying without agreeing to anything.

The last thunderstorm had long passed by us, leaving a smear of wispy clouds turning pink in the east during my drive home. Niki met me at the door with a hug and a kiss. "Couldn't sleep, not knowing if you were coming back or not." She had been working with Colleen for much of the night and reported success at finding Valeria and Nana sanctuary.

I wanted no details. "Talking with the police took longer than I hoped. Nana must wonder what happened to me."

"Take your old red ATV," she said. "Pull off the tracker that's stuck to your hitch and leave it on the floor of your garage, as though it fell off. Unlike your car and truck, there's no way ICE can follow it using its embedded GPS, because it doesn't have any."

That would save time and energy compared to walking. While we reviewed the plan, I changed into a quick-dry shirt and shorts, Keen water sandals, and found my Tilley hat. I brought up a satellite photograph to show Niki the exact spot I wanted Colleen to wait for us. She enlarged the map and pointed to a white area of the river near where it crossed under the bridge at Lukes Road. "What's this?"

"Rapids, which reminds me, I need to bring them life jackets. It's the only one, but we'll have two or three beaver dams to navigate. Have Colleen park in that cleared area west of the bridge where you see that truck." I tapped the truck visible on the satellite photo. "I don't know how long it'll take us. It's only a couple of miles, but the beaver dams will slow us down. We'll pull out before those rapids and walk to the meeting spot. It doesn't matter who gets there first. If we do, we'll wait in the woods for Colleen. She knows how to get to the sanctuary?"

"Our end is under control, Seamus."

I detached the tracker from the ATV, strapped lifejackets for Valeria and Nana onto its rack, filled three water bottles, and kissed Niki goodbye. "Drive safe. With luck, I'll be home before noon and will call you."

"Forget something?" Niki shoved my cellphone into my rear pocket. "Frankly, I'd prefer we didn't require luck."

Eighty-Six

I LEFT THE CANOE PULLED up on the shore where Megan and Valeria had fished and played catch with the eagles. Nana was cooking on the propane camp stove. She spoke Spanish slowly in a raised voice, like for someone you thought was not very bright. Her accompanying gestures showed she wanted me to join them for breakfast. She woke Valeria, who had slept in her clothes. Nana divided the omelet and home fries into three portions. I inhaled the food, which was delicious. Nana ate with more restraint. Valeria pushed hers around her plate.

I told her she should eat. "You'll feel better with a full stomach." I pointed to the bear attached to her wrist. "Iorek wouldn't want your tummy growling later on."

My phone dinged with a text message.

Green Jeep blazed down the road in your direction. Get out NOW!!!

Crap, Agent Carpenter was coming. "Valeria, please let your grandmother know we have to leave right this minute. No time to clean up."

Fear blossomed in Nana's eyes. Fortunately, she had everything packed. I grabbed much of their gear and ushered them before me. Nana shook her head and motioned for me to take Valeria. She ignored my objections and ran back to her tent. I hustled Valeria to the canoe and loaded it with the stuff at hand. I tossed Valeria a life jacket. "Put this on, hon, and snug it tight."

On my return to the campsite, I met Nana hauling a pillowcase stuffed with clothes in one hand and the rifle in the other. I collected the last of their things and ran after her.

The growl of a heavy engine let me know Carpenter was getting close. Valeria had not figured out her life jacket, and I helped her step into its leg straps. I clicked her buckles closed, tightened her belt, and gave Nana's belt an extra tug. As I handed them into the canoe, the truck engine quieted—at the first gate? Given its shoddy construction, it would take him little time to lift the gate off its hooks and drive through.

I settled into the stern and pushed away from shore. The relative quiet ended with the truck engine cranking up—it was heading toward the second gate, which was much more substantial. I sent a "thank you" to the heavens for my foresight in deploying the gates. Their presence had delayed Carpenter and provided us with extra time to escape.

Paddling with the current was easy. Nana picked up the paddle I had left in the bow. With beaver dams in our future, I wanted to be in total control of the canoe. I had Valeria tell Nana to save her strength for later. She tucked the paddle behind her and picked up the rifle. Maybe I should have let her paddle.

Behind us, the engine roared, followed by a sickening crunch of metal on metal. The truck had attempted—succeeded?—to bust through the second gate. The engine was still running. Even if the lock held, he could run to the river in three or four minutes.

We entered a long S-curve that provided cover from anyone upriver. I released my breath, only then realizing I had been holding it, and rolled my shoulders to work out the tension. How had they known? Unless Niki had missed a second tracker on the red ATV, I must have triggered a trail cam similar to mine that forwarded images to my phone. Given how quickly Agent Carpenter got here, he couldn't have been any farther away than Amasa.

Carpenter was waiting for me to make a move, and I had let him play me. I resisted the urge to smack the paddle on the water.

Soon Carpenter would find the red ATV where I left it at the river crossing. How he reacted was key. Once he guessed my plan, it became a race. We had to meet Colleen and for her to escape before any of the bad guys reached Lukes Road. If he wasted time and crossed the river to look for us, he'd find proof Nana and Valeria had been there, but it would add at least twenty minutes to our head start. I could hope.

We would pass several camps before the Lukes Road bridge, and instead of stopping, we could continue through to US 141. They'd have to guess where we planned to leave the river and get there before us. Niki might slow them down. Even if they got past her, they had fifteen miles to Amasa before they could drive the highway north to Lukes Road.

Unless they had people waiting in Amasa.

Or launched long-range drones to follow us.

Or something happened to Colleen.

EIGHTY-SEVEN

THE CURRENT PICKED UP AS we approached a narrowing, and the murmur of water trickling through a beaver dam grew louder. I slowed us going around a bend. Good thing. The dam was right there. I reverse-paddled to break our forward progress and steered the craft to shore.

"Valeria, tell Nana you two have to walk around the beaver dam. I'll haul the canoe over it and we'll get back in."

Nana grabbed the tag alders while I scrambled out and secured the canoe. I helped Nana and Valeria onto the shore. The footing was terrible. "Remember, your ankle is still weak, so be real careful where you walk." I carried Nana's rifle, allowing her to use both hands to maneuver, and led them to a place where we could get back into the canoe. This damn dam was costing us more time than I had expected.

A new text dinged on my phone. Once I had them on stable ground, I checked it.

Colleen on her way

She was ninety minutes away. In returning to the canoe, I missed a step and soaked my left leg to my thigh. Slow down, you jerk—getting wet is fine, but breaking a leg won't help anyone. I tucked my cellphone into my shirt pocket before wading into stomach-high water below the dam and pulling the canoe over. The water was still cool. The sun wouldn't crest the tree line for at least an hour. We should be off the water by then.

Once we passed the confluence of the East Branch of the Net River with Shank Lake Creek, the journey was new water to me. We worked around two more beaver dams. After progressing through a section of the river that on the satellite map looked like a snake, my arms threatened mutiny. I went on full alert as we passed the first camp and underneath a bridge that provided access to it. No ambush.

Soon, my ears pricked at the distant whoosh of another beaver dam. I slowed in preparation, but with each bend, the dam didn't appear and the sound grew louder. And louder. And louder. The first three beaver dams had drops of between six and eighteen inches. This one was *much* larger.

The river widened, counterintuitive since we were approaching an area in which the beavers had constructed their dam. We floated around a curve into a broad valley that the beavers had flooded with a dam at least three feet high. Beyond, great swaths of Canadian shield burst through the soil on a hill that rose seventy-five feet. A log cabin perched on the top of the hill. I remembered this place, having dropped in on the residents years ago on an ATV expedition with my son, Paddy. It was the perfect spot for an ambush. A decent marksman could rock on the porch, spy us coming into the open water, and easily nail us.

Previous canoeists had created a 250-yard-long path to portage around the obstruction. It required three trips to transport the canoe and their gear, but that effort allowed us to stretch our legs. We loaded the canoe, Nana, and Valeria settled onto their seats. I pushed the canoe into the water, keeping only the tip of the stern still on land, and stepped in.

Valeria flung her hand out and shouted, "Look. The eagles!"

The next seconds happened in slow motion. Iorek, the stuffed bear, launched from Valeria's wrist. She grabbed for it, throwing her weight against the canoe's right side. Nana shifted the same way to look for the eagles. The grounded stern acted as an anchor point around which the canoe rotated, shifting my weight to the right. The physics said we would flip if I tried to stay in.

I followed my center of gravity into the water. Soccer players learn how to roll as they tumble to the ground. I tucked my chin into my chest and levered my feet over my head, landing on the water flat on my back. The judges scored my roll as a two on a ten-point scale. My feet settled on the graveled creek bed, and I stood in water up to my waist.

The world was a fuzzy blur. Without my glasses, I can see okay up close, but the big E on an eye chart is only a smudge. I'd saved the canoe from capsizing and kept all their gear from drowning, but at the cost of my vision. Nana jabbered away in Spanish. Valeria cried. I needed to find my glasses. Before my back flop with one-half twist, the river was clear to the bottom. Now, the surrounding water was opaque, filled with swirling bits of forest sediment.

I told Valeria in a no nonsense tone I really wanted her help. "Can you stop crying and translate for Nana?"

To my surprise, she quickly controlled her tears and wiped her nose with her sleeve.

"I've lost my glasses. You've lost your bear. We all need to stay still to let the water clear. When it does, we'll try to spot your bear and my glasses. Can you do that for me?"

Her choked words broke my heart. "It's the only thing I have left from my mama, and Nana put your special stone inside."

Eighty-Eight

WHILE I STOOD STILL, WAITING for the water to clear, the sun peeked over the hill to the east. I appreciated its warmth, but it made it more difficult to see anything underwater. The bottom became visible in fifteen minutes. I stuck my face into the river to eliminate the glare and searched for any blurred hint of gold frames. Nothing.

At my failure, Valeria offered to swim and search.

With the life jacket, she'd be fine. "Here's how to get out of the canoe without dunking your grandmother. Think of yourself as a snake with four legs. Keep low and your hands and feet wide. Good girl. Now one limb at a time move towards the back of the canoe, like you're slithering across the bottom, except only your four limbs touch. You're doing great, nice and slow. Perfect."

"Let's look for my glasses first. If we find them, we can both look for your bear."

Good in theory, and the kid was willing, but she also struck out. Time was ticking by, and Colleen should reach the meeting place soon. Valeria spotted her bear ten feet from me. "Keep your eye on it, and I'll get it for you." I wanted to avoid stirring up the sediment and set my right foot down next to my left—and felt it crunch something.

I stepped sideways, lowered my face into the water, and saw shimmering gold. Crap. They had been underneath me all along. I squatted, submerged my head, and grabbed them. I lowered the glasses with their cracked frame and broken ear piece onto my nose. The world returned to focus—more or less. I held the glasses in place with a finger and walked to Valeria. I handed her my glasses and retrieved her bear. "Trade you," I said. She hugged the bear to her chest.

Valeria swam to shore, and I waded behind her. She used her new four-legged-snake technique to position herself in the middle of the canoe, and I got in without incident. I couldn't paddle and hold my glasses flush to my face at the same time. I had to paddle, I could fake seeing. I tucked my glasses into my shirt pocket.

The pocket that was supposed to hold my phone. Unlike the glasses and the bear, we could not find the phone anywhere. Now we had no way to communicate with the outside world.

EIGHTY-NINE

WITHOUT GLASSES, THE WORLD LOOKED like a Monet painting. I kept the canoe in the main channel of the river. The distant burbling of the rapids became too loud to ignore, and I edged the canoe near the left bank and asked Valeria and Nana to look for a path to the camp that overlooked the rapids. I followed Nana's pointed finger to shore. We landed, and I put on my mangled glasses, bringing some clarity to the world.

"We'll need two trips to bring all your things to the cabin. I see Valeria is limping a little. I'll go ahead. You two take your time." The trail climbed the hill, and my spirits rose with each step. The cabin was only a few minutes' walk away from our meeting spot. Without my phone, I didn't know the time, but I thought Colleen should be waiting. A sixth sense told me to check a side trail that ended at an overlook commanding the rapids and the bridge beyond. I peeked through foliage and my optimism evaporated.

The jacked-up blue Silverado sat on the bridge. Aaron Rogers stood on the road near the cab and Glenn Korpi in the bed, both looking upstream. I tamped down the panic whirling in my stomach. Where was Colleen? Had they discovered her or had she arrived after them?

Even if she were waiting for us, we were on the wrong side of the river. Worse, their allies might be at the cabin we were walking to. I ran and caught up to my fellow travelers, telling them to wait until I returned. A few more steps brought me to the edge of the woods, where I could scan the area around the cabin.

No vehicles. No people. No sound. I placed their things on a wooden deck that faced the river, hustled back to Valeria and Nana, and told them to continue to the cabin. I retrieved the rest of their belongings from the canoe and raced up the hill, praying no one had shown up while I was gone.

Prayer answered. I described our situation and gave them a contingency plan: If I did not return before suppertime, they were to break the glass window in the door, let themselves in, and stay the night. Eat whatever food they found inside. I would not abandon them. Valeria was crying, and

I got down on my knees. "Do you remember this place? You and Megan and I visited here on our ATV ride."

She sniffled but stuttered a yes.

"I want to tell you and Iorek something, a secret just for the three of us. Can we do that? Share a secret?" She nodded. "Iorek has special powers. Whoever holds your bear can never become lost. That's a special skill! But Iorek needs help. So here's what you can do if I can't get back by tomorrow morning. You can lead Nana back to Lake Tranquility. Iorek will help you remember how to do that."

I pointed down the driveway toward Lukes Road and gave her detailed directions to a reference point I hoped she would recall. "Do you remember what comes after that long stretch of standing water?"

She screwed her eyes shut. "The green gate?"

"Smart girl. And you remember where that takes you?"

Her eyes shown with confidence. "To Lake Tranquility."

To reinforce it, I made her tell it all to Iorek. "And now tell Nana about your magic bear and how to get the Lake Tranquility."

I don't know if it was belief in a special bear or feeling responsible or something else, but I knew Valeria would face up to whatever came next. Nana hugged Valeria and shoved the rifle at me.

My mouth went desert dry as I faced the opposing elements within myself. I did not want to be part of a culture that solved problems with guns. And yet, I had used them in the past. I'd bet the people on that bridge were armed. A gun might be the only way for me to rescue Colleen, to keep Valeria and Nana safe. I shredded another piece of my soul and accepted the weapon.

Ninety

I paddled upstream, crossed the river, and beached the canoe. I cut through thick woods and found the driveway to the camp we had passed. It would bring me to Lukes Road at the spot I had suggested Colleen park. Along the way, a red squirrel chattered at my presence—a good sign that no one else was around. Walking down the road whistling Disney tunes was not prudent. Instead, I paralleled the gravel until I spotted Colleen's vehicle backed into the parking area I had recommended.

She would not have parked if she had seen the truck, so what did she do when the Silverado arrived, and where was she now?

I waited for the dub-dub of my heart to quit pulsing in my ears before silently toe-heeling through the woods to get close enough to see into Colleen's car. Empty—unless she was lying on the backseat or hiding in a foot well. I had to check without being seen.

I used her car as a screen from the road and duck-walked to her vehicle. My knees and thighs burned with the effort. Stomach in my throat, afraid I would see a body, I rose and looked inside. The car was empty with no bloodstains and no signs of a struggle. She'd left the doors unlocked with the fob sitting in a cup holder next to a cellphone.

Colleen either planned to return or had left unwillingly. She would have made her presence known if she had been watching her car. My throat constricted, making it hard to swallow.

I inched forward held my glasses to my nose with a finger while I bent down and read the faint vehicle tracks on the ground. She had pulled past the parking area and backed in. A set of wider tire prints had looped in front of her car—the Silverado? Ground too hard to show footprints.

My body was telling me they had her. I released the rifle's safety and returned to the woods. Halfway to the truck, I picked up mumbled conversation, not heated enough for an argument. I inched forward to see the open front doors of the Silverado. The mumbled conversation resolved into WIKB's Telephone Time on the Silverado's radio.

Open doors meant they weren't worried about Colleen escaping. Dark thoughts gnawed at my intestines. They had killed her.

Aaron Rogers came into view walking toward the truck. Over his shoulder, he said, "You want more too?" Korpi replied, "No, it'll only make me pee. Which makes me ask, do we have to walk her—you know, like a dog?"

Rogers leaned into the truck, displaying a pistol strapped to his hip. "Not my problem. She's fine." He exited with a cardboard cup of coffee.

At least Colleen was alive. If Korpi also had only a pistol, the rifle might give me the fire-power advantage. But how to use it to—

Metal jabbed the base of my skull. "If you move, I'll put a bullet in your head."

Ninety-One

"OVER HERE, YOU GUYS," BUNNY Crenshaw said. "I've got McCree. No sign of the fucking wetbacks. Drop your rifle, McCree, and lie face down."

Bunny was the woman who had trashed Serrano's trailer. And probably was the fourth person.

Rough hands patted me down. "Clean," Aaron Rogers said. He jerked my wrists together behind me and zip-tied them. The plastic cut into my skin.

Bunny nudged the sole of my left boot. "Roll over. I want to see your face. Where are they?"

I obeyed, and my glasses settled slightly skewed on my face. I noted the Sig Sauer P226 semiautomatic in Bunny's hand—Niki's favorite model. She had another pistol in a shoulder rig. Aaron Rogers also held a pistol. Glenn Korpi stood a few paces away, holding an AR-15-style rifle. They had me outgunned, outmanned, and outsmarted. Bunny repeated her demand to know where they were.

"I lost it all," I said. "I flipped the canoe at the beaver dam and lost it all."

Bunny kicked the bottom of my foot with the steel tip of her boot, jarring bones up to my knee. "What the hell are you talking about? I want to know where the kid and her grandmother are."

I put on my puzzled face. "What the hell are *you* talking about?" I looked at Rogers. "I saw your drone searching for my grow operation. Doesn't matter now. The whole damn harvest is at the bottom of the river."

My lies led to a confused two minutes of them talking over each other while I tried desperately to think of some way to talk myself out of this situation. The discussion ended with Bunny shouting, "enough," and slicing the air with the knife's edge of her hand. She kicked my foot once more. "Last chance before I drill you. What have you done with the girl and her grandmother? I know you had them." She widened her stance and took a two-handed aim at my head. Korpi retreated several feet. Rogers gave me a wicked grin.

I opened my eyes wide, mimicking that I had experienced a revelation. "You mean Valeria? Valeria and her grandmother. Them? What do you want with them? The kid was friends with my granddaughter. I have no idea where they are. Are you telling me you weren't trying to steal my plants? Did I lose forty thousand dollars of quality product for no damn reason?"

"When did they leave? Where did you take them?"

"Late afternoon Sunday. I dropped them at Tall Pines—in Amasa, you know? Forty thousand." I smacked my forehead on my knee. "For nothing? Ah, man."

Korpi continued retreating, as if to disassociate himself from the current scene. I had to find a way to exploit his weak link. "I can't believe I pissed away all that work and money and you two didn't find it with your drone?"

Bunny gave my foot another love tap. "Shut up about the weed. Where's your canoe?

"I saw the truck parked on the bridge. How'd you know I was coming down the river? Wait a minute. I get it. You sicced ICE on me. Like I told that agent, I haven't seen them since I dropped them off."

"You two check his canoe," Bunny said. "Tell them where you left it, McCree."

I described the place and suggested they follow the shore to make sure they didn't miss it. That would take them longer than walking up the cabin's driveway and cutting in to the river—time when Bunny wouldn't have their guns supporting her.

Bunny shooed them off with instructions to "use your phone and bring me pictures and be on the lookout for the wetbacks." All they'd find in the canoe were two paddles and river water. I needed to disarm Bunny before the guys and their long guns returned.

She took two steps back and ordered me to stand with my back to her. Too far away for me to charge her. She might have read my mind. "I can give a squirrel a new asshole with this baby from thirty feet, so don't try anything stupid. How does your accountant, Colleen Carpetti, fit into all this? Her car's here. Where is she?"

My question, too. If Colleen was nearby and if Niki had given her a gun, the odds might even be in my favor. Big ifs. I kept my movements easy and wracked my brain to sort through the implications of Bunny knowing that was Colleen's car. She had either spotted Colleen, who escaped, and put two and two together or she already knew it was Colleen's car. How could she? I had to keep playing nice and spinning my story out, pretending I was playing "And Then" with Megan, except fending off Bunny's curveballs.

"She was here to collect me and the weed. I assume your guys with the guns scared her off."

Bunny marched me up the road toward the Silverado and said, "Get in the rear."

I waggled my zip-tied hands at her. "Can you open the door?"

"Do it your own damn self."

I backed up to the truck, found the latch, and struggled the door open. I turned around and my legs buckled. Colleen lay hogtied on the backseat with a bandanna stuffed in her mouth.

"Silly me," Bunny said. "I guess I knew where your accountant was all along."

Ninety-Two

UNLESS COLLEEN AND I COULD escape, we were dead. I crawled into the rear seat. Bunny slammed the door, leaving us alone with WIKB playing on the radio. Colleen's eyes were open. "You hurt? Shake your head yes or no."

She signaled no.

That was a relief. "Duck into my hands, and I'll remove your gag."

Easier said than done, but I did it. She coughed and cleared her throat. "Well, here's another nice mess you got me into."

That she could toss out a Laurel and Hardy line was a good sign she had not succumbed to fear. I said, "Not to put too fine a point on it, the guys are temporarily gone. To escape, we need to remove the zip-ties. Can you reach the pocketknife in my right front pocket?"

We aligned our backs, and her fingers slid into my pocket. Pressing into my thigh, she inch-wormed her way down.

"Too tight, but if you remove my tennies, I can slide my hands underneath my feet and see what I'm doing.

With my imperfect vision, it took me multiple tries to remove her double-knotted sneakers. Once I did, she slipped her hands around to the front but still couldn't reach the knife.

I told her to undo my belt.

She barked a tight laugh. "I'm not into kinky sex, or did you want it for self-flagellation?"

Now I got it. Colleen's coping mechanism was to use humor. "To loosen the pants. And pull down the zipper too."

She unfastened the belt, undid the snap, and worried the zipper down. I lay down on the seat and raised my legs over my head, concerned Bunny would see the movement. Still no go.

I dropped my legs on top of her. "Grab my waist and we'll pull the damn pants down to my ankles.

That allowed her to grab the knife. She used her teeth to open it and sawed the plastic zip holding my wrists, apologizing each time she nicked me. My blood-slicked hands separated with a pop covered up by the radio's chatter. I severed her wrist-ties without bloodshed and hauled my pants back up.

I couldn't see Bunny from my position. Colleen leaned forward to look out the front. "She's at the railing looking up the river."

"Get down," I hissed. "If she sees you, she'll realize your gag is gone."

I checked underneath the seats for useful weapons and came up with a tire iron and two Snickers wrappers.

Collen asked if we should rush her.

"Too risky. Keep low and crawl into the driver's seat. When she turns her back, slip out the door and run like hell. If she reacts, I'll draw her attention away from you. Drive like your life depends on it. Soon as you're safe, call 9-1-1, and get the Sheriff's deputies here."

"She'll kill you."

"Not when I tell her I have the thumb drive and haven't given it to the police because I wanted to clear out my marijuana plants first." Seeing confusion on her face, I said, "I'll explain later. It'll buy me time. Maybe I can get lucky with the tire iron. We don't have much for alternatives."

Colleen slithered over the center console and tucked herself low behind the steering wheel. Bunny cocked her head like something on Telephone Time had caught her attention. She took a hesitant step toward the truck. And a second. One more and I'd have to open my door and distract her.

The announcer concluded Telephone Time and cued the minute-long jingle, which they played with extra volume. Bunny gave a little shrug and returned to the center of the bridge and looked at the water.

"Now."

Ninety-Three

COLLEEN WAS OUT AND RUNNING low, the radio commercial providing auditory cover. Next would come the noon news and the daily funeral report. I did not like the implications of that timing on my current situation. Bunny's head swiveled. I yanked down on the handle and flung the door open. I hid the tire iron behind my back.

She held her Sig Sauer in a two-handed grip and hurried toward me. "What the hell do you think you're doing? Get back in there or I'll shoot you."

"I know where the thumb drive is," I shouted.

She slowed but kept the P226 leveled at me. To keep her focused on me, I scooted toward the door, pretending my arms were still tied behind me.

She wagged the gun. "Stay there. What did you say?"

"That I found the pictures of the dead girl." I inched forward, stopped, and added, "I couldn't give the drive to the cops until I took care of my grow operation, so I hid it, but if I go missing or show up dead, people will find it."

She came closer. One or two more steps and she'd discover Colleen was gone. I jerked forward and placed both feet on the running board.

"So where is it?"

"This is where we negotiate, right? We figure out how to guarantee our mutual destruction if either of us talks. Colleen and I keep on living, and you never have to worry about the pictures. Everyone lives happily ever after." I scooched my butt closer to the edge, preparing to jump down. Gears clicked behind her eyes. "This should be easy," I continued. "You know where I live and your associates can kill me if I break my part of the deal. I retain a copy to make sure you keep your side."

With her next step, her eyes opened wide in shock.

Crap. I leaped past the door, losing my balance and my glasses. She fired wide, and I whipped the tire iron at her. She had quick reflexes and ducked under the spinning bar. Before she could bring the gun to bear on me, I employed a move from my soccer days and unleashed a scissor kick at her hands.

She sensed my movement, but her response was wrong. Instead of leaning away from my kick, she ducked again. My toe nailed her neck.

A well-executed scissor kick has a lot of power behind it and leaves the kicker lying on the ground, which is where I found myself. I scrambled to Bunny, prepared to slug her before she could shoot me. That was unnecessary.

She was rigid with pain, grabbing her throat, the gun beside her. I kicked the weapon aside, and my relief changed to horror as she turned blue. I had crushed her windpipe.

Colleen materialized next to me, scaring the bejesus out of me.

"I heard shots." She held out my glasses. "Here."

I shoved my glasses in my shirt pocket and pushed her. "Go get help while I try to save Bunny's life. "

Colleen took root. I punched a hole in Bunny's throat with my penknife. But when I extracted the blade, the hole pinched closed. I tried different attachments and positions. Nothing kept the incision open.

Bunny died a death I wouldn't wish on anyone.

NINETY-FOUR

I CURSED BUNNY FOR DYING on me. And I cursed Colleen for standing around when she should have been calling the police. *Snap out of it!* Rogers and Korpi might be back at any moment, and we can't let them catch us mooning over a dead body. I removed the P226 from Bunny's shoulder rig and handed it to Colleen. I grabbed from the ground the one she had fired at me. "Let's take cover and consider our options."

"No." She expertly checked the pistol. "We're in this mess because you promised to get Valeria and Nana to safety. If we don't do that now, they'll never get out. The police will tie us up for a month of Sundays. There's no place you can keep them. Niki didn't answer when I called her while you were trying to save Bunny's life. It's now, Seamus, or you have to hope the police choose to let Nana go. Which way?"

"But if Rogers and Korpi return—"

"We deal with them if they don't drive off and leave Bunny lying in the dirt. Tick-tock."

We ran to her car, drove it to the chain across the road to the camp where I had stashed Valeria and Nana, and parked it facing out. The faint strains from the Silverado's radio accompanied us as we trotted down the driveway and into the cabin clearing. Valeria's and Nana's stuff was on the covered deck where they had left it, but they were gone. I bellowed their names.

The front door opened several inches. "McCree," Aaron Rogers called out, "what took you so long?"

He couldn't see me because of the door. Where was Korpi? I motioned Colleen into the woods and backed away. "You were expecting me?"

"When Bunny didn't call me after the gunfire, I figured she was a goner. Now you're here, so I was right. She said you're smart. I have two somethings of yours to trade. If it comes to a shootout, I'll kill them and take suicide by cop over life behind bars. Got any brilliant ideas?"

I backed into the woods, looked for Colleen and couldn't see her. Good. I dropped to the ground to minimize my chances of being hit if he sprayed his automatic rifle in my direction. "I need to know they're okay."

"They're alive, bound and gagged. You call the cops, or is it just us?"

Could I make him believe we had a common cause? "You know, I don't give two shits about you. All I want is for the girl and her grandmother to be safe."

"Where are the cops in this, McCree?"

"Cops would just get in the way. My goal is to take the two of them out of state. Bunny and Colleen are both dead. What about your partner?"

"I tied the chicken shit to a tree down by the river. Here's what we do. The four of us walk together to Korpi's truck. I take it and the girl. If no one stops me or follows me, I'll drop the kid someplace safe."

"I can't say I much like that idea. I have Colleen's rental parked at the road. Keys are in it. Take the car and grab the keys to Korpi's truck as you go past. Leave us here."

"And run into a roadblock? No way I'm leaving without bringing a hostage." He offered to take Nana too if I was worried about the girl being by herself.

Nice guy. No doubt, he'd kill any hostages as soon as he didn't need them. Had Colleen finally called the police? And was Korpi really tied up to a tree, or was he circling around to get behind me? The whole situation could blow apart if some innocent drove down Lukes Road and discovered Bunny's body. I had to separate him from Valeria and Nana and time was not my ally.

"You want a hostage? Fine. I'll go with you, except it's mutual destruction if something goes wrong. We take Colleen's car. If I lied about the cops, you shoot me and they shoot you. You drop me off at the highway, and I'll come back and free your prisoners."

I expected an immediate response but heard only my heart pounding. How could the two of us in a car work? Whoever was driving was at a disadvantage because they couldn't watch the road and the passenger. Even though I have quick reflexes, I couldn't respond fast enough if he tried to shoot me while I drove. That means no guns in the car—at least not loaded.

"You think I don't know rentals have tracking devices?"

A little, I admitted to myself. "Fine. Take Korpi's truck. Of course, it's easy to describe. Fact is, any way out of here requires you to get new wheels or arrange for someone to pick you up. Right?"

Behind me, something shuffled through leaves. I pressed a finger to my glasses, flipped from stomach to back, and sat up, pointing my pistol at the intruder. A red squirrel chattered at my sudden movement. I resumed my prone position. The door had not moved. "We've got the canoe. We could paddle out to somewhere you could steal a car."

"That's crazy."

His quick response dismissing the canoeing idea when he hadn't reacted the same way to my suggestion to take a car or truck meant he considered escaping in one of the vehicles at least somewhat plausible. It was the only chance to break Valeria and Nana free of him. "Aaron, you gotta shit or get off the pot. Somebody will discover Bunny, and they *will* call the cops who *will* find us here. If you plan on dying today, just do it already. Otherwise, tell me you have a better plan."

"You sold me, McCree. Come here and we'll walk together to Korpi's truck."

Like I'd get halfway there. "Now you're the crazy one. We need a way to make sure we both behave. Take the grandmother with you to kill if I try something."

"Good idea, McCree. Except I'm taking the girl."

Ninety-Five

ROGERS CLOSED THE DOOR BEHIND him. How would Colleen react to this plan? If she had Niki's skills, I'd want her to take out Rogers before we got to Korpi's truck. But instead, all I could hope was that Colleen made sure Korpi didn't get the jump on me.

The cabin door reopened two minutes later with Valeria visible. Rogers, protected by the door, gripped her arm with one hand, and held a pistol to her head with the other. "Tell him your grandmother is fine."

In a shaky voice, Valeria told me the man had gagged them and tied them to a bed. I asked if anyone else was in the cabin. With no hesitancy, she answered no. Meaning Korpi wasn't there.

Rogers pushed Valeria onto the stoop and pulled the door shut behind him. "Time to get this show on the road."

No long guns. If Korpi got me in his sights with either rifle before I got close enough for mutual destruction with Rogers, I was a goner. I hurried through the woods and met Rogers where the driveway entered the woods. Because I was on his right, it forced Rogers to pull Valeria tight to him with his right arm to keep her between us. His left held the pistol at her head, his finger inside the trigger guard. He was right-handed, but with the gun inches from her, it didn't matter. He couldn't miss killing her if he decided I had betrayed him.

Rogers shuffled down the road using baby steps to control Valeria, who had shut her eyes tight. I faced them, holding the Sig in a two-handed grip and matched his pace to keep my gun aimed at him. I kept far enough away to assure him I didn't plan to make a grab for him or Valeria. To maintain that distance, we steered wide of Colleen's rental.

I could not read Rogers. He seemed patient, methodical, and in control. Unlike me. My heart was clawing its way out of my chest, my teeth ached from clenching my jaw, and a wall of fire rose from my shoulders to the top of my head because I could not envision the next step.

He stopped at Bunny's sprawled body, using quick glances away from me to read the scene. I kept my attention on him, although flies buzzing loud enough to be heard over the truck's radio let me know they had found her. Thank goodness Valeria still had her eyes closed. She did not need to add Bunny's corpse to her nightmares.

"Where's your accountant?"

"Fell off the bridge." I nodded to my side of the road, hoping he would not want to cross in front of me to look. He didn't, but the moment for which I had not yet conjured a solution was upon us: how could we assure his escape while keeping everyone alive?

Ninety-Six

ROGERS HAD APPARENTLY COME TO the same conclusion. "I don't see it working, McCree. You've made it clear you won't let me leave with the girl, and unless I have her as a safeguard, there's no reason you can't shoot me when I let her go. And as you say, if someone drives down the road . . ."

His silence fed my despair. "There's only one way. We have to trust each other, or you're right, this will never work. Truthfully, my only goal is to see no harm comes to the child and her grandmother. Take the truck and leave. I'll go back and release the grandmother, then we'll drive out of here."

Our eyes locked, and I realized he planned to take Valeria with him in the Silverado. His arm tightened around her at the same time I shifted my weight so I could block his path to the truck.

Valeria let loose an ear-piercing scream, and she stomped her heel on Rogers' toes. His grip loosened, and she elbowed him in the nuts, using her momentum to twist out of his grasp. His pistol fired with a single crack—a reflex contraction of his finger. He grabbed for her, giving me a window to shoot him without endangering Valeria. But if I didn't kill him with the first shot, all three of us might end up dead.

I stepped toward him and yelled, "You're dead if you pull the trigger again. Don't do it."

He swiveled his pistol toward me and steadied it with both hands. We stood eight feet apart, death a finger twitch away. He was bent over slightly from pain, and his face expressed confusion.

I pressed for my words to reach him. "Get in the damn truck and go. I told you all I want is for Valeria and her grandmother to be safe. I could have killed you if that's what I wanted. Just go."

"Listen to the man," Colleen said from somewhere behind me and to the left. "You pull that trigger and I'll empty a full clip in you."

Rogers didn't look at Colleen either. "So you lied about the accountant. I can't trust you."

Valeria was safe for now, but there were so many ways this could still go wrong. I took a deliberate step away from the truck. "You're alive, aren't you? I'm moving back." I took another step. "Get in and go. I don't want your death on my hands. Please." I continued backing away, each step making it less likely he could hit me. I hoped Colleen was doing the same, but I dared not take my eyes off him.

Ninety-Seven

VALERIA, COLLEEN, AND I STOOD in a group hug, watching the jacked-up Silverado disappear around a bend. "You're a hero, Valeria. How's your ankle?"

"I'm sorry, Grampa Seamus, I can't walk too good."

I mussed her hair. "You'll heal again. Where did you learn that move?"

"My mother took me with her to a place where they teach women to protect themselves. I got to practice too."

"Right now you get to horseback ride, except I'm your horse. We'll go collect your Nana, and then Colleen will take you to a safe place."

Colleen said, "You two stay here. I can get Nana by myself."

I was glad I had my thinking cap back on. "When Rogers and Korpi left to find the canoe, they had both the AR-15 and Niki's rifle that they took from you. Rogers left the AR-15 at the cabin, but Korpi might wait with Niki's rifle to ambush whoever comes for Nana."

"No, Grampa Seamus." She pointed in the direction Rogers had driven. "That man left two rifles in the cabin with Nana. He and the other man had a big argument after they tied us to the bed. He hit the other man in the head with a frying pan and dragged him out of the house. I never saw him again."

Had Rogers killed Korpi? Tied him to a tree, as he claimed? Something else? "Until the three of you are on the highway, we're sticking together."

I hoisted Valeria onto my back. In short order, we released Nana from the duct tape holding her to the bed. I used some of it—handy—to repair my glasses. Colleen found Niki's rifle leaning against the wall next to the AR-15, both loaded. Neither smelled like anyone had fired it. The frying pan lay on the dining room table. I didn't pick it up, but I couldn't see any signs of blood or hair on it. I hoped Korpi was alive, but worrying about him needed to wait until Colleen was safely off with her precious cargo.

We stored Niki's rifle in the trunk, and, on the off-chance Rogers was lying in ambush, I carried the AR-15 on my lap as we drove down Lukes Road to the highway. He wasn't. I gave Valeria and Iorek smooches on the tops of their heads, shook hands with Nana, and gave Colleen a big hug. "Good luck. Two miles north and you're out of Iron County."

I stood there, the AR-15 strapped over my shoulder, an unfamiliar emptiness in my heart, and watched their car disappear over the distant hill.

Ninety-Eight

I HAD BEEN SO FOCUSED on getting Colleen on her way with no interference from Rogers that I had not thought to use Colleen's cellphone to call Niki—or the police. I considered walking to the nearest house and asking to borrow a phone. But I didn't know where anyone lived, and they might not be home, and I convinced myself the best course was to walk back and use Bunny's phone to call the cops.

It wasn't until I reached the bridge and Bunny's body that I remembered I had tossed her phone into the Silverado Rogers had escaped in. My stomach threatened revolt at the buzz and constant motion of insects around the body. The gravity effects of livor mortis had drawn her blood away from her front, leaving her face and neck preternaturally pale under the dried blood remaining from my attempt to keep her breathing. That sight would fertilize a million bad dreams.

What now, Seamus?

Find Korpi. If he was injured, I could give him aid. If he was dead, at least I could lead the police to him.

I followed drag marks from the cabin and found Korpi prone, secured to a tree behind the outhouse. Rogers had looped Korpi's belt around his neck and buckled him to a tree. He had stuffed part of Korpi's torn shirt into the guy's mouth and used the rest to tie his hands behind his back.

Korpi had heard me and was kicking the ground to gain my attention. I pulled the shirt from his mouth but left him tied to the tree in what had to be an uncomfortable position. "I'm glad to see you're alive, Glenn. Let's have a little chat." I sat with my back against another tree and rested the AR-15 across my legs.

Fear bloomed in his eyes. "Where's Aaron?"

"Bunny's dead. Aaron took your truck. That leaves you holding the bag." To pry open the guy I considered the weak link, I told him I knew he was a minor player who'd gotten involved in something bigger than he'd expected. The real culprits were everyone else. I aligned myself to him by sharing some truth. "That whole story I told about the marijuana patch and trying to leave with my product? Total bullshit. I was protecting the little girl and her grandmother from Bunny. Did Bunny tell you what she was looking for?"

"Nuh-uh," he stammered. "I just did errands. Drove for them."

"Exactly. You're not one of them. But let me tell you how deep the shit is that you're in. Bunny wanted a thumb drive that contained pictures of a murdered woman. The person who took those pictures disappeared. Her name is Katrina Serrano. Friends call her Kat. The little girl is her daughter. Now, Bunny didn't know this, but the police have that thumb drive. Anyone they link to the murder is going down hard. That's you, my friend, unless you can help me."

His unfocused eyes shown white with fear. I pressed on. "You help me, and I'll convince the police you did not know squat. That Rogers kidnapped the girl and her grandmother. He knocked you out and tied you up because you wouldn't go along. But," I made an exaggerated shrug, "you don't help me, I won't help you. Simple, right? You understand what I'm saying?"

"But I wasn't any part of that."

I brought up my hands to suggest surrender and enunciated my words. "Glenn, I totally understand, but the cops . . . I'm trying to help you, but I need information." I tilted my head and scratched it, like I had come up with a new idea. "Well, never mind. I guess you don't know anything after all. Problem is, I need time to take care of some things. My only choice is to leave you here. Scream loud enough and long enough, maybe someone will hear you."

"You can't," he whimpered.

He was right. I couldn't, but I needed him to believe I could. "Let me ask something you do know. How did you learn I was canoeing down this river? Did that ICE guy tell you?"

"Bunny figured it out. She was sure you were hiding them. She had me and Aaron use a drone to scout the properties you own. We found that spot on the small lake you camped at, but you were gone. Then she got that ICE agent involved. I don't know what she has on him, but it must be good. She snaps her fingers, he jumps. He put trackers on your stuff and called her this morning to tell her you went to your river property. I was following your accountant, and she—"

"Wait, why were you following my accountant?"

"Bunny told me to. 'Glenn,' she said, 'you get to the motel early—before dawn—and tail the broad wherever she goes.' She and her husband were comparing notes, and she figured out the accountant was the same person the Silver Fox hired as a dancer. So, I'm doing what she told me when Aaron and Bunny catch up to me and signal for me to pull over. They join me in my truck, and we find the accountant pulled off before the bridge. Anyway, she figures you're making a run for it by the river. That's it, man. I just drove my truck where they told me."

That all made sense, and I'd bet once Rogers got out of the woods, he'd trade the jacked-up Silverado for Bunny's car. Not my problem. I had Korpi talking, and I had a pinkie-swear contract to fulfill. "How'd she figure out I had the girl?"

"We searched the woman's trailer for whatever Bunny was looking for—you tell me it's a thumb drive. When she couldn't find it, she decided the kid or old lady had it. On our way out from searching the trailer, we passed you going the other way. Bunny paid someone to learn who you were from your plate number. When we saw you heading to that arts camp in Amasa, she was sure you had the kid and went crazy when we couldn't find them."

How did Bunny learn of the photographs? From Kat? "You know where Kat Serrano is now?"

His eyes flitted everywhere, avoiding looking at me. "I never seen her."

"That wasn't my question. Look at me, Glenn. So far, I've believed everything you said. I'm helping you avoid prison. Don't screw this up. Where is Kat Serrano? Is she alive?"

"I swear, I don't know nothin'."

I leaned into him, putting my nose an inch from his, and stared into his eyes, not blinking for a minute. He broke.

"She's dead. Leastwise, I think so. I heard Aaron and Bunny talking. They drugged her to get answers. And it sorta sounded like, you know, like she died. Honest. That's all I heard. You gotta believe me."

"Where did they take her?"

"I don't know, man. Someplace out where no one could find her. I didn't have nothing to do with that."

I was ninety-five percent sure he was telling the truth, and nothing I could do right now could increase the percentage. While I had him talking, I asked if he knew anything about those two guys who got whacked and dumped at my place. "Were they involved in manufacturing meth?"

His face lost its color. His Adam's apple worked up and down, like he was swallowing bile. "No. No, man. I had nothing to do with killing them.

That was Aaron and Bunny. They just got me to drive their stuff to your place and set up that equipment on your propane tank."

"Where did they kill them?"

"I don't know, man. I don't want to know." He started crying, his body shaking with his sobs.

"Stay with me here, Glenn. Are you telling me that besides running a high-class prostitution ring, Bunny was manufacturing meth?"

"No, man. Randy discovered those two yahoos near where they bring guys and her girls for weekend retreats. I've never been there. Hear tell it's a sweet setup. Anyway, Randy stole their operation. Bunny found out and chewed him a new one because she didn't want police coming anywhere near her deal with the girls. Randy supposedly told them to stop. I don't know that he did. Either way, those stupid meth heads kept stealing propane and cooking product. Aaron lured them somewhere, and they whacked them."

He segued into a shaggy dog story about him and his wife arguing over money. He went to blow off steam at the Silver Fox. Ended up hooking up with a dancer, doing some drugs, falling more behind in money. One night, Aaron Rogers suggested he do a little security work on the side to pay them back. Before Korpi knew it, he was in trouble and dependent on them.

Similar to how pimps got girls hooked on drugs to keep them needy and compliant. I interrupted and asked if he had a phone.

"In my truck. You can borrow it."

He had forgotten his Silverado was gone. I couldn't leave him where no one might find him if something happened to me before I called the police. I told him I'd undo the belt, and we'd walk to his truck. If he tried to escape, I'd catch him, strip him, and leave him to starve to death, if bears or wolves didn't eat him first.

He blathered from the moment I released him until he spotted Bunny sprawled on the road. His feet shuffled to a stop. He leaned over and threw up.

I prodded his back. "Don't look at her. You forgot Rogers has your truck and your phone? I brought you here so the police could find you, but I need to secure you to the bridge with your belt until they arrive. Either that, or I shoot you in both legs."

Ninety-Nine

WHEN I JOG, I COVER six miles in forty-eight minutes. Normally, I could walk that distance in ninety. But I was so whipped, it took double the normal time. Three hours of second-guessing everything I had done and worrying if everyone was okay. I reached my property so bushed I could barely put one foot in front of the other.

Cresting the last hill and seeing only my F-150 and the Outback, still up on a jack, was like a slap in the face. I had convinced myself Niki would be waiting for me when I got home, and I'd have my answers. I rarely miss not having my cellphone, but now I desperately wanted to talk with Niki and to verify with Colleen that she had escaped with Valeria and Nana. One of my mother's favorite proverbs popped into my head, "If wishes were horses, beggars would ride."

Niki's SUV not being here meant she was fine. She had responsibilities in St. Paul—business and family responsibilities she had not wanted and had accepted largely because I had encouraged her. She and Colleen and even Mom had done more than I had any right to ask. But I hadn't yet done everything I'd asked of myself.

I retrieved the hidden spare key to the house and found a note from Niki on the dining room table.

Seamus,

I'm dealing with federal bureaucracy. Call me and I'll fill you in.

Niki

I wished she had time-stamped her note so I knew when she had left. It occurred to me the replacement trail cam I had installed on Shank Lake Road would tell me that. I traded my damaged glasses for a spare I kept at the house and retrieved the memory card. I reviewed the pictures while scarfing down a bowl of cereal, a hunk of cheese, and an apple.

The camera caught Agent Carpenter's green jeep heading in, and minutes later, Niki trailing him. Nothing for two hours. Then, a fire department rescue truck drove past. It and Niki returned after an hour.

Niki stopped at the house and then headed toward town. The last human was me, dragging up the road.

I told myself Niki was fine. She shot Agent Carpenter and summoned the closest thing we have to an ambulance to transport him to the hospital. Except police weren't involved. Or maybe she didn't shoot him. He injured himself attempting to crash through the second gate to the river. Okay, Seamus, you have no clue what happened. Get yourself into town, call in Bunny's death, and leave before the Sheriff's department shows up.

I removed the tracking device from the truck and stuck it to the Bobcat, just in case it stopped sending signals if it didn't remain attached to metal. Paranoid, I'm sure. But I did not want anybody to follow me where I planned to go.

Glenn Korpi thought Kat was dead. He might have misinterpreted what he heard, and Bunny still held Kat prisoner. While I was free, I would use my time to fulfill my oath to Valeria to try to learn what had happened to her mother.

I loaded the truck with snacks, a fresh can of mosquito dope, and my camera supplies. I realized I should change clothes, did that, and scribbled a quick note below Niki's telling her I was going to Crenshaw's compound—just in case she returned. Not that I expected it.

Not knowing what else I might need, I collected bolt cutters, pry bar, chainsaw, come-a-long, and block and tackle, and threw them into the truck bed.

I raced down to Tall Pines where I used their phone to report Bunny's death and Glenn Korpi's detention. I hung up on their questions. As much as I wanted to call Niki and Colleen, I scratched buying a phone at the Verizon store in Iron River. A replacement phone would take too long to port my information from the cloud to a new one, and a burner phone did me no good because no one would know how to reach me on it. Plus, I relied on my phone's address book and, with a burner, wouldn't know anybody's number to call them.

I was running solo and incommunicado with the police surely looking for me. If anything went wrong, I had no safety net.

One Hundred

ON THE FOREST ROAD LEADING to the Crenshaw compound, where I now suspected Bunny had taken Kat to question her, I paid attention to the two-track trails I passed. Glenn Korpi had said the meth dealers worked nearby, and, sure enough, a mile before Crenshaw's property line, I noticed one with recent traffic. I stopped and examined the tire tracks. They included wide truck treads and a distinctive set that I figured came from a passenger car. The truck tracks came and went. The most recent passenger car track was heading in. I filed that information away and continued to the locked gate that guarded the Crenshaw property.

I put on work gloves to assure I left no prints. Two snips of the bolt cutters removed the lock, which I chucked into the woods. Littering, yes, but keeping it in my truck as incriminating evidence did not sound like a good idea. I closed the gate behind me and arranged the chain to mimic a locked gate, then drove to the house and was pleased to see no parked vehicles.

The pry bar forced open the rear sliding glass door. Inside, my nose wrinkled at the stench of massive disinfectant use—more than required for a standard cleaning. I called out, asking if anyone was here, and got no answer. With all the people wandering around the first floor over the weekend, the upstairs and basement offered the best hope of finding signs of Kat's captivity.

Upstairs, I counted six bedrooms and a bunk room that could house a dozen. The place was spotless; even the corners were free of dust bunnies. I checked bedroom closets, under beds, in drawers. Loungewear and women's gowns—much fancier than what Kat and the murdered woman had worn at the party given in the Menominee Rapids Resort's private room—filled the closets. Sex toys crammed the bureau drawers. The bathrooms contained only over-the-counter medicines for headache and upset stomach, extra tissues, and toilet paper. Stacked fluffy towels and high-thread-count sheets filled the linen closet shelves. Nothing suggested Kat had been here.

I found an entrance to the attic through a closet ceiling. I dragged a bureau into the closet to stand on and popped the ceiling panel up and out of the way. With no obvious light switches or lights, I retrieved a flashlight from a kitchen drawer and used it to illuminate the area: thick pink insulation cozied between ceiling joists. Nothing stored, and no hidden rooms. I replaced the panel and positioned the bureau feet to fit the original rug indentations. I scuffed the rug with my foot to hide the drag marks.

That left the basement. I opened its door and a wall of disinfectant odor greeted me, even though I had become accustomed to its smell. A light switch at the top of the stairs controlled all the lights. The stairs showed no dust. The devil suggested I was a fool to leave Bunny's P226 and the AR-15 lying next to her for the police to find. I should have them in reach. Until recently, I would never have generated that thought. I told the devil to return to hell and stay there. I swear he snorted.

The main basement area contained a freezer massive enough to hold a body and shelves filled with nonperishable food items. Heart in my mouth, I opened the freezer door and gagged at the sight of hanging slabs of meat. I settled my stomach and inspected each slab, labeled as beef, deer, and elk.

Three padlocked rooms jutted out from one basement wall. I raced to the truck, grabbed the bolt cutter, and removed the first padlock. The door opened to reveal a disinfected bathroom containing a standalone sink, commode, and shower stall. A mold problem in a closed room might require the disinfectant, but I soon discovered that was unlikely the reason for the extreme cleaning. A narrow bedroom lay beyond the second padlocked door. Here, the tang of feces added to the overpowering disinfectant stench. Pushed against the far wall was a single bed, stripped to a plastic mattress cover. An empty chamber pot sat underneath the foot of the bed.

With a bathroom next door, you'd only use a chamber pot if someone had locked you in. The flashlight illuminated several dark brown or rusty spots in one corner that looked more organic than mineral. Disinfectant had burned away my ability to smell even with my nose to the floor. A crime lab could confirm if it was blood.

I unzipped the plastic mattress cover, hoping to find hidden treasure. Nothing. I flipped the mattress up to examine the box spring. One corner had the outline of a stain left by dried liquid.

Breaking into the house, I had been sure I would uncover evidence, but so far, I had discovered nothing that would warrant summoning the police and their forensics. A combination lock secured the third room, which was tucked into the corner and larger than the other two. The bolt cutter made quick work of it, and I entered my last hope.

This space had no internal lighting. The flashlight's beam revealed the walls lined with metal shelves filled with ziplocked storage bags. I slid my feet to make sure I didn't trip on anything, retrieved one bag, and brought it into the light of the main room.

I'd never used cocaine, but I'd seen plenty during my days on Wall Street. This powder had a crystalline structure similar to coke, but yellow shaded its white, unlike the pure white or pinkish tinge I remembered the traders lusted after.

The bag weighed about a kilo. No one locked up bags of detergent. Best guess, this was the meth Bunny had supposedly been furious about. I returned the bag to its place and shut the door on a seven-figure stash of illegal drugs. Now I had something the police would find exciting.

And a problem.

How could I entice the police to raid the place without admitting to B&E?

One Hundred One

I LEFT THE BASEMENT AS I had found it, except for the locks I had removed. I couldn't lock the damaged French door from the outside, so I secured it from the inside and left the house using the front door, which locked behind me. It was dusk, but the sauna and garage still beckoned. I made myself a deal: if I found the doors locked, I'd leave. I returned the bolt cutter and pry bar to my truck to assure I didn't cheat.

The sauna was secure, but the garage was not. God's will. To let in maximum light, I screeched open both garage doors. Kat's rusted Ford Ranger had not been there earlier, but I still registered disappointment to not see it. I weaved around the side-by-sides, past the tractor with a front bucket and a backhoe attachment and examined everything on the workbench that ran across the rear wall. No bloody hatchets, no cellphones, no clutch purses.

Headlights coming down the driveway swept through the garage. Had I triggered a silent alarm and someone from town was checking on the compound? Well, I sure couldn't hide with my F-150 parked in full view. I rushed outside, smacking my shoulder against the backhoe attachment along the way. Randy Crenshaw's blaze orange Caddy Blackwing pulled up next to my truck. I approached as he got out of his car.

He cleared the door and pointed a pistol at me.

I froze. "Randy, it's Seamus. I didn't expect you here." That was true. "Your dad told me to feel free to look around." Total Bullshit. Would Randy call me on it? I resumed walking toward him and offered my hand to shake.

He lowered the gun to his side. A lefty, like his dad, his right remained free to shake mine. He made no move to do that. "Dad didn't say anything about that."

I dropped my hand. "He was exploring options. I don't think he'd decided. I got the impression he didn't come here often. Nice bunch of toys." I waved toward the open garage and brushed my shoulder. My hand came away dirty. *The backhoe.* I wiped my hand clean on my pants.

His eyes jittered, losing focus. Nerves? Drugs?

"You have a key to the house? I peeked through the windows. It looks super in there, but I'd love to see the upstairs."

"Not today." He motioned with the gun toward my truck. "Time to leave. We'll sort this out with dad at a later date."

"Yeah. Sure. Okay." I shut the garage doors. "Could use some WD-40."

He was already walking toward the front stoop. I hopped in my truck and engaged the ignition. While turning the truck around, my lights illuminated his car. I focused my binoculars on his tire tread. I'd bet it matched the automotive tracks I saw entering that two-track a mile before the Crenshaw compound gate. Curiosity got the better of me, and I shifted my focus to the interior. My attention passed over the two-tone leather driver seat, noted a cellphone lay next to the black stick shift, and stopped on seeing dozens of freezer storage bags filled with a yellowish powder on the passenger seat.

ONE HUNDRED TWO

HOW WOULD CRENSHAW REACT WHEN he discovered I had broken into the house and found the drugs? I checked my rearview mirror for him.

Never mind what *he* planned, Seamus. What do *you* do? Because if those drugs escape to the wild, *you're* responsible for the lives lost.

I sped to his gate and parked between the posts to block the driveway, trapping Crenshaw. Now what? The only phone available to call the police was in Crenshaw's car. I sprinted back, hoping I could make it before Crenshaw came back outside.

He opened the front door while I was still fifty yards—six seconds—away.

First three seconds: he raised his head in awareness, retreated two steps, and stopped.

Twenty-five yards to go.

Second four: he leveled his pistol.

Brain calculating: Fifteen yards. Even people trained with pistols have a difficult time hitting a target at any distance. I needed that phone and began an erratic weave.

Second five: he fired three shots.

Second six, I ducked behind his hundred-thousand-dollar beauty.

He sidled left to get an angle. I scooted past his blackened rear window to the front door and looked inside. The phone was a billfold.

"Castle doctrine," he yelled. "I've got every right to kill you."

Bully for him. I'd survived my confrontations with Bunny and Aaron Rogers. Three in one day was pressing my luck. I wanted to keep him here after I escaped so the police could catch him. I extracted my Swiss Army knife and, remembering Niki's advice to take out two tires, not just one, stabbed the awl through the sidewalls of the front and rear tires. Each wound yielded a satisfying hiss. I stayed low, and using his car as a shield, zigzagged to safety behind the garage.

He threw two more slugs in my direction before retreating inside. He could call reinforcements. I could not.

One Hundred Three

I BROUGHT THE F-150 TO a sliding stop scattering gravel, hopped out, and yelled to the folks streaming into the parking lot from the Northwoods Second Coming of Jesus Christ Church, "Anyone got a phone I can borrow?"

The women scattered, either locking themselves in their cars or retreating inside the wooden church. The men gathered in a bunch.

I presented my hands in prayerful supplication. "Please, I need to borrow a phone to call the police. I don't mean to frighten anyone, but it is urgent."

The youngest, smallest guy there walked over and handed me his phone. "You okay, brother? You're bleeding. Press emergency and it dials 9-1-1."

The operator identified herself and asked the nature of my emergency. I was looking down at my arm, which was bleeding, and the first words I spoke were "Holy shit, I've been shot." That got the operator's attention, but not in the way I had intended. My frustration with rules boiled over because she wanted facts about the wound, which was only a crease, and I wanted her to focus on who had done the creasing. Progress went faster when I relented and let her ask her questions.

The operator asked where I was. I handed the phone to the kid to give directions. *Hell, the church is on the highway. Use your head, Seamus.* I leaned against my truck, energy draining through my feet. Now that I had to wait, my body wanted to collapse. Directions complete, the kid said the operator needed my name.

"Seamus McCree."

He repeated my name into the device. His eyes widened. "I understand, but I gotta get home before my curfew." He hung up and jogged to an older guy in the group.

What the hell?

The guy listened to the kid and stepped forward. "You're sure you don't need the hospital?" Behind him, the men were backing toward the church, eyes wide with fear.

"I'm good. Is there a problem I don't know about?"

"We're a Christian community, and if you want help to get medical assistance, I'll take you. But the 9-1-1 operator told young Justin that we should consider you armed and dangerous and to get to a place of safety. I don't know what's going on, and I don't want to know. We believe all people have good inside them. I'm familiar with your work setting up a foundation to help local crime victims. You've shown your positive attributes. I beg you, in the name of Christ our Lord, not to harm any of our flock."

Guilt burned my face and neck for causing innocent people to be fearful. I laced my fingers over my head. "There's a Swiss Army knife in my pocket, which I'm happy to give you. I never intended to make anyone feel threatened. How can I make this right?" I pointed to the picnic table in the side yard, well away from the parking lot. "If I sit there and wait for the police, can everyone go home? I am sorry to have inconvenienced or frightened anyone."

He looked me in the face. "I believe you, brother. Keep your knife. You mind if I wait with you?"

I sat at the picnic table with my back to the parking lot and my legs tucked between the seat and the table. He sat facing me, called someone inside, and told everyone to leave. His name was Christian Fletcher, and he was the church's lay leader. No relation to the HMS Bounty mutineer. He asked if I would pray with him.

I loosely use the term "prayer" to mean sending good thoughts to others or hoping for a good result, like not getting stuck in a mud hole. Christian meant something entirely different, and while I don't believe in an all-powerful God who intercedes on our behalf, it would do no harm. I bowed my head, let his words wash over me, and reflected on my fervent wishes that Colleen and Valeria and Nana and Niki were all safe on their journeys.

And that Randy Crenshaw's poison would never leave the compound.

ONE HUNDRED FOUR

AN IRON COUNTY SHERIFF'S CRUISER, supported by an Iron River patrol car, pulled into the lot, lights flashing. The officers exited their cars, guns drawn, using their doors as shields. "Seamus," Iron County Sergeant Tex said, "keep your hands on your head where we can see them."

I complied and cranked my neck enough to see him. "Tex, everything is cool." I told Christian that the police would feel much better once he was away from me, and he should take a route that didn't put him between the police and me. "Thank you for staying with me. Please give my apologies to anyone I frightened."

Christian told the officers what he planned to do. I yelled at them to hurry. We had a crime to stop.

Tex snapped cuffs on me. "Next time answer your damn phone."

"I can't. It's sitting on the river bottom."

"That's the first time I heard that one." Tex claimed he wasn't arresting me, but that I was a person of interest. *Right, a person of interest with his hands cuffed.*

"You're lucky on that wound. Only a graze, but there's a lot of dirt in it. When did you have your last tetanus shot?"

I lashed out. "Will you stop worrying about me for one minute and focus on the drug bust you need to make?"

Tex contacted Sheriff Bartelle, who reluctantly gave him permission to drive to Crenshaw's compound for a look-see at the supposed drug operation I had spotted. "Block the road if you think you should, but under no circumstances will you approach any suspects until you have backup. And McCree stays caged."

"You heard the man. Into the back." Tex ducked my head under the frame. "I can't wait to hear this story."

Very crafty of my friend. He hadn't asked a question, meaning Miranda didn't apply, and they could, and would, use anything I said against me. I had lots I wanted to tell him, but given I had killed Bunny, let Rogers go, and broken into the Crenshaw compound, I'd be stupid to say anything without representation present. Hell, I'd already been a fool to point Tex to the compound to investigate Randy Crenshaw.

On our way to the Crenshaw compound, I pointed out the trafficked dirt road. "Have your drug guys check down there. I suspect you'll find they've been cooking meth."

"You know this how?"

"Friendly ravens told me."

A red glow painted the clouds as we came closer to the clearing. Tex accelerated down the narrow road and stopped at Crenshaw's gate. Waves of heat poured from the inferno that had been the house. The roar was so loud he had to shout at his phone to call in the fire. The calm night, recent rain, and the distance between house and woods made it unlikely the fire would spread. I might not believe in prayer, but leaving nothing to chance, I prayed the red gouts of sparks shooting into the sky wouldn't start a forest fire.

Randy Crenshaw's car had not moved. The heat had blistered the paint and melted much of the plastic. The garage doors remained open. I pointed out the spot a four-wheeler had occupied, and Tex called dispatch again and issued a BOLO for Randy Crenshaw.

Tex left me in the back seat with my thoughts, which spiraled around everything that was happening. In one sequence, I acknowledged how lucky I was that Randy had only grazed me, tried to picture the circumstances of my most recent tetanus shot, failed and obsessed about the dirt in the wound, remembered the fresh dirt on the backhoe, and pondered the bare area in the garden.

When Tex finally returned to the car, I begged him to let me show him something. Bartelle's orders wouldn't permit it. "That's fine," I said. "You'll need a search warrant, anyway. Check the bare patch in the garden. I could be way wrong, but there's a good chance they buried one or two bodies under there."

ONE HUNDRED FIVE

THE DOCTORS AT THE HOSPITAL cleaned my minor gunshot wound and gave me a tetanus booster. We reached the Iron County Jail at three o'clock Wednesday morning. They took an hour to process me into the facility. The mug shot was not my finest.

They woke me for breakfast and took me from there to the interrogation room, where they read me my rights, but claimed they had not charged me. I made it clear I had nothing to say until I spoke with my lawyer. Years ago, Iron County had arrested me for murder. My attorney then was a force of nature from the Traverse City area. My call found her in Petosky, looking for its famous stones. She'd be here late that afternoon. Irene Frankel had to be in her mid-seventies, but she looked much as she had in her sixties. A cropped helmet of gray hair now replaced the dreadlocks she used to wear.

It took me two hours to share the complete details of everything that had happened. Afterward, should they need it, I engaged Irene's services for Colleen—whose whereabouts were unknown—and Niki, who Irene determined was attending a Pendergast Holdings board meeting in Minnesota. "That's fine," she said. "But if it comes to a conflict of interest, you are my client. I'll make sure they get excellent representation."

That made me feel a little better. "Thanks. Now tell me all the reasons I should not give the police the full truth?" Her reservations caused me to avoid saying anything about breaking into the Crenshaw compound.

My interrogation Thursday morning ran for three hours. Their questions focused on how I "claimed" to have become involved with Bunny and Randy Crenshaw and my version of a timeline of events during the last two weeks.

We broke for a long lunch. Before the afternoon session, Irene had a few minutes alone with me. "Colleen's back. She was successful. A doctor examined Valeria. The meds are working well on her Lyme's disease. By the by, she invited me to stay with her at your place. Generous, don't you think?"

I laughed, the first time in days. "Don't let her fool you. She's an accountant and knows about billing by the hour and travel expenses. She's trying to reduce your charges."

Her eyes twinkled. "Back to business. I have news on your case. Not all the Iron County police think you should be in jail. At least one is feeding info to Niki. She also contacted some FBI friends who confirm the Bureau is looking into the Chicago connections.

"Mike Crenshaw ratted out his son, Randy, who claims the whole thing was Bunny's doing. Randy says he discovered she was manufacturing the drugs and storing them at the compound. He was there to destroy them. They found his prints everywhere in and around the trailer where you guessed they were cooking the meth—not exactly supporting his story. Police recovered several portable generators and the battery bank stolen from your neighbor."

"Did they arrest Mike Crenshaw?"

"Not yet, but the more important question is whether they will arrest you. They can hold you today until they finish talking with you, but they can't keep you overnight without charging you."

The afternoon session concluded at six p.m. I had gone over everything multiple times, showing them on plat maps where the events occurred, including the river segment where I had lost my phone. They had mined everything I planned to tell them, and they knew it. Two hours later, Irene informed me the prosecutor had charged me with involuntary manslaughter, obstructing an official police investigation, and a bunch of other miscellaneous crimes tacked on to use as bargaining chips in a plea agreement.

She had other news. They had uncovered Kat's rusty Ford Ranger in the garden plot. Underneath it, they found the bodies of Kat Serrano and Peggy Dowson, the woman choked to death at the motel.

I hadn't wanted to be right, but at least now we knew, and I had kept my promise to the kids. I told Irene that I hoped Colleen could pass the information to Valeria and Nana.

At the bail hearing, the prosecutor recommended no bail because I was a flight risk. Irene observed to the judge that I had had plenty of opportunity to flee the area if that had been my desire. Instead, I had continued my investigation, without which the police would not have uncovered the burial of two women, a prostitution ring, and a drug operation.

She softened her voice. "And why, you may ask, did he do this? Because he promised his granddaughter and her friend he would try as hard as he could to find out what happened to her friend's missing mother. Not just a promise, a pinkie swear. This, more than anything else I can say, proves my client is a man of his word."

Returning to regular volume, she continued. "If your honor wants to question character witnesses, I have several citizen volunteers in court ready to testify. Frankly, your honor, that's a waste of everyone's time. But I'm willing. I get paid by the hour."

She waited until the chuckles subsided. "We ask for no bail. Mr. McCree will surrender his passport and not leave the state without the court's permission. If your honor decides it's warranted, my client consents to wear a monitor. The defendant wants the court and the prosecutor to understand that he insists on his rights to a speedy jury trial. We will brook no delays."

One Hundred Six

Two Months Later

A WEEK AWAY FROM HIGH color in my part of the U.P., the oranges and reds of the maples burned in the bright sunlight at Lake Tranquility. The extended McCree clan had conspired to gather for a long weekend. Colleen's bail—they charged her with obstructing an official investigation—required her to remain in Michigan. I gave her the main house to allow her to work remotely twenty-four/seven and retreated to my unimproved guest cabin.

Megan, her parents, and their dog, Atalanta, drove up that morning from Chicago. They had invited my mother, but she claimed a darts exhibition prevented her from coming. I suspected Mom had had all the wilderness she wanted and preferred her city life.

Colleen and I had shuttled food, extra camp chairs, and hammocks to Lake Tranquility. Once Megan and her parents arrived at the rocks on Lukes Road, we brought them the rest of the way by ATVs, Atalanta loping ahead, her Golden Retriever tongue hanging from her mouth. Megan, with Atalanta at her heels, convinced Colleen to check the trail cameras. Paddy and Cindy, happy to entrust their daughter to Colleen, canoed the lake, leaving me to wait for Niki's arrival.

To keep busy, I built a fire for those less enamored than I of the cool autumn day. My new phone chirped—I should say my primary phone. After losing the one, I vowed never to be without a phone again and had purchased a dozen burner phones for emergencies. Niki's message asked me to bring the two-up to the rocks blocking Lukes Road. Could I also have Paddy come with another ATV? I couldn't imagine why she required both ATVs, but figured I'd soon learn.

Colleen returned with Megan and the dog in time for me to substitute her for Paddy. We arrived at the rocks to find Niki and Valeria (with a signed paper giving Niki *in loco parentis* status for the weekend). "Surprised?"

Colleen helped Valeria onto her ATV for the ride to Lake Tranquility. Niki hopped on behind me and gave me a hug. "Nana is doing well. She wishes she could be here too, but we agreed it was unwise, at least for now."

I plugged my ears to mute the squeals celebrating Megan and Valeria's reunion. They hugged and jumped around one another. As they settled down and I unplugged my ears, I realized I was hearing more than their shrieks. Wheeling above us were George, Martha, and Gonzo. They must have heard the girls. I had continued the eagles' training, adding a special act. I handed the kids fishing poles and told them bait was down in the boat house. They had hungry eagles waiting.

The adult humans gathered around the fire, sipping wine and popping beers. I demanded of Niki, "What's happened with Valeria and Nana?"

"A lawyer who supports the folks harboring Nana persuaded Texas to issue Valeria a birth certificate. That proves she's a US citizen. She's making friends in school and doing splendidly. The organization arranged for her to visit a child psychologist. Her ankle has healed, and the antibiotics did the trick against the Lyme's. All good news."

"Indeed," I said. "And Nana?"

"At least with this administration, Nana isn't the type of person they are targeting. How it plays out long term?" Her shoulders rose and fell, and she let out a sigh. "One gigantic piece of wonderful news, Seamus, is your mother was right about Nana's wood carvings. The organization helped her set up an online store. She's already making enough money to support herself and is accepting special orders."

"Excellent." I caught Paddy and Cindy trading meaningful looks. "Okay, you two, what's up? I haven't seen that much silent communication since you told me you were expecting Megan."

"Well . . ." Cindy prodded Paddy with her elbow.

They were pregnant? "I thought—"

"No medical miracles, Dad," Paddy said. "But we are looking at adopting. We have Nana's permission to adopt Valeria. It's a long process, but the lawyers believe there's an excellent chance it will succeed. Neither girl knows. We don't want anyone getting their hopes up."

"Later," Cindy said, "we'd bring Nana to live with us. Not as an employee, just to stay. Remember, mum's the word around the girls. Have you guys heard what happened to that ICE agent Carpenter who harassed you?"

Colleen and I had not.

Niki's evil chuckle caused Atalanta to raise a questioning head and almost made me sympathetic to the asshole. "On the day he tried to catch you at the river, he made one huge mistake. After seeing how flimsy that first gate was, he thought to save time he'd crash through the second one."

I laughed. "Except, I had embedded those poles in concrete."

"Now he knows," Niki said, "and he'll have a permanent limp to remind him of his stupidity. But that's not where his troubles end. I saved his life that day, which I thought gave me the right to talk to a guy I know who's pretty senior in government."

Yeah, like the assistant director of national intelligence with his strong connections to Homeland Security and ICE.

"I mentioned that Agent Carpenter had a cowboy streak and suggested management should reevaluate his work. Surprise, surprise. To justify the warrants to search your property and put trackers on your vehicles, he fudged facts and exaggerated the situation to the judge. I know this investigative reporter in Chicago." She and Cindy Nelson, my daughter-in-law, high-fived it.

Cindy continued the telling. "And I uncovered evidence that suggests he's part of a rogue group of ICE agents we suspect have links to human trafficking rings. Still not a hundred percent. What is certain is that Vincent Otto is brother-in-law to Bunny Crenshaw. Sources say that before she married Mike Crenshaw, she ran an escort service in Chicago. She never stopped running it. We're pretty sure Vincent Otto is the money behind it. I bet he's feeling heat and lashing out."

She drank a slug of beer. "Drew Dombey, the pimp? Found him in a sewage lagoon with two small-caliber holes in his head. I've tracked down several of the party women you photographed. Some are talking now that Bunny and Dombey are dead. The Feds are also looking at this. We keep crossing each other's trail. We'll be ready for our exposé in another month."

I asked, "Anything on Aaron Rogers?" Everyone looked at everyone else. "In the wind, I guess." I wondered what name he was using and where he was. "So far, they haven't arrested Mike Crenshaw. I hear he has the motel, the resort, the Silver Fox, his house, and all his land for sale. I wish I could've added some of his forest property to Megan's trust, but he won't sell to me given I killed his wife and got his kid arrested for producing and selling meth."

Paddy said, "I thought the house fire destroyed all the evidence you found."

My opportunity to provide information. "Randy left traces of meth on the front seat of his car. His tire tracks went to a travel trailer in the woods a mile away where they cooked the meth, and his prints were all around the trailer. As part of our legal discovery process, we received redacted transcripts of police interviews with Glenn Korpi. He claims Bunny went ballistic when she discovered the two guys stealing propane were also cooking meth for Randy. She ordered him to shut down his operation to protect hers. Randy didn't. Korpi claimed Bunny killed those two local guys to warn Randy and had them dumped at my house to cause me trouble. We know one of the Sig Sauer P226s I took from her was the murder weapon."

Cindy said, "The thing I don't understand is why the prosecutor hasn't dropped charges against you two."

Colleen said, "Irene, our lawyer, speculates that he believed we would cop a plea on a lesser charge. Can you believe they offered me a deal to squeal on Seamus? Failing that, he counted on having the extra time to find evidence to build a case or charge us with something else. Three times wrong. Most defendants try to defer the trial. Irene had told them from the get-go that we'd fight any delays. We want our day in court, and we want it now."

"So," Cindy said, "Irene's confident she'll win—even the obstruction charges?"

My throat tightened, recalling Irene's caution that juries come with no guarantees. "What she said was that she planned to call Sheriff Bartelle, Tex, and the Michigan state officer as hostile defense witnesses. None can testify that any of Colleen's or my actions actually hindered their investigations, even if technically we interfered. And that without the information I provided, they would not have broken up the prostitution ring, solved the propane thefts, cracked the meth operation, etc."

Niki slapped her thigh. "The police will despise the prosecutor if he puts them in *that* situation."

"Which," Colleen said, "is why Irene thinks he will drop all charges. And if it goes to trial, the worst we'll get is a hung jury. But—"

From the lake, the kids yelled, "We got fish!"

Paddy and Cindy wanted to see the girls and their eagles. We tied Atalanta to a tree and made a semicircle of the chairs we carted down to the shore. The eagles were circling overhead, calling with their jittering kri-kri-kri. The kids took turns flinging the fish. Martha snagged hers from the air. George and Gonzo missed and grabbed their fish from the water. Megan had the last fish, which was for Gonzo. Trying to launch it "super-duper high," she threw it behind her. It landed at my feet.

"You do it, Grandpa Seamus." And Valeria chimed in, "Yeah, Grandpa Seamus, you throw it."

I grabbed the fish's tail and held it vertically above my head. "I'll show you something better." Gonzo came swooping in and grabbed it from my hand.

Paddy said, "That is one of the stupidest things I've ever seen you do."

Cindy said, "And we've seen you do a lot of dumb stuff. Do you remember the time . . . "

No way I could defend myself; it was pretty stupid. But it was damned exciting to have an eagle eat from my hand.

Niki came to my rescue. "Valeria, did you have something from Nana you wanted to give to Grandpa Seamus?" Niki pulled a bag from her knapsack and gave it to Valeria, who handed it to me.

Tissue paper covered a heavy object eight inches long. I unwound the wrapping and my eyes stung with tears. From a single block of maple, Nana had carved two bald eagles, wings spread behind their backs, their talons extended and linked by their rear claws.

"Turn it over." Valeria grabbed it from me and flipped it. "Read the bottom."

The base had a brass sliding plate with the etched words "Pinkie Swear."

"Open it, Grampa Seamus." Valeria shoved it into my hands. She was twitching with anticipation.

I slid open the plate. Nestled inside was the granite stone Niki had given Valeria to signify my oath. My heart swelled and pressed against my chest. I couldn't speak. How was I so lucky to have Valeria and Nana enter my life? I motioned Valeria to me and wrapped her in my arms. I regained control of my voice and whispered, "I can't tell you how much this means to me."

Her arms pulled me in tight. "I love you, too, Grampa Seamus."

I hope you enjoyed reading this story. To help me reach other readers, I would appreciate your posting a short review of *Granite Oath* on your favorite retailer or review website.

Author's Note

THIS BOOK WOULD NOT EXIST had it not been for you, my readers. You asked for another story with Seamus and his family, and you wanted it set in Michigan's Upper Peninsula. A special shout out to my Reader's Group who helped pick the name for the "G" novel and choose (and improve) the book cover from several options.

Most of the roads and geography referenced in this story are real. I've spent many enjoyable days exploring the interconnected logging roads, skidder trails, lakes, and rivers of Iron County, Michigan often accompanied by my son, Brad Jackson. Recently, I've been spending more time exploring the adjacent sections of Baraga County accompanied by Lisa, Craig, and Dani Cherry and Courtney Ainsworth. Despite that detailed knowledge, I have taken liberty with the exact locations and numbers of camps, beaver dams, gates, and trails. Lake Tranquility lives only on these pages.

Although I have used many real businesses in this tale of fiction, I have invented several others. The motel in Iron Mountain, the Menominee Rapids Resort, and the Silver Fox are complete figments of my imagination and not based on any existing establishments. You won't find the Northwoods Second Coming of Jesus Christ Church among Iron County's many fine religious establishments. Nor can you reserve a spot for your child or grandchild next summer at the Amasa Summer Creative Arts Academy.

The story refers to several actual police organizations. Over the years I have talked with many professionals from the Iron County Sheriff's Department and the Michigan State Police and watched them work. I've always found them to be great professionals. This is not a police procedural, and I've taken liberties with normal investigation practices.

Gabriel Belanger won a silent auction that benefited The Friends of the Crystal Falls District Community Library. Instead of having me name a character after himself, he chose to give his mother, Kim Belanger, that "pleasure." Neither had a choice in which character I picked, but I did make sure Kim was okay with the idea.

Carl Dickson looked over the Spanish phrases I used. Debra Goldstein told me that it didn't matter how I spelled bupkes/bubkes/bupkis, someone would complain, and I should go with whichever one I preferred. My two eagle-eyed early readers, Carol J. Baldridge and Dottie Caster, prevented me from committing many abuses of the English language. Jan Rubens is always my first, last, and best reader. After all their hard work, I make further "improvements," and so I take full responsibility for any mistakes.

I love to hear from readers. Drop me a note and let me know how you liked the story or that you found a typo so I can correct it for future editions. My email is jmj@jamesmjackson.com.

James M. Jackson
Amasa, Michigan

James M. Jackson authors the Seamus McCree and Niki Undercover Thriller series.

Jim has also published an acclaimed book on contract bridge, *One Trick at a Time: How to start winning at bridge.*

He calls the deep woods of Michigan's Upper Peninsula home. You can find out more about Jim or sign up for his Readers Group newsletter at his website, https://jamesmjackson.com.

9 781943 166329